FINDING BRIAN

A NOVEL

TIM NORBECK

outskirts
press

Outskirts Press, Inc.
http://www.outskirtspress.com

Paperback ISBN: 978-1-9772-6937-9
eBook ISBN: 978-1-9772-7190-7

Library of Congress Control Number: 2023923195

Cover images © 2024 www.gettyimages.com and Pexels. All rights reserved - used with permission.

Outskirts Press and the "OP" logo are trademarks belonging to Outskirts Press, Inc.

PRINTED IN THE UNITED STATES OF AMERICA

Praise for *Finding Brian*

Finding Brian kept me mesmerized throughout a thought-provoking, enjoyable, entertaining, and even educational read. There are so many takeaways from this interesting novel. Tim Norbeck manages to weave in some very cogent and introspective quotations and anecdotes into a fast moving and riveting story. I couldn't put it down.

Edward Smoragiewicz,
Attorney, Connecticut and Florida

Author Tim Norbeck has done it again! He has written a book with a captivating antihero. Brian, in a bad marriage, will amaze you with his wily ways. The story line has a way of drawing you in and leading you on as you try to determine how he will continue to survive. A very good read!

Anthony Romanovich,
retired steel company executive,
and avid reader

Other books by Tim Norbeck

Two Minutes

No Time for Mercy

Almost Heaven

Also

A Guide to Better Hockey Coaching and Play –
For Players, Coaches, Parents (1969)

In Their Own Words – 12,000 Physicians Reveal Their
Thoughts on Medical Practice in America (2010)
(Co-author)

Dedicated to Joseph Kevin Cooney (1950 – 2022),
who brightened everyone's day, showed remarkable courage in the face of enormous adversity, and whose daily mantra followed John Wesley's "Rules for Life":

Do all the good you can,
by all the means you can,
in all the ways you can,
in all the places you can,
at all the times you can,
to all the people you can,
as long as ever you can.

Rest in peace, my esteemed friend!

CHAPTER 1

Can things degenerate any further when it appears that suicide is your best option?

His life simply didn't matter anymore. And that was assuming that it ever had. It certainly didn't to his wife. Is there anything on earth more hurtful to a human being than to be considered totally irrelevant? A sense of utter hopelessness permeated his psyche. How could anyone in Brian Hart's situation, who had a good job and enjoyed excellent health, feel such despair? Four centuries before, John Milton, the author of *Paradise Lost*, had the perfect answer. "The mind is its own place," wrote the venerable blind poet, "and in of itself can make a heaven of hell or a hell of heaven." Truer words were probably never spoken.

Divorce didn't seem like a viable option. Brian didn't want to lose everything he had worked for and start all over again in a cramped and dingy apartment, something he had experienced years before when working his way through law school. He wasn't a wealthy man and didn't have many possessions, but he didn't want to lose those he had. And there was something else – something important. He didn't want Carol or Barry to feel that he ran out on them. In fact, they might have been the real reason that Brian had even married Margaret in the first place. His relationship with his own father had been a sour one at best and he felt compelled and desperately needed to make up for it. By being a loving and attentive father to his stepchildren, he could atone for his own father's dereliction. It was complicated, but that was how he felt about it. Divorce was off the table. He couldn't risk even having them entertain the idea that he would be willing to jeopardize their cherished relationship in such a way.

So that was what Brian had told a few of his friends about his marital woes, and almost all of them urged him to have an affair. But that was a non-starter, too. While not being overly virtuous, still his moral compass wouldn't allow it. He was a man of his word and he had taken a vow. His womanizing friend, Harold Stapleton, told him that he just hadn't met the right woman yet. Brian was amenable to counseling but Margaret didn't see any sense to it.

Margaret and Brian had been polar opposites from the first day that he met her. That fact had stood out like a gigantic red flag to him, but too often men thought with another part of their anatomy and didn't always think with their brains. They disagreed on all things political, and she didn't share his sense of humor. But she was pretty and voluptuous, and that red flag dissipated rather quickly.

Years into their marriage and when his stepchildren, whom he had formally adopted, entered college, Margaret immediately immersed herself into any group or cause she could embrace. She was a good mother but probably not as close to her own kids as was their adopted stepdad. His wife began treating him with indifference and apathy if not actual disdain. It wasn't so much the empty nest syndrome with her as much as it was an apparent anger with him. At least, that was how he interpreted it. She seemed to enjoy disagreeing with him on any opinion he might offer, even those unrelated to political issues. And it appeared that she took particular pleasure in putting him down in front of his friends. Sometimes treating someone with disinterest or detachment can be more damaging to someone's psyche than harsh words or intemperate actions. One spouse totally ignoring the other can be the most unkind cut of all, as Shakespeare's Anthony described the wound given to Caesar by his close friend Brutus. She also took pleasure in playing with his mind, gaslighting him on occasion. Sometimes it would be something out of place like his car keys, or when he was certain that he had left a book by his bedside table, only to discover it downstairs in the study. If the kids weren't away at college, perhaps he could tolerate her humiliating and sometimes bizarre behavior. She would never talk about it.

So, Brian Hart was at a very important crossroads in his life. Harold Stapleton was certain that all his friend needed was a suitable female companion. But Brian's history with women was not exactly a satisfying one. In his four-plus decades, he'd had precious few encounters with the opposite sex. He was a respected lawyer, an accomplished athlete, and enjoyed many friendships. But when it came to being woman-savvy, his résumé was thin.

His future options would have to be limited to either a suicide or disappearance. Suicide would undoubtedly result in some dishonor to his family, he reasoned, and he lacked the courage to actually do it. A vanishing act was looking more viable to him.

CHAPTER 2

Female relationships had never come easy to Brian Hart. From the early age of eleven or twelve, when boys really start noticing girls, he had an innate sense that they were not interested in him. There was no specific incident that he could pinpoint or remember that prompted such an instinct, but just an overall feeling that there was a lack of interest on their part. Later on, in high school, when he was old enough to process it, he attributed it to his lack of confidence around them. Of course, a lack of confidence only served to beget a greater lack of confidence. He had very good friends who were very comfortable around members of the fair sex, but that poise never seemed to rub off on him. In fact, their assurance around girls had the opposite effect. He didn't really know what to say when he was in their midst. Brian would hear tales from his high school buddies about having sex, or "scoring," as they put it back then, with their dates. The very thought of getting that far was absolutely incomprehensible to him.

His first and only really serious relationship before he married was with a striking eighteen-year-old blonde who moved with her family next door to his best friend in Buffalo. She was from Pennsylvania and beautiful enough to have won local beauty pageants. But he was only sixteen and Joanne was two full years older than him. And yet she seemed to really like him. One of his biggest mysteries and something that was never fully resolved for him, even as an adult, was why she really liked him. She could have had any pick of the litter, so to speak, but she chose him. While Joanne was gorgeous, she was not full of herself and had a wonderfully engaging personality that drew everyone to her. And she loved to laugh and had a marvelous sense of humor. So, for Brian, it was a heady experience to have such a beauty fall for a sixteen-year-old kid. They often double-dated with his best friend and Joanne's younger sister, Marlene, and he couldn't ignore the double takes of other guys when they saw her with him. All these reactions only served to reinforce his own feelings of doubt. He just knew these other guys who saw them together had to wonder what she was doing with him. Brian wasn't a bad-looking guy by any means, skinny as he was, but no way did he deserve to have this beautiful woman as a girlfriend. It was very much akin to the scenario of a very attractive woman walking down the street or in the mall with some regular-looking guy. People, especially envious men, would invariably comment to a friend walking by: *"What the hell is she doing with him?"* The super envious and callous would always attribute it to the fellow being rich. His personality, whether good or bad, would never even be part of the equation.

The second week after he met her, Joanne told him that she had planned to enter a convent the following year and had committed herself to the Lord. He thought and hoped as the couple's relationship grew closer during that next year, that she might change her mind. She didn't. On their last night together before she left, they hung out on the couch just kissing, nothing more, and exchanging endearments. On the positive side of the ledger for him, Joanne appeared sincere in her feeling for him and confessed that she would really prefer to remain in Buffalo with Brian. They both cried a lot and held each other. He would see her again only once, and many years later. She fulfilled her commitment to the Lord for the next three years while he was in college. They wrote each other for two years and then the letters stopped. During that almost halcyon year of his youth spent with her, he was perhaps too callow to fully comprehend the mystical and magnetic force that drew her to the Lord, but at that time he was just a nerdy nearly eighteen-year-old who had lost a girlfriend. And she wasn't just a ladylove, she was incredibly beautiful and kind. His psyche was torn about their time together. On one hand, there was this movie-star glamorous and nice woman who seemed to genuinely love him. On the other hand, he didn't have the confidence to grasp what she saw in his persona. Was it that she had been new in town and didn't know anybody? He wasn't sure.

Actually, Brian had experienced an earlier meaningless romance, if you could call it that, when he was fourteen and a junior counselor at a boys' camp north of Toronto, Ontario. The camp doctor had a very attractive niece who lived in the area, and he asked her over to attend a joint dance with a nearby girls' camp. Calling all the boys over to the lodge where the event was to be held, the doctor lined them up against a wall. Then Lucy made her appearance and was introduced by her uncle to the girl- hungry young men. "Lucy, pick out your dance partner," he suggested. She proceeded to walk in front of the group as if she were a commanding officer reviewing the troops. Most of the boys were timid souls like Brian and said nothing. But a few assertive types stepped forward and urged her to choose them. Then she stepped in front of Brian and said: *"I choose him!"* If he was surprised, he could only imagine the look of astonishment on the faces of his friends. Unfortunately for him, his euphoria was ephemeral. One of them exclaimed: "You've got to be kidding." Undeterred, she grabbed his hand, and the music began. For a few minutes, they were the only couple on the dance floor. Brian expected someone to cut in, but to his shock, no one did. Soon the other girls entered and everyone began dancing. He felt like a king, but that elation didn't last very long. His self-doubt soon crept in and he wondered how it was possible that she chose him instead of the others.

As shy as he was, she seemed to be his opposite. Very attractive, with short black hair, a pert nose and enchanting green eyes, Lucy was the full package. Only fourteen herself, she had a woman's body and even exposed some cleavage behind her black blouse. She was six inches shorter than his five feet and eleven inches, but feisty and self-confident. She was pretty well everything that he wasn't. He was captivated by her warm smile, which displayed almost perfect teeth. They talked about where she lived, the weather and the beauty of Canada. Rather, she did. He mostly listened. At the end of the dance, she gave him a kiss, which nearly floored him.

"When should we meet again?" she asked aggressively. He had never met a girl like her. They had danced for the entire two hours, and she actually wanted to see him again. Brian walked her to the doctor's cabin where she would spend the night, and she latched onto his hand during the quarter-mile stroll, which took about ten minutes. He was enthralled, captivated, and beguiled all at the same time. No female in grade school had previously demonstrated even a scintilla of interest in him, and here he was now at fourteen with a luscious young babe who seemed to really be into him. And best of all, she actually picked him, Brian Hart, out of all the other guys. What an ego builder that should have been! Except it wasn't. This wasn't any run of the mill, full of piss and vinegar, fourteen-year-old kid ready to impress the ladies. This was Brian Hart. Lucy had asked him when they should meet again. He didn't even have to ask her.

Literally, it should have been a chest-pounder for him, as it would have been for most male adolescents. If she had asked him to jump into shark-infested waters, just for the heck of it, he probably would have done it. That was the extent of the momentary hold she had on him. It wasn't even so much that she was a beauty; it was that she chose him.

To go and see Lucy would not be that easy. Not only did she live almost five miles away, he didn't have a license to drive. Worse than that, he had no car, nor did he know how to drive one. Visiting her in Dorsett meant paddling across a big lake for about a mile and then walking the rest of the way. But it wasn't your everyday walk. This was almost four miles on a dirt road before he hit any pavement. And that dirt road meandered through a heavily wooded area full of Canadian North Woods animals. Big animals, like bears! But Lucy wanted to see him and that was that. They had jointly decided on the very next night for their meeting...the general store in Dorsett.

As a junior counselor, it was Brian's job to "tuck in" the younger boys and be certain that they were all asleep before he could leave the cabin. As he crept out as silently as possible, he could feel his testosterone kicking in. No one heard him as he entered his canoe and paddled softly away from the dock. The only illumination, on a very dark night, came from the moon. He wasn't even frightened. That's what full-mode testosterone can do for a revved-up fourteen-year-old boy. Especially one with no experience but who possessed an active and creative mind. Upon reaching the dock on the other side of the lake, he tied up his canoe. It was about 9:00 and as dark as a mine shaft. Still no fear. Brian walked uphill on the dusty road for about 500 yards until it leveled out. All he had was a flashlight. Then the road sloped down suddenly. He had to be careful not to trip. He could hear rustling in the brush, which was unsettling. But, undaunted, he resolutely continued forward. This went on for another hour as he quickened his pace, figuring somehow that he would be safer that way. Several cries and howls could easily be heard in the distance, but still he was undeterred. Canadian nights tend to be breezy, even in July and August, and that was the only thing that prevented him from soaking his tee shirt.

Finally, at a little after 10:00, he saw her on a large rocking chair to the left of the front door of the general store. Stores like this one in other small Canadian towns often stayed open late, especially on weekends. It was a village hall kind of thing and its citizens enjoyed mingling there. He couldn't believe that she was sitting there waiting for him. Lucy was wearing a light-blue halter tank top with navy-blue shorts which were definitely on the too-short side. But who was he to complain? The deep neckline of the halter top revealed cleavage and a pretty good view of her ample breasts when she bent down. He couldn't believe that she was only fourteen, but clearly she seemed out of his league. She moved over in the old-fashioned swing chair of the times, which could accommodate two people. Without waiting for any preliminaries, Lucy kissed him on the lips as he nestled in beside her. Except it was very unlike any kiss he had ever received. This was a wet one with plenty of tongue! She had obviously done this before. He hadn't.

They kissed for a few minutes and then Lucy got out of the chair. "Let's move it around to the side," she suggested.

He knew he was in way over his head. "Okay," he stammered, while repositioning the heavy chair. Brian was dumbfounded as to what his next move should be, but she helped him out. She led his hand under her top and then to her nipple. She sighed while he squirmed uncomfortably. It was the first time he had ever touched a female's breast – at least the first time he could remember it!

"You can kiss it, if you want to," she invited him. He was actually afraid and looked around nervously and apprehensively as if he were breaking the law. She sensed his discomfort.

"Don't worry, nobody is coming over here."

Apparently, this was not her first rodeo. But it was his! He gently rubbed his thumb over her nipple and then softly kissed it while watching the porch with one eye. She moaned her approval, and by now he was almost praying that someone would come by and interrupt them. Something was going on inside his pants. His prayers were answered when a voice yelled out to Lucy that the store was closing. He looked nervously at his watch and the time indicated 11:00. *Saved by the bell*, he thought. Lucy said that she was available for a rendezvous the following night, but Brian lied and said he couldn't make it because of a camp tennis tournament under the lights. They didn't even have outdoor lights, but that didn't matter. Anything to avoid what was almost certain to be third base and home plate the next time around! He hadn't even been ready for second base. She gave him her home phone number to call when he was next available. Brian wasn't sure when that would be because he was frightened of that little vixen. She was pretty, sexy, and alluring, but she definitely seemed demanding and interested in an endgame. He was pretty sure what that was, and he had never done it before. Not even close. Brian wasn't even a dilettante in those kinds of things. But he knew he'd better produce if there was a next meeting.

On the way back to camp, Brian was angry at himself. He knew that any of his camp friends would have jumped at the same opportunity that so intimidated him. Maybe intimidated was the wrong word. Perhaps unnerved would be more like it. But the bottom line was that when the chips were down, or her panties in this case, he was afraid to deliver. If he ever told his friends, they would mock him and think that he was the greatest wuss to ever walk the earth. He would be totally humiliated. Here was a voluptuous and very sexy young woman who clearly wanted him, and he sat helplessly in the chair with her hoping for someone to come by and rescue him. Brian felt lower and worse than a wuss, whatever that might be. He was just a kid and hard on himself.

The only person at the camp that he could tell would be Bruce Putnam, a tough bodybuilder, and head counselor. He could disclose the entire Lucy charade to him without fear of ridicule or disparagement. That was because Bruce respected him. The reason was simple. Although much smaller in stature and lacking Putnam's bullish strength, Brian made up for it in his dexterity and quickness. He was very difficult to pin despite his larger friend being a good wrestler. Very simply, Putnam, a hulking and physically strong eighteen-year-old, had a difficult time pinning down a skinny fourteen-year-old. Brian served as his sparring partner, and the two would be seen very late almost every afternoon wrestling over bunkbeds and tables in practically every cabin in the camp. While his younger foe lacked his strength, he was so nimble and adroitly slippery, that Bruce had to work very hard in order to pin Brian. Consequently, they were good friends. Deep down, Putnam was a nice guy, but he appeared surly and in ill humor. No one messed with Bruce Putnam. And no one, by inference, fooled with his friend, Brian Hart, either.

It was the very next day after Brian's first date with Lucy that he asked Bruce to talk with him after lunch.

"What do I do, Bruce?" he asked. "She seemed to want to have sex with me."

"Here's what I suggest," his muscular friend replied. "Send me in your place!" They both convulsed in laughter.

"Seriously," Bruce continued, "exactly what is the problem?"

He hated to admit to his sparring partner that he had no clue what to do. "I just don't want to make a fool of myself."

"You won't. It sounds from what you've told me about her that she will bring a condom for you and that she will lead you through the process. Just follow her," he urged. "She will lead you to the promised land!"

Even Brian had to laugh at that remark, and he appreciated the advice. He would roll with the punches, so to speak, just as Bruce suggested. With his friend's encouragement over the next few afternoons at their wrestling sessions, the girl-shy kid from Buffalo felt his confidence level rise. The ball would be in her court. He called Lucy the next afternoon and made a date for as soon as he could get to the store the following night. Brian had explained to her that he couldn't leave the camp until the kids under his watch were asleep. Sometimes that was 8:30, other times it was as late as 9:00 or even 9:15. That important night it was 8:30, which he interpreted as a good omen for what would follow. He was at the dock by 8:35 and across the lake by 8:50. Somewhat nervous, but eager to see Lucy, he semi-jogged the remaining almost four miles left in the eventful trip. Breathing hard, he clamored up the steps where she was waiting. The big clock by the front door of the general store indicated that it was 9:40. The first thing she did in greeting him was to deliver a French kiss.

"Did you bring a condom?" she whispered in his ear.

"No, I, ah, assumed that you would have it," he answered.

"Well, I don't," she said, visibly annoyed. They sat together and kissed a few times but that was it. She didn't offer her bosom, nor did he make any such overture. He wasn't sure if her coolness toward him had anything to do with the three young men who had just entered the store, but the feeling was palpable. They sat together there for about ten minutes and then, without warning, she popped out of the rocker and disappeared inside the door. When she returned five minutes later, he was gone.

They never saw each other again.

The walk back to camp was long and tedious. While he was oblivious to the animal sounds and cries on his way to meet Lucy, he was aware of every single one on his joyless return trip.

He was in bed before midnight, a little perplexed and a tad embarrassed. He knew that he had learned a lesson. What it was, he really didn't know. But there must have been one. At least subliminally! The potential Lucy romance now shelved, Brian concentrated on enjoying the camp life and carrying out his responsibilities as a junior counselor. And he continued in his effort to avoid being pinned by Bruce Putnam. That was the extent of his experience in the world of romance, other than with Joanne, until he got to college. The one with Lucy never really got off the ground, while the relationship with Joanne was such that he would always fondly remember her.

CHAPTER 3

In college, Brian had the occasional blind date but never even came close to finding someone he really cared about. Rarely does the imperfect man win the love of a perfect woman. After he graduated from Cornell Law School, he didn't have the time to go looking for a future Mrs. Hart. He was too busy studying, learning the process, finding a job, and then litigating, to date very much. The perfect one for him was probably Joanne, and he let her get away. Or maybe she let him get away. The letters just stopped. Perhaps he was always comparing his future dates to Joanne, and they were always found wanting. Maybe that was his problem, and he never really got over it. Whatever it was, Brian had the benefit of far too few female relationships when he met Margaret Harrington.

It was the summer of 1989, when he was thirty-five and she was thirty-four. A couple named Sam and Nancy Morton knew both of them and suggested a dinner and a movie together where they all lived. The Mortons lived down the street from Phil and Margaret Harrington before the divorce, when Phil moved to Philadelphia. Brian's first thought upon seeing Margaret at the restaurant was that she looked like Joanne but had dark hair. He was immediately drawn to her innate shyness and genteel bearing. She had gone to the University of Pennsylvania and worked for a Providence public relations firm. The four sat down together in a booth and the Mortons exchanged knowing glances and smiles which indicated that they might be successful matchmakers. Margaret didn't say much, which left the door open for Brian to lead the conversation between the two. He found out that she had two children, Carol and Barry, who were nine and seven, respectively. To some men, the children might have been a turn-off, but not to him. Margaret's eerie resemblance to Joanne was intriguing, to say the least. Both had full lips, a pert nose, and an engaging smile. Joanne's hair was shorter and curly blonde versus Margaret's long black and straight hair. The two shared generous shaped eyebrows over high cheekbones and almost the same flashing blue eyes. They could almost pass as sisters, although Joanne's head was a little more oval shaped than Margaret, and her ears were smaller. Both had soft, gentle voices that they hardly ever raised.

Brian and Margaret went out with the Mortons one more time and then solo a few times. When she felt confident about him and his interest in her, she was eager to run him by her kids. Their approval of Brian would be a must if the two were to make it as a couple. But he had his own deal-breaker. She was a smoker, and she would have to stop the habit for him to continue their relationship. Kissing her was not the pleasure he envisioned because of her tobacco breath. His Joanne never smoked; it would not even have occurred to her.

Brian auditioned before Carol and Barry at a county fair followed by dinner one sticky Rhode Island afternoon in late August. They went on the rides together and enjoyed the clowns. At nine and seven, they were still into that kind of thing. At dinner, Brian excused himself, ostensibly to go to the restroom, but the real reason was to allow the three of them time to talk about him. He apparently passed muster, and therefore his only potential obstacle for her was no longer relevant. Not so for Brian, however. The smoking issue loomed large for him, and it was an issue not so eas-ily abandoned.

He would bring it up at their next meal together. It wasn't that he was obsessive about the subject, but the habit was undesirable to him. He hated to be around smoke. It burned his eyes and he detested the smell. Margaret was a two-pack a day smoker, and as almost anyone knows, it was not an easy habit to break. On their third date together, he tried to put it as firmly but as politely as he could.

"I don't know how important smoking is to you," he implored, "but I just don't enjoy being around cigarettes or the smoke. You have every right to smoke, of course, but if we have a future together, it will have to be without cigarettes." It was probably the first time in his thirty-five years that he had ever stood up to a woman. Surprisingly, she took his ultimatum quite well and said that she intended to stop the habit. And, to her great credit, she actually did. They still had a number of other obstacles to overcome. Both shared good educations, he at Cornell and she at the University of Pennsylvania. But that is where the comparisons and common interests ceased. He was a Republican of conservative bent and she a Democrat of liberal persuasion. Brian loved sports; athletic activ-ity was not her bag. In fact, she detested his favorite sport of all, hockey, because the violence appalled her. He was not a big fan of opera or the ballet, but she loved them both. The issue of women's rights was something they both agreed on, but he felt that later on in their marriage she had become too much of a zealot.

Perhaps her biggest assets were her children. Early on in his relationship with Margaret, he developed a deep fondness for Carol and Barry. Not close to his own father, he relished the chance to have another opportunity but as a parent this time. She was delighted by Brian's obvious affection for her children as well as theirs for him.

Marriage probably seemed right for them, at least according to their friends. It became inevitable as each drifted into the other's web. A friend of theirs, who didn't have a clue what he was talking about, once falsely observed that *theirs was a match made in heaven.* To one with keen insight, nothing could be further from the truth.

They married in the spring of 1990 with the usual hopes for a long and fruitful union, but the cracks began to show when Carol went off to Williams College in the fall of 1998. Brian actually missed her more than her mother did. By this time Barry was a junior in high school. The two guys did a lot together, sometimes driving up to Boston for a Red Sox game or hanging out at the gym or playing tennis. Margaret became more involved in community activities and started a book club.

CHAPTER 4

Brian took pride in his physical condition. He still had that chiseled face, those piercing and intense blue eyes, and the body of an athlete. His short brown hair was just starting to go slightly grey at the temples. While he sustained a number of lacerations and some deep cuts in his face over the span of his hockey career, only two scars were actually visible to the human eye. One of them ran directly between his eyes at the top of the bridge of his nose. The other was just under his chin. A recipient of over 100 stitches received on his face, the result years later wasn't that noticeable. No woman would mistake him for being handsome, but he wore average-looking pretty well. He viewed football and hockey as give and take sports, but definitely preferred the give part. His nose was pronounced and his square jaw housed a fairly straight set of pearly whites, thanks mainly to an orthodontist familiar with sports injuries like broken teeth. From ten feet away, he looked like every other forty-four-year-old man. Up very close, however, it was apparent that his face had blocked a number of objects over the years.

He always looked back on his college years with a great deal of fondness. There were so many wonderful experiences on the hockey rink and football field for him, and he still kept in touch with some of his teammates. If in need of extra cash, Brian waited tables at his fraternity and did some maintenance work, which included repairing windows. He became an entrepreneur during his sophomore year when he discovered a spray can shoeshine product. It cost him only about one dollar per can, and he could clean at least twenty pairs of shoes. All he had to do was spray the fluid on each shoe, and it would gleam like a military shine. Everyone in his fraternity became a customer for one dollar a pair, and soon the word spread to others as well. He was clearing close to $100 a week until a major problem arose. It seemed that the substance used in the spray, after two or three applications, would dry and crack the leather. The resulting disfigurements sometimes cut all the way through the leather, leaving unsightly holes. Needless to say, his business closed after about a month, leaving him about $400 richer but with some very angry customers.

Brian Hart was a complicated man. He had a rather unhappy youth which, by some miracle, didn't seem to scar him—at least to the outside world. His older sister, Linda, was a lovely person and close to his heart. Both their mother and father smoked and imbibed more than their share of alcohol. Unfortunately for the marriage, both got nasty after they consumed too much of the demon liquid. It's been said by many observers that a marriage of people who drink too much on a regular basis can still survive, provided that one of them got silly rather than nasty. Two nasties aren't going to make it, but one silly and one nasty actually have a chance.

Brian saw firsthand what alcohol could do to a relationship, and it was never good. The fighting, bickering, and arguments went on increasingly and, as a young boy, he couldn't get away from it. Several times, his parents' quarrels got so heated that he was afraid that something bad would happen. He didn't know or want to think about what that might be, but it scared him. It wasn't as if he could just leave, especially when he was only eight or ten or even twelve.

His mother and father were good people; they just drank too much. When sober, which was most of the time for her, she was supportive of him and encouraging. His father, undoubtedly an unhappy man, was a good provider for his family and a very hard worker. But when he came home from work in the early evening, the cocktail hour began. And it wouldn't last for just an hour. At dinner every night (and back then, families actually ate their meals together), his father always smoked a few cigarettes. Young Brian wanted so much to say to him: "Dad, would you mind not smoking, because I'm choking here and it's killing my appetite?" He knew that if he dared to say something like that, he probably would not have made it through the night. Respect for your elders was paramount to his father, and such disrespect would have been dealt with harshly. Once when Brian was fourteen, he felt it necessary to physically stand up between the two whose squabble was escalating out of control. His mother appreciated the gesture; his father clearly did not. No blows were struck, but the incident did not help endear Brian to him.

Sadly, he could never remember, not even a single time, when he and his dad had a man-to-man talk about anything. Just about every father and son had a few talks about the birds and the bees, or growing up and becoming a man. Didn't they? But not Brian and his father. Even when he went off to college, there was no such conversation. He acknowledged and rationalized that things were tougher, grimmer, harder, stricter, and more solemn and austere in those days. Men worked longer and felt acute pressures to provide for their families. Women, before many entered the work force, felt the brunt too, not having the benefit of microwave ovens, modern washing machines and dryers, and other conveniences. Men and women in that era were probably more the product of their own upbringing and early environments than were their children.

Brian knew that his father had a very difficult childhood of his own, and knowledge of that helped to explain the old man's diffidence, irascibility, and inability to bond with his son. In fact, his father's childhood must have left him with a terrible void and profound sadness. His dad's mother and father had been divorced when he was only six, and he and his sister had been shipped off to Wisconsin to be brought up by their grandparents. Brian met his grandmother just two times, and she was the coldest person he had ever met. She was dressed in a dark navy or black dress both times and she looked like the grim reaper dressed in a shroud. Aunt Liz seemed to have handled her childhood quite well compared to her brother. She was lovely, and she was a talented fisherman, horseback rider, and magazine writer. It was Brian's Aunt Liz who took him to his first major league baseball games in Philadelphia, and she appeared sincerely interested in him.

In a moment of candor, Brian's father once confided to him that he had been promised a trophy if he had earned straight A's through each of his four high school years. No one apparently had ever accomplished that feat. He actually achieved that honor, but the school reneged on its promise to him, leaving him a bitter and disillusioned young man. The incident helped Brian to better under-stand his father's distrust of the system and people in general. Unfortunately, it didn't serve to bring them together. But the real pain came later.

While visiting his father in Florida, just after Brian had gotten married, he noticed during a walk that people would call the older man by name, but their friendliness didn't elicit any response. It was clear that the old man needed a hearing aid. Miraculously, Brian talked his father into an appointment with an ENT physician and, amazingly, it was scheduled for the very next day. The ear, nose and throat doctor confirmed his problem and they talked about getting the hearing devices on the way back to his father's apartment. Brian expressed his willingness to extend his stay and complete the task, but his father suddenly got agitated and angry. The subject was abandoned. After packing his clothes the following day for the return trip home, Brian again offered to lengthen his visit so that the hearing aid issue could be laid to rest. Sure enough, the old man's rancor rose anew, and the discussion was over. The next night, while at home, the dutiful son called and asked his father whether he had gotten the hearing devices yet.

"You miserable sonofabitch," were his first words and the softest and mildest ones. The rest was a diatribe consisting of every swear word Brian had ever heard plus some new ones. The bottom line was that he should stay out of his father's business, period! And then, to add to the indignity, the old man hung up on him.

Just five hours later, at 3:00 the next morning, Brian received a phone call from Florida. His father had died in a fire that he probably had accidentally started with a burning cigarette. Brian knew from talking with him earlier that he was intoxicated at the time. Later that day, Brian was ushered into the morgue to identify the body. There his father lay with a tag around his left big toe. The respectful son identified him and silently thanked his Lord that his father's irrational outburst – the last conversation ever between the two – had been directed at him and not his sister Linda. She would have been psychologically destroyed by his invective. Perhaps not so strangely, he didn't shed a tear at the small funeral he and Linda had arranged for their father – although she did. Sadly, she also passed away a few years later.

The entire incident probably left a mark on Brian, but he didn't think so. This was the man who married Margaret Harrington, and a man who few people really understood. He had many nice friends, who despite their own problems, were never desperate enough to think about the actual act of disappearing. But some were definitely in the throes of a midlife crisis, whatever that was.

Tom Wood had grown tired of his stockbroker job and let Brian know at one time that his actual preference would be to move to Maine by himself and become a writer. The problem for Tom was two high school kids, whom he loved, and who were looking forward to going to college. He knew that successful writers don't just pop out of nowhere; they must have talent and then be discovered. That scenario wasn't likely, and just like the numerous, aspiring young actors and actresses he envisioned were waiting tables in New York City restaurants. Any one of them might win an Oscar someday, but first they had to get the opportunity. That meant actually getting a part! What were their chances? Almost zero, and about the same as they were for Tom Wood to become an acclaimed novelist.

Bill Depew was another of Brian's friends with dreams. He was a financial consultant, a good one at that, but working for his father-in-law. He never knew deep inside how successful he might have been out on his own.

And what about Don Smith? Here he was, at the tender age of forty-four, worrying about dying. He had one child before he was twenty-two. He had read an obscure study from some Scandinavian country indicating that a man who had fathered a child before reaching that age, had a 26 percent chance to die between the ages of forty-five and fifty-four as opposed to men who waited until they were at least twenty-five. No one else had ever seen that study or even knew if it was an accurate one, but poor Don stewed over it and worried. Another study he cited suggested that shorter and lighter men lived longer lives than their taller and heavier counter- parts. At 6 feet 3 inches tall and weighing 225 pounds, Don had two studies to worry about. Brian was a sympathetic friend to all, but he considered their worries to be foolish. He would be damned if he was going to give such concerns any credence. As long as he got to the gym, ate properly and did not abuse his body with too much booze, Brian was comfortable with rolling the dice.

But he did have a salient problem, and her name was Margaret. Despite the obvious difficulty and her seeming disregard and indif- ference toward him, he was not going to emulate Harold Stapleton and chase after women. As far as Brian knew, Kathy was a loving and caring wife. But that hardly mattered to Harold. Balding and the possessor of a considerable paunch, which was described as a Milwaukee tumor by his friends, he must have felt that he had something to prove. He needed to know that members of the oppo- site sex found him attractive, regardless of how Kathy felt. So, he cheated on her whenever and wherever he found the opportunity. Brian didn't have that problem, because he both recognized and accepted that women were not that much "into him." Consequently, there was no need to prove himself. He did look upon Harold with disdain because of what he had done to his loyal spouse.

The Hart story was different, much different. Margaret seemed to treat Brian as a necessary imposition. That's not exactly a tonic for one's ego. He had actually saved her life, or at least would help to prolong it. Perhaps she resented him issuing that "no smoking" ultimatum. That was a real possibility. If it wasn't that, what was it? He was sure that she had fallen out of love with him, and that mani- fested itself in so many different ways. She didn't value his opinion anymore, it was always so easy for her to point out his faults to others, and clearly it didn't matter to her whether they spent any time together. In fact, she sought out every opportunity to occupy herself in other endeavors so that they didn't. The two stopped going to dinner with their couple friends because it became painful for him to watch others respect each other while the Harts bickered throughout the meal.

Maybe Margaret Harrington Hart was just as complicated as Brian. But this is where they found themselves in early September 2000 when Brian was forty-six and Margaret forty-five.

As for their children, Carol was a junior now at Williams and Barry had entered his freshman year at Lehigh. She was leaning towards a career in real estate while he, like so many of his first-year male peers, hadn't given much thought to it yet.

CHAPTER 5

Brian came home from work one Wednesday afternoon and went to the kitchen in search of a cold drink. Margaret came in and told him very matter-of-factly that she would be starting law school and would be attending Tuesday, Wednesday, and Thursday nights each week. It wasn't that he needed to sign off on such a salient event in her life, but he thought that it might have been nice if she had asked for his input. He recognized her absolute right to do such a thing, but she could have asked for his opinion – even if it wouldn't have mattered to her. She would be driving up to class three nights each week with three of her friends. That was it. It was that simple. Of course, he would have had no problem with such a plan, but it might have been fitting for the couple to at least sit down and discuss it.

"Sounds like a plan," he responded. "Good for you to go for it."

Perhaps hoping to elicit a different and negative response from him, she looked disappointed. Maybe it was her way of telling him that their marriage was over. He wasn't sure, but that's exactly what it seemed like to him. It appeared to Brian as if she had thrown down the gauntlet, but he didn't let on that he had gotten the full extent of her message. With that said, Margaret disappeared upstairs.

I need to get out of this marriage, he thought, *but how?* He didn't love her anymore and wasn't sure that he ever had. But he did have great affection for Carol and Barry, and a divorce would probably shake them to the core. He often felt that he had a closer connection with them than they ever did with their own mother. Her needs seemed to always come first. Theirs were next, and then his were farther down the line – much farther.

Brian would never forget Laura, nor how he first met her. It was exciting and exhilarating, and he seemed to come alive again when in her presence. Maybe Harold had been right all along. It was like his own resurrection. He had not seen her in several months and resigned himself to the strong likelihood that he never would again. Their affair lasted only ten months, but it was a life-altering experience for him. Laura would never understand that she was the catalyst that moved him to seek a new life.

It had been only a week after Margaret had announced her intention to attend law school when Brian stepped into the elevator in his office building. He was returning from lunch to his seventh-floor office on a dismal and otherwise unmemorable afternoon. The elevator door was closing when suddenly a hand reached in and the sensor stopped it. In walked a tall, willowy, and lovely dark-haired woman wearing a black-and-white striped dress. She moved in next to him and smiled. He hoped that she didn't notice that his jaw dropped a bit. Probably about 5 feet 8 inches tall, svelte, and with flashing green eyes, she exchanged looks with him as she exited the elevator on the third floor. If it was possible to be smitten with someone after barely a glimpse, this was it. As she stepped out, he couldn't help noticing her shapely legs. He wondered if she was there visiting someone or whether she worked in the building. If it was the latter, she had to be relatively new because there was no way she would have gone unnoticed by him.

Brian would now be on alert for her until he had the opportunity to actually meet her. It was 2:15 p.m. and he visited the men's room on the third floor at that same time for the next few days. Unsuccessful in that gambit, he hung round the ground floor lobby each day before work the following week. Just when he was convinced that he would never see her again, she appeared one morning while he was talking with Tony, the newsstand proprietor. It had been eight days since his first sighting of her and he had almost given up. Flustered for a moment, he was unsure of what to do. He raced to the elevator and just made it on as the door was closing. He took a position across from her. This time, she was wearing a green dress that matched her eyes. If she recognized him from their past very brief encounter, she didn't let on. When the mystery woman exited the elevator on the third floor, he wanted to follow her off but he had no clue what he would do or say. Instead, he stood there like a deer frozen in the headlights. At the seventh floor, he headed for his office, a bit disillusioned.

Over the weekend, Brian had a lot of time to think about this elusive woman. By this time, Margaret had been in law school for a week and decided to do most of her studying on her two nights off with a classmate at the town's library. Carol and Barry were away at college and he was left alone with his thoughts. He felt like kicking himself for not noticing whether she wore a wedding ring. Harold Stapleton would have noticed. In fact, that was probably one of the first things he would check. *What was her name? What did she do for a living and who did she work for? Where did she live? Where was she from?* These were his repetitious thoughts both Saturday and Sunday. They were driving him crazy, and he resolved to meet her the following week by hook or by crook. Monday and Tuesday came and went with nary a sign of her. But, lo and behold, just as he was heading back to his office on Wednesday afternoon after lunch with a client, there she was entering the lobby elevator. The woman who had captivated him in her zebra dress that first day was now wearing a canary yellow fitted dress that revealed a very ample figure. The door closed before he could get there, but she saw him and smiled. That, in and of itself, was a victory!

It wasn't until Thursday afternoon the following week that Brian saw her again. Not that he didn't try. He did go to the Men's room down on the third floor on several mornings, but there was no sign of her in the hallway. Failing in that effort, he took to spending nearly twenty minutes of his lunch hours at the newsstand in the lobby with one eye on the newspaper and the other carefully monitoring each elevator run. Still no success. His fortunes soon turned for the better. His stockbroker friend, Tom Wood, and he grabbed a quick lunch that day at the tower restaurant in their office building. While he was sipping an iced tea and chatting with Tom, sure enough, she appeared. A man Brian estimated to be about his age accompanied her, and they sat about four tables away. Brian looked at her and she looked back. Expressionless when he first saw her, he now managed a smile. After lunch, as the two men got up from their table and walked to the restaurant's exit, Brian stopped briefly and turned to glance at her once again. They merely exchanged smiles, but he felt that he had gained some important ground. Tom Wood hadn't a clue as to what had just transpired.

Over the weekend, Brian had much time to himself but, then again, it had become the routine. Margaret was a member of the local school board and needed to prepare for an important meeting the following Monday night. It seemed that she was always busy involved in something. He really didn't begrudge her community involvement—nor should he, he reminded himself. It bothered him more since the kids had gone away to college. Heck, he was a public-minded citizen too. He had done his part coaching little league, working with the Cub Scouts, and he presently served on the Cancer Society's Board of Directors. *Paying his dues* was the way he put it. But, in his mind, Margaret appeared to make a bloody career out of serving others. Well, everyone but himself, he lamented. He knew that he shouldn't resent her efforts to fulfill herself, but part of him couldn't help it, and he did. There were too many nights that Brian spent home alone. He liked to read, but not every night. This was now part and parcel of her persona. It seemed that the less time she spent with Brian, the better.

Resentful at being left alone so frequently and with seeming impunity, it started to filter into his psyche and gnawed at him despite his efforts to try and contain it. It wasn't that he would actively seek companionship, because that would run afoul of his marriage vows, but he realized that Margaret wouldn't even care if he did. And now, the coup de grâce – law school. He struggled within himself. Brian felt pangs of guilt whenever he felt sorry for himself for what he perceived as neglect, but didn't he deserve real companionship? *Why couldn't she have gone to law school after college like most normal people? I can't begrudge her the opportunity to pursue a goal,* he thought, *but why can't she cut back on other things so that we could still spend some time together?*

He was vulnerable, and he knew it. With very little else on his mind, his thoughts wandered to the banal matter of determining the true identity of his mystery woman. For some reason, he hoped that her name wasn't Debbie, because that moniker just sounded so young. He was angry at himself for engaging in such trivial deliberations.

For distraction, he walked over to the large pond behind his house in Barrington and stepped into his canoe for a short paddle out to Lookout Point where the trout usually assembled that time of year. It was an unusually sticky afternoon, hot and humid, and the sun beat down mercilessly on those exposed to its rays. Normally there was a cool breeze circulating around that pond, but not on that day. The water was rather deep, and one of the residents had actually drowned there some twenty years before. It took a full week before the body was recovered. Children were warned to never go out in a canoe or rowboat by themselves.

As Brian paddled out near his destination, a soft, gentle breeze sent out tiny ripples, which forced the inevitable water bugs drawn to the fishing hole to alter their course accordingly. He took off his shirt and waved to neighbor Jim Dakins, who was passing by on his Sunfish. For a moment he envied Jim, whose wife, Doris, was almost always at home waiting for his arrival. She wasn't that vivacious or attractive, but she was home. No frozen spaghetti dinners for Jim Dakins. Like Margaret, laughter didn't come easy to her, and both women practically had no sense of humor. To the contrary, both Jim and Brian did, which helped to foster their friendship. Brian laughed out loud at the thought of Jim recently telling a joke, which predicably left their wives with deadpan expressions. It was one of the funniest jokes he had ever heard. The four were at a seafood restaurant one night waiting for their drinks to be served. Jim said that he had heard a great joke that day in the office.

"Three thieves went into a bank," he began, "armed to the hilt with an arsenal of weapons including AK-47s, but without masks. They ordered everyone in the bank to lie down, and above all, that no one should get even a glimpse of their faces. Almost everyone did as they were told, but the teller stole a quick glance while giving one of the them the money. He was immediately shot dead. Just as the thieves were walking to the exit, one of the security guards caught a look of the three and he, too, was summarily executed." Jim had already started to laugh as he told the rest of the story. "So, with their hands on the door to leave the bank, one of them noticed a little old Italian man waving his hand while cowering on the floor next to his wife in the back of the room. Greatly annoyed, one of the robbers went over to him and said:

" 'What the hell do you want, old man?'"

" 'Well, I thinka mya wife, she gotta a glimpse!'"

Jim and Brian practically doubled over in raucous laughter, but Doris and Margaret didn't think it was even amusing. So much for a sense of humor! Back then, ethnic humor was okay as long as it was not mean-spirited. It became passé as the years went by.

While caught up in thought, he barely noticed the slight tug on his line. The trout appeared to be no bigger than the palm of his hand, and he removed the hook and watched the little fella swim away, relishing his newly found freedom. He always released anything he caught.

The weekend was uneventful, but then again, all of them were. If Margaret were home, she would either be reading a best-seller or prepping for some presentation she would be making. The thought of law school could only exacerbate the already tenuous situation at home. He didn't mind so much making his own dinners, despite his ineptitude in the kitchen, but it didn't seem to be what he signed up for when he got married. One didn't get married in order to be alone. Whenever he started to feel the resentment building, his sense of guilt would soon kick in and would nullify it. Such thinking was chauvinistic. He recognized that it wasn't all about him, and that she deserved to do things that made her happy. But why—all of a sudden, it seemed—why now?

Was Brian the stimulus for her sudden interest in law? Did she want to get away from him that badly? Was trudging off to night law school classes more meaningful for her than spending an evening with her husband? Apparently so. The way she had been acting toward him lately made him think that any option would do – just as long as it didn't include him.

Somewhere along this marriage divide was a line and it seemed to him that it was crossed too often. It really wasn't either one of their faults; they had merely drifted apart. The things that first brought them together either didn't matter so much anymore, or perhaps both had moved on in different directions.

Margaret seemed to be content in a rather loveless arrangement; not so much for him. That was the pickle he was in. Brian had talked enough with his friends and even some acquaintances to know he was far from the only man who experienced such frustrations. Far from it. He always laughed to himself when he remembered his friend, Jack Ford, being asked if he and Molly would have any more kids. Jack's response, "No, you have to have sex to have kids!" It might not surprise anyone to know that a rather large percentage of marriages had lost their original glow and had dissipated into a boredom of mere convenience and fear of the unknown. Maybe, maybe not. But that's not exactly where he was. More importantly, it was where she was.

CHAPTER 6

Monday morning came on like gangbusters. It was an unusual hot, hazy, sunny early September day with absolutely no breeze. It was the kind of day that everyone dreads, except perhaps for the ducks on the pond behind his house. Rhode Island could be hot sometimes in the early fall, but there was usually at least a balmy breeze to offset the heat. Not on this day.

As he guided his Lincoln Town Car out of his driveway, he was not feeling very good about things. It wasn't that he would miss her at night; it wasn't even that he would be responsible for almost all of his dinners. It was just that Margaret must have thought so little of him. He couldn't believe that she didn't even want his blessing as she embarked on this new career. Had she asked, of course, he would endorse her new venture, but she hadn't even asked.

Automobiles never meant much to Brian. The only reason he had leased a Town Car was that he occasionally took clients to lunch, and it provided for a comfortable ride. If he had been in the trades, worked for himself as a carpenter or electrician, and didn't take people to lunch, he would have opted for a Chevy or Ford. To him, automobiles were merely a mode of transportation – nothing more and nothing less. Never one to "keep up with the Joneses," he thought it ridiculous to have a new car every year or two. That certainly might have been good for the economy, he reasoned, but not for him. "I don't need to make a statement," he would say to his friends and colleagues whenever the subject came up.

He was decked out in his favorite outfit of light beige slacks and a crisp white shirt and a lightweight blue blazer. A bright tie with white, beige, and blue stripes brought the entire outfit together. His shoes were spotless and often the subject of jokes in the office. Manny's, the dry cleaners where Brian did his business, knew that he wanted the sharpest crease possible in his trousers. He didn't even own a short-sleeved dress shirt because he had read somewhere that a well-groomed business look did not include the less formal short sleeves – no matter how hot it was. He once kidded an associate for wearing a navy-blue raincoat, quoting several surveys which indicated that the blue coat conveyed a weaker image compared to the more conventional tan trench coat.

Brian took one last breath of fresh air, warm as it was, before entering the main floor of his office building. His eyes swept through the lobby for the sight of his mystery woman, but to no avail. For some reason, he was particularly anxious to see her this morning. Passing Tony's newsstand, he smelled the unmistakable remnants of the cigar he must have just smoked outside. That acrid and pungent odor permeated his stand. *"Good lord,"* he murmured to no one in particular, *"how the hell can someone smoke a stogie at eight o'clock in the morning?"* Never having been a smoker himself, he had little tolerance for the smell, but he reserved his greatest criticism for cigar smoke. He was guilty of being more than just casually opinionated on the subject. He steadfastly, but silently believed that everyone who smoked a stogie had an ego problem. His reasoning was rather simple and shallow: they really craved attention and derived a feeling of power from contaminating everyone's air with that foul weed! Cigar smokers would undoubtedly disagree with that assessment. He was very careful with whom he shared that theory, however, because some of his good friends enjoyed their Coronas. Brian held his breath while he purchased the morning paper from Tony and then sauntered over to the bank of elevators. He looked around carefully one last time, his eyes in full panoramic mode. There was no trace of her. He was disappointed, yet he had a feeling the time would come for their meeting in the not-too-distant future. It just hadn't arrived yet.

The day slowly passed. Fellow lawyer, Harold Stapleton broke up an otherwise monotonous Monday morning for Brian by requesting a discussion over lunch about a rather perplexing problem he was having with a client. Harold wanted to go to Homer's, a place best known for its big-breasted waitresses.

"You won't believe the cleavage on these women," Harold said lasciviously, trying to persuade him to go. But Brian opted for the restaurant upstairs in the Tower. "Geez," Harold whined, "you would love Homer's!"

"Keep it in your pants, Harold," Brian snickered. He didn't reveal the real reason for wanting to go to the Tower. They proceeded to the restaurant, and a casual glance was indeed rewarded with a sighting of his mystery woman lunching with a female friend. Brian brushed off an attempt by the maître d' to seat them in a quiet corner and instead steered the confused host to a table nearer the object of his obsession. *This time*, he admonished himself, *she will not elude me.* She was too absorbed in conversation to notice as he sat down with Harold. An overwhelming sense of disappointment gripped him. It wasn't long, however, before those blazing green eyes found his, and the happy look on her face left no doubt as to her feelings. He flashed her a warm smile and turned back to Harold, pretending that she was just an innocent acquaintance. Lecher that he was, Harold was cognizant of the brief exchange and winked at his dining partner saying, "Hey, not bad old boy, not bad at all. Too bad she's married." That last word hit him like a thunderbolt. It felt like a cold dagger thrust right into his gut. Brian wondered how Harold would even know that, but then he realized that men like him instinctively knew those kinds of things. Brian's eyes darted immediately to her table and, sure enough, she appeared to be wearing a wedding ring. Now feigning disinterest, he murmured that she was a friend of a friend. "Whatever," was Harold's response, maintaining the same smug look on his face.

As they ate lunch together and discussed Harold's legal problem, and the reason for their lunch date, Brian couldn't help thinking about how he really disliked Harold as a man. He remembered all those tacky times when he came on to waitresses, always calling them "honey" or "sweetie," and making lewd suggestions to anyone he was with. During their business discussion he glanced over to mystery woman's table occasionally just to assure himself that the electricity wasn't all coming from him. It wasn't. She never failed to return his look with one of her own, complete with a warm smile. He remembered reading a magazine article which talked about body language and how a woman primping her hair, licking her lips, or holding a gaze just a tad too long were all signs of sexual interest. She did all those things, and clearly, Brian was smitten. At that moment, her companion got up accompanied by a slight goodbye wave, a sign that she was vacating the table and that lunch was over for her. Since the two men had just finished, Brian told Harold that he just wanted to say hello to the friend of a friend he had mentioned earlier. Of course, Harold winked approvingly.

"It's not like that, you dirty old man," he responded with an aggravated smile. Brian rose from his table, and attempting to look debonair, meandered over to her table. He felt more than a twinge of guilt about being a married man going over to a supposedly married woman's table – especially someone he didn't know. But he didn't feel it enough to prevent him from completing the journey. *For God's sake,* he thought to himself, *what am I going to say?*

"Hi," he greeted her with a smile, "mind if I join you for a moment?" She nodded her enthusiastic approval. Brian threw back his shoulders, sucked in his stomach, and sat down.

"I've seen you so many times, that I'm afraid you've become a mystery woman to me." *Say your name, you damn fool,* he admonished himself. She tossed her head back with a gentle giggle while he blurted out, "I'm Brian Hart."

"Delighted to finally meet you, Brian," she put him at ease, "I'm Laura Parker."

"I must confess that I wanted to meet you ever since I first saw you on the elevator a while back." He looked at her closely for a reaction.

"I remember that day," she smiled, "and I wondered who was that handsome man!" That was all he needed to hear. Blushing slightly, he leaned forward and in almost a whisper asked her to join him for a drink after work.

"I'm so sorry Brian, but I have an appointment then." Crushed, crestfallen, embarrassed, and humiliated all at one time, his face flushed and he felt like a fool. She interrupted the awkward silence saying, "but I'd love to on Thursday." Saved by this reprieve, he beamed his relief. They agreed to meet at 5:00 p.m. on Thursday in the Tower lounge. With that exchange, he rose from his seat at her table, smiled and wished her a nice day. He wondered if Laura knew that he was married, inasmuch as he didn't wear a wedding ring. *Did she notice or even care?* he asked himself.

Margaret had wanted him to wear a wedding band when they

first got married, but he was adamant in his refusal. He tried to assuage her by pointing out that he had never worn a ring of any kind before, and that he felt uncomfortable wearing any jewelry – except for his leather-banded watch. Brian knew that some men purposely avoided having a wedding band because they wanted to appear available. Howard Stapleton was the perfect example of that! But Brian had also read an article or two about women feeling more comfortable when seeing visual evidence that a man was married. But not wearing a ring had nothing to do with such mind games for him. He flat out did not like to wear a ring – any ring. At first, Margaret had been hurt by his refusal to honor her request, but she came to understand his reasoning and eventually got over it.

On his drive home, Brian felt a deep sense of guilt but was also energized by his foray into uncharted waters. He knew it was wrong and against his principles. But he rationalized all he could in order to justify it. *What have I done?* he asked himself one last time as he pulled into his driveway. Not surprisingly, he and Margaret quarreled that night. It was another one of those "you're on your own" dinners, and he fixed a salad to go along with some chicken and rice soup. He wasn't even sure why they had argued, inasmuch as the altercations appeared to be more frequent in the past few months, but this one might have been on him. Perhaps it was the guilt quietly consuming him, he wasn't sure, but clearly, he would rather be somewhere else. Maybe it was because his step-kids, nineteen-year-old Barry, and twenty-one-year-old Carol, hadn't called home from college in several weeks. He missed their last calls when he was away on business. Their biological father had died in an auto accident when they were just five and seven years old, and Brian and Margaret had married two years later after a brief courtship. He had become close to Barry, soon to be a sophomore at Lehigh, and relatively close to Carol, almost a senior at Williams. He missed them.

Both Brian and Margaret were quite cognizant of the "empty nest syndrome," that well-recognized and pervasive feeling of loneliness that affects parents when their child goes away to college. Most couples endure such a phenomenon and some relationships grow even stronger because of it. But not theirs. Margaret dealt with their absence, if in fact she was lonely, by filling her calendar with endless community commitments. It seemed to work very well for her, but Brian was less fortunate. He really missed the kids despite not being their biological father, and there was no filling the void. All couples with college-bound children must deal with the experience; single mothers or dads even more so. It often ends up being a real test of exactly how deep their relationship extends. Unfortunately, at least for him, that missing part exceeded his connection to his wife. Perhaps if she stayed home occasionally, he mused, their marriage might endure despite the challenges. But she chose another avenue, to always be busy, and that seemed to work for her. And she continued to ignore him. It didn't work for them, however, and it didn't work for him – but it clearly worked for Margaret. And yet, Brian couldn't begrudge her that. As annoyed as he would be by her frequent absences and her indifference toward him, he knew that this might have been her way of coping. He was simply too good a guy to openly resent her behavior, at least initially. But a quiet discontentment, despite his effort to contain it, was very much at work.

Brian could not control his building resentment and the sense that no one needed him anymore. It surely hadn't always been that way. Barry and Carol were good kids with good values, but they were no longer dependent on their stepdad. Fortunately, he thought, they grew up before the advent of rewarding kids for simply participating. Trophies for everyone soon became the ideology, so that no child would be disappointed. Some of their older couple friends had grandchildren who experienced that new ethos of the time. Margaret thought it appealing and wise, so that everyone could share in that exhilarating sense of success and not the letdown which attached itself to failure. Perhaps it was the athlete in him that passionately resisted this well-meaning but foolish reward system. At least, that's what he thought. He used to argue with Margaret a number of times about it, but to no avail.

"How can kids learn to deal with defeat and failure," he expressed so fervently, "if they get trophies for merely participating? The adult world," he continued, "is full of disappointments. How will they learn to deal with them if they are coddled, spoiled, and pampered throughout their childhood?"

But Margaret wasn't having any of it. "Kids eight or nine years old," she responded, "don't need to have their hearts broken. They can learn all that later on during their lives."

And so it went. Soon, a major division in what he considered to be a rather fundamental issue contributed to the schism in their personal relationship. But then again, they never seemed to agree on anything. He thought it a growing and important problem for the country that children and grandchildren were being raised with a strong sense of entitlement. But she considered him to be antediluvian and way too judgmental in his thinking.

Barry and Carol were just seven and nine years old, respectively, when Brian and Margaret married. The kids were wary of their "new" dad at first, but soon learned to accept and then love him.

Brian suspected early on that Margaret might have married him more out of giving her kids a father than because she loved him. Increasingly, he became more convinced that she had used him in that way. He resented her for it, but he truly cared about both Barry and Carol. Then again, he probably married her for the same essential reason – because she had kids that he didn't.

The rest of the week was slow and uneventful. He spent an inordinate amount of time thinking about Laura. *Is she thinking of me? And what about her marriage? Is it a good one, or just like mine? Just because someone wears a ring on that particular finger doesn't necessarily mean they're married though, right? Maybe this is just a simple and totally friendly dalliance to her. Who knows, perhaps it is to me, too.* The unknown and mysterious nature of it all made it interesting. Lord knows, any intrigue in his life had disappeared years ago.

It was a dreary-looking Thursday morning, yet nothing could dampen Brian's spirit that day – even despite sleeping very little the previous night. He was too transfixed by intermittent feelings of euphoria and the omnipresent sense of guilt to manage even a modicum of sleep. After all, he had never transgressed like this before. This was all so new to him. He never envisioned that he would ever be tempted to break his marriage vows. Perhaps Laura wasn't interested in anything more than being a friend. But then again, he thought, maybe that wouldn't be so bad. He could use one. *Was he starting to get cold feet?*

He felt confident in a dapper-looking blue blazer, crisp white shirt, and sharply creased beige trousers. But his stomach was churning. He feared that his inexperience would result in some inevitable failure. For one brief moment, he even considered asking the resident lecher, Hal Stapleton, for his advice. But that thought was never seriously considered.

The afternoon passed dreadfully slowly. The hour's wait for him between four and the rendezvous time at five was nothing less than interminable with competing rushes of anxiety and excitement. He spent the last fifteen minutes alternately watching the clock, pacing his office floor, and trying to think of clever things to say to her. The more he tried, the greater his frustration. He was gripped by the realization that he would have to rely on being himself. As the clock struck five, Brian bounded out of his seat, looked in the mirror to adjust his tie and check his hair, bid farewell to his secretary, and headed for the elevator. He arrived in the Tower Lounge just a few minutes after five, sat at a table and ordered a Canadian Club and water. There was no sign of her. Ten minutes passed and still no Laura. Just as he was fearing the very worst, she appeared from behind him. He immediately noticed how beautiful she looked, in a Kelly-green velour dress which was the perfect match for those enchanting eyes. Brian rose quickly to greet her and held out her seat at the small table that had a view of downtown Providence.

"You look absolutely radiant," he heard himself say. With an alluring smile, she thanked him and sat back comfortably and confidently in her chair.

"Sorry I was late," she began, "but a client called just as I was leaving my office." The waitress came by, and Laura ordered a glass of the house chardonnay.

Brian learned during their conversation that she was a fellow barrister and had gone to Brown University where she had met her husband, David. They had married right out of college and she went on to Yale Law School while he launched a sales career with a plastics firm. His company had moved to Providence from Baltimore barely a year ago, where Laura secured a position with a small law firm in Brian's building. She was thirty-two and seemed to be full of bountiful energy. Good observer and listener that he was, Brian sensed that she was not very happy. Her zeal to talk took him by surprise. *But maybe she's a bit nervous, just like I am*, he thought. He had to admit, for a man, he was a pretty good listener. His mother had once remarked to him that the words silent and listen had the exact same letters but arranged differently. She also schooled him, "If you are silent, you will be a better listener." He never forgot that advice, and Brian certainly abided by it now as Laura continued to tell him about her family. So, he sat back and listened intently.

Laura's father was a rather prominent attorney in Boston; her mother had died three years before from a rare cancer. She had one sibling, an older brother who was also an attorney and with whom she was very close. She was not as close with her father. Brian got the distinct impression that she became a lawyer in order to please her father, although she didn't exactly put it that way.

"I was often at odds with him and got the idea at a relatively early age that he might have taken more interest in me if I had been born with a penis!" She smiled sheepishly when she noticed he had winced at hearing that word.

"I really admire your candor," he chuckled. At that point, the waitress appeared, and they each ordered a second drink.

"Please forgive me if I'm talking too much," she blurted out. He gently stroked her hand and urged her to continue. Laura went on to describe how she felt she was never able to satisfy her father, whatever her achievements, and his indifference had only driven her on to greater heights.

"I was only one of a few women to make Law Review," she said with a slight frown, "but it didn't appear to matter to him."

"I'm sure it did," he interrupted while briefly squeezing her hand again, "but he just didn't let it show. Fathers back then kept their emotions to themselves. I know my father did."

Laura continued their one-sided conversation by telling him that she and her husband had been seeing a marriage counselor for the past six months. "He had an affair and has a girlfriend," she explained sadly, yet matter-of-factly, "and you can imagine what that has done to our marriage."

"Why didn't you—why don't you—just leave him?"

"I should, and my father and brother have urged me to do just that, but I can't bring myself to go through all of that."

Brian looked her directly in the eyes and asked, "Do you still love him?"

"No, I don't think so, but I guess I'm a procrastinator." She took a sip of her chardonnay and continued her tale again. She had been seeing a psychologist weekly for the past four months and had learned a great deal about herself. Brian squirmed ever so slightly in his seat when he heard that information, as he was not a "believer." His father had ingrained in him at an early age that "strong people solve their own problems." Perhaps sensing his unease, she said that her husband would not join her in those therapy sessions.

"What is it with you macho men that you refuse any outside help?" She suddenly looked at her watch and exclaimed, "Oh my goodness, it's almost seven! And here I am talking about myself the whole time! I'm so embarrassed. Forgive me. There was so much I wanted to ask you." He took her hand in his again and assured her that he had enjoyed their conversation.

"Maybe we can get together again, and I can fill you in."

"I'd like that, I really would," she replied.

"May I call you?" he asked.

"Oh, please do," she responded as she pulled out a business card from her purse. He stood as they said their goodbyes and he sat down to finish his drink. When she was a few steps away from him, she turned back, smiled, and thanked him again for the drinks and conversation.

He was still feeling a little guilty, so he sat for a few moments to gather himself. He liked her, there was no question about it. She was very modest, without any hint of arrogance or elitism. It was easy to feel sorry for her, but in doing so, he also felt sorry for himself. She was gone now, but he was confident that they would see each other again.

CHAPTER 7

The following day, a cooler and more typical mid-September day, he was sorely tempted to call her but decided against it. He didn't want to appear to be too eager. Brian was also troubled by the not-so-minor notion that a married man had no business cavorting with another woman, especially a married woman. A gut feeling told him that any further contact with Laura would result in something inappropriate and should be resisted. But he also really wanted to see her again. The best he could do was to ward off the temptation until the following Tuesday.

Sure enough, Laura Parker's cell phone rang at 1:30 but she didn't answer it. He debated about whether or not to leave a message but after hearing the beep, hastily decided that he would. "Hi Laura, this is Brian." He tried to sound as casual as possible. "It was wonderful meeting you the other night. Please give me a call at 240-2022 when you get the chance. It would be great to see you again. It's about 1:30 on Tuesday."

And so the suspenseful wait began. He was nervous for the next hour, wondering if she would call back. The thought occurred to him that she may have intentionally let his call go into her voice mail. *Maybe she's having second thoughts about me or her situation,* he mused, and it was probably a natural reaction for him to come to that pessimistic conclusion. While outwardly conflicted, he didn't really expect a call back, but not so deep down, he did.

That night as he drove home, he was anxious, irritable, and feeling guilty, and he was smarting for an argument with Margaret. But, of course, she wasn't home. This was a law school night for her and another lonely night at home for him. *All the responsibilities of marriage,* he pondered, *and none of the benefits.* Margaret arrived home after eleven while he was watching the Red Sox game on television. She admonished him for leaving some dirty dishes in the kitchen sink. He responded in kind, grumbling that he had to fix another dinner while his friend and neighbor, Jim Dakins, "didn't have that problem."

"Is that what you want," she snapped, "a wife like Doris? She wouldn't know the difference between a deficit budget and a tuna casserole. She probably thinks," she piled on, "that the Falkland Islands are a new salad dressing!" When vexed, Brian remembered that she could get downright nasty. They argued for several more minutes and then she turned on her heel and went off to bed. He snorted to himself and watched the rest of the game. The Sox lost in extra innings to Cleveland, which made him even more annoyed. Margaret slept in Carol's bed that night, while he resolved before retiring that he would make another attempt the next morning to reach Laura. He wasn't exactly sure when. He also decided, that very night, to stash some money away, and to do it regularly from that point on.

CHAPTER 8

The next morning, Brian trudged down the stairs a bit weary from his restless night. Margaret had already left the house. A quick oatmeal and coffee breakfast and he was out the door himself and en route to his office. He waited until 9:20 and then dialed Laura on her office line. Her secretary explained that she was out of the office and would probably return by 11:00. He debated for a split second about leaving a message, and decided to leave his name and cell phone number. *The ball is in her court now,* he told himself, as he sat back with a cup of coffee and the *Wall Street Journal. I won't call again.* Three calls came into his office over the next hour, but all were from clients. He felt himself getting edgy as the clock moved inexorably toward noon. Suddenly, at five before the hour, his cell phone rang and he reached for it instantaneously. He caught himself before answering it in a weak attempt not to appear too eager. On the third ring, he casually said, "Hello."

"Hi Brian, it's Laura." Her voice seemed full of enthusiasm. "I've been thinking about you, and I'm so glad you called."

"Could we get together tonight for a drink," his voice seemed to implore, "even for a short time?"

"I'm sorry, Brian, but we have to go out tonight." A brief silence ensued while he tried to conceal his obvious disappointment. Perhaps sensing it, she quickly changed course. "Well, maybe just one drink," she chimed in, "but I have to leave by six." Greatly relieved, he said he would meet her upstairs at 5:00. The rest of the day was a total waste for him. He might just as well have taken the afternoon off and played golf.

The bewitching hour of 5:00 finally arrived, and with it, a new bounce to Brian's step. He bounded away from his desk a few minutes before the hour, bid adieu to the office staff, and practically sprinted to the elevator. She was already there waiting for him at the very same table they had occupied the previous Monday night.

"Hi," she greeted him warmly as he approached, "our drinks are on the way!" She was wearing the same zebra-striped dress that she had worn the first time he had ever laid eyes on her.

"That dress," he stammered, "that's the same one you wore on the elevator that day."

"I know," she acknowledged with a slight smile, her face turning a few shades of red. Their pleasantries lasted only a minute because of their eagerness to converse while cognizant of the time constraints. Soon the waitress appeared with a Canadian Club and water for him and a chardonnay for her. They clinked glasses and he toasted, "To friends."

"Brian, this time I want to learn about you." She leaned in to give him her attention.

"Well, it's pretty boring, I'm sorry to say," he began, trying to sound humble. He described his childhood growing up in Buffalo, New York and revealed that both of his parents had died years ago – within three weeks of each other. For a moment, he considered telling her about the grisly way his father had died and the whole sad scenario that immediately preceded it, but something convinced him that this wasn't the appropriate time to share the tale.

"My father was a very tough man, and I never really got close to him. He had played football at Pittsburgh and got me started in sports when I was very young. Ted was his name," he continued, "and he was a sales executive. They lived in Milwaukee and Chicago before moving to Buffalo. My mother, Jane, was a very sweet and gentle woman who gave up college to marry him, and she was mostly at home to take care of me and my sister. Let's see, what else?" he mused. "Well, I don't have any children of my own, but I do have two great step-kids. Carol is twenty-one and will be a senior at Williams, and Barry is nineteen and entering his sophomore year at Lehigh. They really are great kids," he exclaimed, "and I have a close relationship with them."

"OK, enough about me!" Brian raised his hand to signal the waitress to ask for another round of drinks. Laura declined the offer, reminding him that it was already 5:50 and that she had to leave shortly. "Do you play tennis?" he asked. Her face broke into a wide smile, and she nodded. "How about getting together for a game next week?" he blurted out. "Inside or outside – depending on the weather."

"That would be fun," she said, "but it might be difficult to do it at night."

He thought for a moment and then suggested the following Wednesday at 3:00. "Could you do it then?" She quickly checked her calendar and indicated that she could. "Wednesday it is," he declared with renewed vigor. "I'll call you Monday with the details." It was now just before six and she had to leave. As they entered the vacant elevator, he considered giving her a kiss but decided against it. They walked to her car, and again he felt an urge to kiss her but rejected the impulse.

On the drive home, he thought that she might suspect that he was married, especially since he had mentioned his stepkids. He vowed to tell her on Wednesday. He couldn't help thinking how wonderful it would be to hold her in his arms and kiss those magnificent lips. Brian was fairly certain that she liked him. But did she like him enough? Was she as fond of him as he was of her? *Time will tell,* he assured himself.

He maneuvered his Town Car up the driveway and, sure enough, the garage was empty. It was another of Margaret's law school nights and he would dine alone again. Yet, he thought, it would also provide him with ample time to ruminate over the events of the past several weeks.

Everything seemed to be going along reasonably well until the past couple of years. Was it his fault or hers? Can it just happen that people fall out of love with each other? He remembered seeing an article years before about actress Elizabeth Taylor saying something about marriages ideally lasting for only ten years...or something to that effect. Maybe there was some truth to it. But how does one explain how some couples are happy together for sixty or even more years? *Are they the exception, or did they persevere harder than the rest of us to make it work?* As he stood over the kitchen counter to make himself a BLT, he wondered where he and Margaret had gone wrong. Not a man normally given to introspection, this apparently was the moment for it and Laura was the likely catalyst.

Margaret was certainly a good person, he conceded, but so was he. *We hardly knew each other, he thought, so how could we be expected to make a lifetime commitment? Not only that, we are completely different from each other.* Was he rationalizing this major challenge to his fidelity? He had never as much as looked at another woman before, and now he felt himself drawn inexorably into an illicit relationship. The more he thought about Laura, the guiltier he felt. *How does Harold Stapleton do it?* He remembered an absolutely repulsive story that Harold had related to him, and yet the reprobate appeared to have been proud of it. It seemed that Harold had set up a meeting at a bar with a woman he had recently met. According to his miscreant friend, after two drinks and some bar snacks, it became apparent to him that the woman was not interested in having sex. On the pretense of visiting the men's room, he left her sitting at the bar and walked out of the establishment – sticking her with the bill in the sordid process. And he didn't seem to regret any of it. *But,* Brian surmised, *that is par for the course for people like Harold Stapleton.* Although he himself was a stranger to infidelity, he knew more than a few men, besides Harold, who were not. Always critical of them for such behavior, now, given his own situation, he wondered if he had judged them too harshly. Maybe they were good men too, but unhappy circumstances drove them to such illicit behavior. *Who am I to judge anyone, anyway?* he thought.

This rumination lasted throughout his makeshift dinner and almost until Margaret's return at 11:00 p.m. The Red Sox game saved him from thinking too much, and this time they were winning. When she returned, she didn't go overboard in her response to his greeting, merely saying "Hi. I'm tired and going to bed." He watched the game until it ended and was pleased that the Sox scored twice in the top of the ninth to win 7 – 6. But instead of retiring for the night, Brian poured himself a beer, sat back in his easy chair, and did some more thinking.

His friend, Joe Rogers, whom he called JR, lived halfway around the lake from the Harts, and the two had engaged seriously in a number of conversations about their marriages. His wife, Cindi, was in the same book club as Margaret, but the two women saw little of each other besides those monthly meetings. As a couple, the Rogers were undoubtedly in a better place than the Harts, although Joe had complained more than a few times about their lack of intimacy. The two men forged a deep friendship from the very first week that the Rogers had moved in, some five years before. They first met at a men's group tennis outing and became fast friends almost at once. Just short of six feet tall, with a rugged build, Joe was a handsome man in his mid-forties, with closely cropped brown hair that was greying at the temples. He had blue eyes, a ruddy complexion, a strong nose, and prominent cheekbones. Brian's good neighbor was a competitor, another thing they had in common. *Perhaps it is time for a chat with Joe*, Brian thought.

To say that the next few days were a wash would have been an understatement. The wait for the Wednesday tennis game with Laura seemed like an eternity. It felt like the more Margaret pulled away from Brian, the more distant from her he became. He wondered if she ever thought about seeing another man. When he realized he really didn't care, it was a clear signal to him that his marriage was nearly over.

The first two days of the week seemed to be as pointless to him as had been the previous weekend. It was the same old meetings with clients. His mind was fixated on Laura Parker and he didn't like it. He was feeling as if he was held hostage by a woman, and the feeling of not having any control over it disturbed him.

Wednesday came. It was an early-October day in Providence with the temperature hovering in the sixties. He was relieved somewhat because the good weather would allow for them to play on outdoor public courts, obviating the need to risk being seen at an indoor facility. He called her at about 10:00, and they agreed to meet at the courts in a park in East Providence only about fifteen minutes away. He arrived first and was hitting balls against the net when she appeared.

"You have to hit the ball a little bit higher," she teased him through the open car window while parking. Her comment was accompanied by a twinkle in her eye and a matching smile.

"Thanks a lot!" he retorted. He did a double take when she emerged from her vehicle wearing short, but not too short, yellow tennis shorts and a matching tank top. Her long tan legs looked even better than he remembered. *No question about it,* he thought to himself, *she is definitely a knockout.* After a few minutes of chit-chat and retrieving balls, they began their initial rally. He was impressed by her ball-striking skills. "Boy," he exclaimed, "you can really rip the ball. Where did you learn to play?"

"My brother used to hit with me, and I played some club tennis at Brown."

"I'm impressed," he muttered out loud as she blasted a ball by him.

They hit for about an hour then sat down on a park bench to cool off before heading for a Dairy Queen. He indulged in a chocolate milkshake and she settled for a lemonade. While they sat at an outside table enjoying their drinks, Brian leaned in toward her and said that he had a confession to make.

"I'm also married," he acknowledged. He was somewhat confounded by her response.

"I knew you were," she replied.

"How did you know that?" he stammered.

"Call it woman's intuition if you want, but I just knew. You're an attractive man with no discernible character flaws," she continued with a coquettish smile, "and I figured that you were either married or had been. And your stepkids didn't come out of nowhere.

Besides," she added, "I think all the good ones out there are already taken."

"Please, don't think of me as one of those guys who fools around. I have never done this before. Something mysterious or serendipitous is going on because I find myself very attracted to you – and only you."

She blushed for a moment and then reached across the table to grasp his hand. "I know the feeling. I'm also attracted to you."

They looked intently at each other for a moment, neither one knowing what to say. Finally, he broke the silence by telling her how he had clandestinely followed her from the elevator that first day. After a few more minutes of casual conversation, they both smiled and clasped each other's hands and got up. "We have to do this again," he offered, and she agreed. As they headed to their respective cars, they set another date for the following Tuesday afternoon. He wasn't certain how she felt about him, but the tennis date only served to considerably heighten his interest in her. Kissing her someday jumped to the top of his "TO DO" list.

He arrived home just before six, early for him, but there was no sign of Margaret since she was at law school. It spared him having to lie about where he had been and with whom. A hot shower felt good, especially after a vigorous workout on the court. After making himself a dinner of cold cooked chicken, a baked potato, and iced tea, Brian sat back in his favorite easy chair and contemplated what might come of his relationship with Laura.

The rest of the week seemed endless for Brian as he attempted to focus on his legal practice. But he just couldn't stop thinking about her. Watching college and pro football got him through the weekend.

He called her on Monday and asked if she could have dinner after their Tuesday tennis outing. Laura said that she probably could because David was attending a meeting in Boston that night. As for Brian, he didn't care what Margaret thought about his absence that night. Then again, she had a law school class to attend, so she wouldn't even know.

Their tennis game went well but his thoughts were on the dinner that would follow and how he would handle the conversation. Friar Tuck's was an out-of-the-way restaurant near Cranston. They each drove their own car to the destination. Very little was said over cocktails.

"Let's face it, Brian," she began the earnest part of the conversation. "We're both married. It would be bad enough if only one of us was attached, but we both are."

"Laura, I understand what you're saying. But I also think that we owe it to ourselves to get to know each other better. I know it's difficult, but life is too short not to take a chance. Let's face it, neither one of us married the right person."

"What if we become too fond of each other? What if we get caught?" she interrupted.

"What if after dinner we walk into the street and get hit by a truck?" he countered with a slight hint of a smile. She laughed and he labored on. "What if it turns out that we had something special together—something, I might add, that we don't have now?"

"Brian, you are pushing it."

"I'm sorry. I'm also a little nervous. But I know how I feel when I'm around you."

With that expression of endearment, she reached across the table and took his hand in hers. "Now tell me," she almost commanded him, "your story. You started to over drinks one time, but then I had to leave early. You know mine, but I want to hear about yours."

"As I said before – it's boring," he warned.

"Let me be the judge of that."

"Well, as you heard, I was born in Buffalo—a great city, by the way—and went to Cornell for my undergrad and then also law school. The reason my face isn't so pretty is that I played hockey and football and took a few high sticks to the face, leaving a few scars."

"I can't even tell," she said while getting closer to inspect his brow.

"Nice of you, but I can assure you that they are there. I married late—in my mid-thirties, because I now realize that I was eager to be a dad and she had two young kids from an earlier marriage." She arched her eyebrows quizzically. He noticed the look and went on.

"I never had much of a relationship with my own father," he explained, "and I really wanted so much to be a dad." She squeezed his hand hard, as she could discern from his voice that he was choking up from emotion.

"My wife and I are polar opposites, and stupid me knew that going in. But I grew very attached to her kids and married her more because of them than my feeling for her. She basically ignores me and obviously considers me irrelevant – especially now since she's started going to law school." She squeezed his hand even harder.

"But that's all for now," he stated rather abruptly, and she didn't protest. Then, sensing an opening, he pursued it.

"Laura, if you don't feel anything when we are together, I will get up right now and leave you alone. I don't want to push myself on you."

She continued squeezing his hand and started to speak. He

wasn't good at this and had little experience when it came to romance, but a sixth sense told him he was making headway. He cut her off. "We'll never know unless we give ourselves a chance. If just one of us was happy with our spouse, I would never even suggest it."

"Brian..." she began to stammer, "I, OK, I feel the way you do, but I'm scared."

"So am I. But I can't help thinking about the words of John Greenleaf Whittier." Without waiting for a response from her, he repeated the words made famous by the Quaker poet and abolitionist. "For all sad words of tongue and pen, the saddest are these, 'it might have been.'" Her eyes clouded up and tears formed in each corner. He knew right then and there that his closing argument had resonated. While scoring low marks in the romance department, Brian Hart was a lawyer and trained in making compelling arguments.

Most of the electricity in the room seemed to be generating from one table. It was so pervasive that he didn't even notice the waitress by his side.

"Sir...sir," she muttered. Finally, he noticed her.

"Oh, sorry," he apologized.

"Would you like anything else?"

"Yes," he answered for the both of them. "Two coffees, please." He didn't want the discussion to end, especially at that point where so much was still unclear. She didn't seem to mind, and it was evident even to him that she seemed to care for him.

"Okay," she nodded while sipping her coffee, "we'll see where it goes and if it goes." Her comments were music to his ears.

When they reached her car, she opened the door but stood there waiting, wanting, expecting something to happen. The moon seemed full and totally theirs. She looked up, almost teasing him with those inviting lips. Whatever time it was in Rhode Island, or anywhere else for that matter, the clock stopped then for the two of them. Their hands worked in unison as both moved them to the other's shoulders. Neither spoke a word. Brian gently stroked the nape of her neck and drew her toward him. She offered no resistance. He wondered if she could hear or feel his heart racing. Laura closed her eyes as their lips met. After kissing her softly, he withdrew for a moment and murmured softly, "Laura, sweet Laura. I have waited for this moment."

Her eyes fluttered open and she responded, "I've been waiting too." Their lips found each other again and their bodies followed willingly and almost desperately as the two clung to each other. In another setting, the relationship would have escalated to another level.

When he got home, he poured himself a knuckle of Crown Royal and settled into his easy chair. All he could think of was kissing Laura. By design, they had both decided not to communicate with each other for the next few days, giving themselves time to think about their blossoming relationship.

CHAPTER 9

It was near the end of the month and a Friday when Barry and Carol returned home from college for a week-long break. They arrived in the afternoon and promptly called their stepfather at his office. Brian quickly finished his business and jumped into his car for the short ride home. It seemed strange, but he realized that he loved his stepchildren considerably more than his wife. And they returned his affection in kind. In some ways, especially in the humor department, they had much more rapport with him than her. Brian always made them laugh, something that was beyond his capability with Margaret. Her not having a sense of humor had something to do with that.

As he maneuvered the Town Car into the driveway, Carol was the first to greet him. She seemed to jump into his arms at the precise moment that his feet hit the pavement. "Hey," he teased her, "have you been putting more lemons in your hair? It seems a tad blonder than it did two months ago when you left for college."

"Oh, Daddy," she pretended to pout, "you know that I don't use anything on my hair." She was a tanned and blonde version of her still attractive mother. At 5 feet 3 inches she was slightly shorter but about five pounds heavier. Carol seemed to be universally happy, loved to laugh, and her enthusiasm was infectious. Her small nose, full lips, and dancing blue eyes were the perfect complement to her narrow face. A perpetual smile which showed off her gleaming white teeth also made her appear even more beautiful than she probably was.

Barry appeared and gave his stepdad a hug. At 6 feet 2 inches he was as tall as Brian but had not filled out yet. He had the tall, slender look of a marathon runner. Barry wore his bushy brown hair on the longish side, and had matching eyebrows that dwarfed his hooded hazel eyes. The young man was an artsy-craftsy type who had headed up the drama department at camp and carried that interest with him to college. Strangely enough, his mother disapproved of his interests, while Brian had no problem with whatever made Barry happy.

After a sumptuous dinner which included corn on the cob, the four repaired to the family room to continue their conversation. Margaret retired a little after 9:00, but the three remaining Harts talked until midnight, accompanied by some Billy Joel and Elton John music. A little Barry Manilow was thrown in to satisfy the old man.

With college-aged kids, family discussions often eventually turn to attractions for the opposite sex, and this conversation was no exception. Soon Carol was telling them that she had met a nice guy, a junior at Williams, but she made sure that her father and brother knew it was nothing serious. Barry had encountered an interesting young woman who was a freshman at Lehigh. He admitted that she had intrigued him for a while, but then she had exhibited some bizarre behavior – at least according to him.

"Well, Sarah dressed like a gypsy, was a tad spacy, and didn't believe in deodorants," Barry explained. "I probably could have gotten through all that, but she didn't shave her underarms, and man, that was a huge turnoff!" Some of the other girls he knew at school reminded him that such a thing wasn't at all uncommon in some European countries, but he had countered that "this is Pennsylvania!"

Before the trio went to bed, Brian succumbed to his evening-long temptation to needle Barry about his long hair. "I see that you managed to save money on haircuts this fall," he chided with a broad smile.

"Just trying to save your hard-earned cash, Dad," he quipped with a mischievous grin of his own. The three always enjoyed these give-and-take encounters, but Margaret rarely, if ever, participated in them. She didn't see the purpose to the banter. As for the length of Barry's hair, Brian really didn't care, and it wasn't a big thing to him. But he pretended that it mattered because he felt that every child needed some form of victory or independence over their parents. Better that it be long hair than drugs or alcohol, he reasoned. *Let Barry think that he was getting away with something,* was the way he explained it to his friends.

Despite being almost a senior, Carol still wasn't sure what she wanted to do with her life. Nursing school interested her, but so did a career in real estate. Deep down, Brian hoped that she would opt for the nursing career because she would be doing God's work, as he put it. Always seeming to take a different tack, Margaret thought it made more sense for Carol to be a realtor. In fact, a good friend of the family, Sally Anderson, had a successful realty business in Providence and could give her a job. Barry, on the other hand, didn't know what he wanted to do out of college. But neither did his stepfather at that age.

Meanwhile, Laura became a little jealous that Brian had so many family goings-on while her activities were very limited. The two met for lunch and tennis once, but he wanted to see his step-children as often as possible before they returned to college. On the first night after Carol and Barry returned to school, and when Brian took Laura to dinner, she was initially very cool and diffident towards him. But he understood why. He figured she was struggling with some jealousy, recognizing on one hand his need to be with them, while on the other wanting to spend time with him herself. She wasn't being selfish, just practical. It took two glasses of wine to settle her down, but once she did, they were both comfortable again. He kissed her hand and told her how much he had missed her. Laura needed to hear that, and suddenly things between them warmed up considerably. David would be out of town two weeks from the following Tuesday night and that set the stage for a dinner and whatever else might follow.

CHAPTER 10

After Margaret had been at night law school for two months, Brian discerned a further change in her demeanor and interactions with him. And it wasn't a positive one. She became even more critical of him, more petty, and irrational. At first, he thought that her ill-tempered behavior was due to the kids being away again, but soon traced it to her law school classmates. Margaret had mentioned after that first night that she was carpooling with three other local women. All three were divorced from their cheating husbands, two of whom had remarried their younger secretaries. The third had recently become engaged to a woman twenty years his junior. Margaret had confided once that the conversation to and from law school had centered around male infidelity and practically nothing else. In other words, her fellow commuters were man-haters and such a thing didn't portend well for Margaret's opinion of Brian.

Her disposition, never positive to begin with, gradually became bilious and more disagreeable, and Brian's attempts to fend off her increasing array of insults fell on deaf ears. It had only been a few weeks of her commuting when she made a caustic comment to him about not keeping the house clean. That was the catalyst for him to badger her back about the influence that her man-hating classmates were having on her. That night, Margaret was the angriest and nastiest that he had ever witnessed in their entire marriage. She called him an idiot and a fool, among other things, and that he "probably belonged with an insipid younger woman half his age who doesn't know shit from Shinola." Brian's only response before heading to the family room was a weak "That sounds pretty good to me." .

Margaret slept in Carol's room that night and they didn't exchange a single word over the next two days. Neither apologized when they did speak again, both preferring to act like the ugly scene never happened.

Brian talked with a few close friends, including Jim Dakins, about Margaret's increasing hostility toward him. They all agreed that the Harts should see a marriage counselor if he wanted to continue the marriage and that divorce seemed to be the only viable option.

"Do you think she met someone?" asked Jim.

"No, I'm sure she hasn't," Brian opined, "but to be totally honest, I'm not sure that I care."

"If that's the case," Jim offered, "then divorce is probably your best bet."

"Frankly," Brian shrugged, "I don't think it would matter to her if I had a girlfriend."

"If that's the case, then maybe a marriage counselor is a waste of time and money," Jim declared. "Divorce may be your only option, my friend."

It seemed to Brian that it might be, but he couldn't bear the thought of telling Carol and Barry.

The long-awaited Tuesday night rendezvous with Laura came while Brian was still very agitated with Margaret. He had made the dinner and motel reservations but felt guilty about it. Laura wore a black skirt and matching turtleneck and when she joined him at the table, he thought she was the sexiest woman he had ever seen. He wore his usual attire of tan slacks, white shirt, and blue blazer.

"You look incredible!"

"You aren't so bad yourself, mister."

He was very nervous but hoped she wouldn't notice. He was somewhat taken aback that she didn't appear flustered at all. Canadian Club on the rocks helped to calm him down. Laura ordered a glass of wine and nursed it throughout the entire dinner. Another CC arrived for him, but he took it with water this time. His nerves needed to be steadied, but not at the expense of not being able to perform. Their conversation over dinner was a bit more stilted than usual.

This was his first rodeo; he certainly wasn't a Harold Stapleton who was always looking for an opportunity to stray. Despite feeling angry at Margaret, guilt was still his enemy as he sat and smiled at his dinner partner. He had checked into the motel earlier to avoid any embarrassment later, and collected his key to room 107. The cash transaction probably gave away his intentions. After all, how many people arrive with no luggage and pay cash for a room in mid-afternoon? He laughed to himself as he hoped that somebody named "Arnold Porter" wouldn't mind if Brian borrowed his name for an evening!

The final ten minutes it took to get from the restaurant to the hotel seemed inexorably longer than it had earlier. Brian wasn't sure what Laura's exact thoughts were, but he was in desperation mode himself to somehow rationalize what he was about to do. Yes, Margaret was combative, quarrelsome, and truculent. Yes, she was not a supportive wife; he couldn't remember the last kind word she said about him or to him. And yes, he thought that she was getting worse. The change was especially discernible during her past few weeks of law school. She was still carpooling with the spurned three women, and he no longer wondered if they had anything to do with the change in her behavior.

Despite these thoughts, he was still feeling guilty when he maneuvered his Town Car into the motel parking lot and guided it into the space reserved for the occupants of Room 107. They emerged from the car and quickly entered the room, as if they feared that someone might see them from the road. As he closed the door behind them, there it was. The elephant in the room in the shape of a queen-sized bed adorned with a worn, ugly green color bedspread. He vowed right then that if there was a next time with Laura, it would be in a nicer place.

He immediately took her in his arms as if he was afraid that either one of them would change their mind. She went with the flow and they fell on the bed groping each other. Soon that offensive bedspread was removed along with their clothes. Their intense love-making lasted nearly twenty minutes and left them soaked in sweat and in each other's arms. Laura was the first to speak. "That was so good," she cooed. He held her tight and then squeezed her to indicate his similar satisfaction. They lay there quietly for at least another ten minutes without uttering a word.

"I guess we should have a smoke," Brian chuckled and smiling, he finally let go of her.

"Very funny, Mr. Hollywood," she retorted while gently elbowing him in the ribs.

They got up, turned on the TV, and had a glass of wine from the bottle he had brought along for the occasion. *Jeopardy!* was something they both enjoyed, and it had just started. They snuggled and nestled in amongst the pillows.

"These two men," the first question began, "are the only people who have ever presided over the US House of Representatives and the US Senate." None of the contestants knew the answer and Laura admitted that she had no clue.

"I know the answer," Brian shouted out. "John Nance Garner and Schuyler Colfax!"

After a few seconds, host Alex Trebek confirmed those names. "I'm really impressed," Laura exclaimed. "How on earth did you know that?"

"I just read it somewhere and it seemed interesting enough that I thought I should remember it."

"Well, it's especially impressive that none of the three contestants knew the answer."

"Every once in a while," he snickered, "even pigs can fly!"

She laughed and nudged him to turn off the TV. It was time for another round of intimacy. Laura had a stunning body with firm breasts and he felt a little embarrassed by contrast with his slight paunch. She either didn't mind or notice and they lay together again as close as two lovers can. When it was over, they held each other tight as if to extend the encounter as long as possible. They had another glass of wine while taking a bath together. Neither wanted the evening to end, but there was no option other than to return to their respective homes. They kissed deeply before leaving the room and getting into Brian's car. He dropped her off at the restaurant and they both drove out of the parking lot together but in opposite directions.

The guilt hit him as soon as he was on the road. *Margaret doesn't deserve this,* he admonished himself. *She may not even be close to the model wife, but she doesn't deserve this.* He also knew that the past four hours had been the best he could ever remember or at least for many years.

The garage, empty when he arrived home, he moved to his spot on the left and turned off the ignition. He figured that Margaret would probably be home in the next thirty minutes. He changed into a t-shirt and sweatpants and washed his face and neck just to make sure he got rid of any lingering trace of Laura's perfume. A surge of guilt hit him again.

In a possible sign of contrition, neither Laura or Brian spoke right away about meeting again after their tryst. *It is probably easier for her to rationalize it since her husband had at least one affair,* he mused. To his knowledge, Margaret had not cheated on him and this was his first transgression.

He turned on the TV and awaited her arrival. Sure enough, within the half hour she walked through the door. It had been her turn to drive.

"How'd it go?" he greeted her.

"How do you think it went?" she replied acidly.

"Just asking," he muttered.

Recognizing how hostile she had sounded, Margaret explained that one of the "girls" had gotten sick in the car. She didn't apologize to him for her tone, it wasn't in her DNA. She had never apologized for anything. After their brusque interaction, suddenly Brian felt better about stepping out on her. *It's obviously an effort for her to even be civil to me,* he thought. He knew that their relationship had certainly been struggling before she went to law school, but in just that relatively short time, it had deteriorated even further. Brian was sure he knew why. Her three law school classmates had all gotten divorced in the past three years, and their stories were sad. In a rare moment of candor, Margaret had related to him the circumstances of each. Ellen's husband was a serial cheater. Mary's husband divorced her to marry his secretary, who was twenty years his junior. Peggy's husband had gambled away their life's savings, drank too much, and then had the temerity to marry his secretary. Brian could just imagine what his own wife was contributing to the feeding frenzy. If only she knew about that very evening. He had a feeling that Margaret's carpool consisted of three man-hating women and a fourth who was almost to that point. He couldn't blame her classmates for their obvious contempt for their husbands, but he didn't deserve such condemnation. *Or did he?* Margaret chose to sleep in Carol's bedroom again that night. He wasn't sure why.

CHAPTER 11

After work the next day, Brian hit the gym for a vigorous work-out. He now had a real reason to get rid of his slight paunch. He ran into Ed Bloom, one of his tennis buddies. A tall, muscular man with a friendly face and generous but close-set brown eyes, he was one of the few black men that Brian knew and considered a real friend. Not because he didn't want more friends like the ami-able Ed, but he just didn't come into contact very often with them.

"Nice six pack you have there," he smiled to his friend.

"Sorry I can't say the same for you," Ed chided him. "In fact, are you pregnant? That paunch is a little bigger than the last time I kicked your scrawny ass in tennis!" Brian loved his buddy's sense of humor and they always had fun teasing each other.

"I'm working on it, Eddie," he responded in kind. "If he is a boy and as ugly as you, I might name him for you." Ed tossed his head back in laughter. In truth, Brian thought that Ed Bloom was not only a magnificently conditioned athlete at age forty-five, but probably the most handsome of all his friends. Ed had to go shopping with his wife, so the two men bid each other goodbye. Brian made his way through the lobby on his way to the locker room and passed three very attractive female thirty-somethings busily engaged in conversation. He nodded his head in recognition but was disap-pointed that they didn't even seem to notice him.

Ed must be right, he thought, as he looked in the bathroom mirror and pinched his stomach. *I have some work to do.* Not one for much introspection, he thought about it for a minute and had to reluctantly admit that he had lately fallen victim to the "fat and lazy syndrome." Whether those three ladies' unawareness of him had anything to do with it or not, he had one of his most vigorous workouts in memory, and he really felt good about it. A steam room and shower later, he felt like a million bucks. He even posed in the mirror when no one was looking and thought, probably wishful thinking, that his paunch was actually smaller. On his way home from the gym, he was tempted to stop for a cheeseburger, fries, and a shake, but realized that he would totally nullify the good efforts of his workout. Instead, he settled for a tuna sandwich, frozen peas, and a glass of water at home. Margaret arrived about an hour after he had finished his dinner and immediately admonished him for not using a coaster under his glass of water.

"And welcome home to you, too," he chirped sarcastically.

"You men are impossible," she spat out her response. Once again, she retreated to Carol's bedroom for the night.

Brian couldn't wait to call Laura the next morning. Out of respect, if you will, for their respective situations and their mutual understanding, he had allowed things to cool off and hadn't called her the day after their rendezvous. He asked her about getting together that week but she nixed any possibility of a repeat of their recent experience. She sensed his disappointment.

"Not because I didn't enjoy it, Brian," she attempted to assuage his hurt feelings, "but because David will be back in town."

"How about lunch tomorrow?" Somewhat comforted by her reply, lunch sounded like a fair compromise.

Margaret was curt again that night upon her return home, and he was sorely tempted to call her out on it, but didn't.

Lunch with Laura went well the following day, but neither one seemed comfortable talking about their motel tryst. Finally, he addressed it.

"The other night was magical," he said as he clutched her hand for just a moment.

"Yes, it was wonderful," she agreed, "but I can't help feeling guilty about it."

"Me too," he assured her, "but it's not like we were out there looking for an opportunity. We found each other for a reason."

"True. I guess you're right," she answered, "but it's still diffi-cult." The conversation didn't improve any over the rest of their lunch, and both left the table far from satisfied.

A thorough workout at the gym after work seemed to take the edge off for him, but he was disappointed that Ed didn't make it that night. When he got home, Margaret criticized him for leaving his dishes in the sink, but he resisted the impulse to respond in kind. Clearly, something was eating at her.

CHAPTER 12

It was late October and the nights were getting chilly. After a few more lunches, Brian felt that Laura still seemed diffident toward him, and it annoyed him. He wasn't sure what was going on in her head, but with things going so badly between Margaret and him, his patience was wearing a bit thin. *"I'm done with women,"* he exclaimed to himself on his drive home that night. Right then and there he decided to cool it with Laura. He was reading a novel that a friend had suggested when Margaret arrived home. *"I wonder what she'll bitch about tonight? The dishes are done and there is no mess."*

"Our garage is filthy," she declared upon seeing him.

"And good evening to you, too," he responded with a slight smirk.

"Well, it is," she snapped and marched to the stairs in a huff.

The more he became involved in Edith Wharton's novel, *Ethan Frome*, the more he identified with the book's main character. Margaret was looking more like Ethan's wife, Zeena, with every page. She seemed to be more whiny and shrewish with each passing week. There was no interest from her in discussing her classes with him despite his questions. Nor was she interested in talking about her classmates. He had never met them but disliked them for their perceived negative effect on his wife. Brian had ruled out an affair for her. *Where would she find the time?* He rationalized that she must have become a man-hater, just like the gals in her carpool. She had taken to spending all her nights sleeping in Carol's room, and there had been no intimacy between them in over a year. When he asked her if everything was okay, she would always grunt an almost incoherent "yeah."

As Christmas approached, he still hadn't called Laura. He assumed that their relationship, if that's what it was, had come to an end. His feelings remained strong for her, but clearly she either couldn't handle it or had gotten back with her husband, David. He was done with women. That he knew for certain!

The snow came and went without any thaw in his relationship with Margaret or with Laura. Springtime brought a plethora of rain, but his home remained a toxic and hostile environment.

CHAPTER 13

As summer neared, Brian found himself longing for Carol and Barry's return from college. Although they had spent some time at home during the holidays, they were often off with their friends. And, frankly, they didn't seem to sense the tension between him and their mother. At this point, Brian was grateful for that.

With nothing but work, the gym, and tennis, even traces of his paunch were gone and he felt like he was in the best shape of his life. But that was the only good thing going on for him. He and Margaret barely spoke and merely tolerated each other. Laura had been out of his life for many months now. Brian had no feelings for his wife, and it was obvious that Margaret felt nothing for him either. While he realized that they had gradually become alienated from one another, he attributed the real catalyst being her going to law school. He wouldn't have objected to her going—how could he?—but it might have been nice for her to have at least talked with him about it. It hadn't even been a month into her first fall term when he began to feel like the enemy. Initially, he had felt sorry for her carpool classmates when he found out that they had scumbags for husbands. But that wasn't his fault. He wasn't a scumbag. He did, however, have a brief affair. Did that make him a scumbag?

It was a hot and muggy July afternoon in Providence. Brian had just gotten into his office building's elevator. Things weren't great but were okay. Carol and Barry were home from college but were working summer jobs. Margaret was a little less cantankerous than usual, but that wasn't saying much. *Time away from her classmates*, he reasoned, *must have done her some good.* Suddenly a woman's arm stopped the elevator door from closing and she stepped in. It was Laura. Their eyes met right away and he was gripped with a wave of anxiety. He decided to ride up to her floor with her. Upon disembarking together, he said hello but couldn't make out her muffled response. She began walking to her office without even looking at him. But before she could get too far, Brian placed his hands on her shoulders from behind and turned her around as gently as he could. Laura looked awful! Her hair was a mess, those once flashing green eyes were bloodshot, and her face was sallow and almost catatonic.

"Are you okay?" he asked.

"What do you care?"

"I care a lot!"

"Yeah, right."

"No, I truly do. I haven't called you because I thought you were done with me."

"I thought you were done with me," she pouted.

He kissed her right then and there outside her office door and didn't care if anyone saw it.

"I have to go." She pulled away.

"Meet me at 5:00 tonight for a drink," he implored. "If, after that, you don't want to see me, I will never bother you again."

Without answering, she disappeared behind the door.

It was almost 5:30 when Brian was certain that she was going to be a no-show. As he was paying the bill, she crept up behind him and sat down next to him. Pleased, but startled, he quickly seated himself and asked Laura if she wanted a drink. Merlot was her choice, and he had a second Canadian Club and water. They talked incessantly for an hour. She had taken his failure to call her as a personal affront and a definite sign that he no longer cared for her. He repeatedly shook his head no, but she continued. She cried during the telling of her tale, and he just sank lower and lower, cowering in his seat.

"I'm so sorry," he replied, taking her hand in his. "I'm so sorry. I thought that you didn't care for me. You were so lukewarm the last time we met for lunch that I thought you were brushing me off." She started to say something, but he cut her off by holding his palm up in front of her face. "So many times," he said earnestly, "I wanted to call you. But with each passing day, it got harder and harder. I didn't think that you gave a damn. I even thought that maybe things were better between you and your husband."

It was her turn to grab his hand. "I never stopped caring," she stammered. There were four moist eyes at the table. She looked at her watch and said that she had to go but was free for dinner the next day – if he wanted. He did, and they agreed to meet at Angelo's at 6:00.

That night while looking for some crackers in the lower kitchen cabinet, he came across something that puzzled him. It was a vodka bottle that seemed to be hiding behind a few discarded and almost empty boxes of spaghetti noodles. He had never noticed it before, but then again, he had never looked for it. To his knowledge, Margaret had always limited her drinking to a glass of wine while out for dinner, and even then, just a single glass. The bottle was nearly empty, which perplexed him even further. She was gone practically every night, so she must have been taking a few nips during the day. Occasionally he might have a CC and water at home, but it was always at night and he didn't make any effort to conceal the bottle. Any liquor, beer, or wine they had for entertainment purposes was stored in a small cabinet in their living room. Brian was careful to place the bottle back where he had found it. *Could the bottle belong to either Barry or Carol? They had been home for the summer and they hadn't spent any real time together.*

Margaret gave him a very unenthusiastic hello when she stepped in the door that night and then just continued on her way upstairs. Their marriage appeared irreparably broken. He wasn't sure how deeply he felt about Laura, but his affection for Margaret had reached a relationship nadir. Their borderline contempt for each other ate at him, and he didn't know where to turn. A week later, he searched again for the vodka bottle and discovered that there were about two fingers more than when he had first come upon it. That meant, he figured, that she had consumed almost a full bottle. He had read somewhere that vodka was generally the drink of choice for drinkers because it looks like water and they think that their breath won't give them away. *She must have been right on that one,* he mused, *since I have never smelled vodka on her.* But then again, they hadn't kissed in a long time, so how could he tell?

As July turned into August, Brian's Red Sox seemed to be going nowhere. The Yankees were running away with the American League East division, and Boston was mired in third place, barely ahead of the Toronto Blue Jays.

He and Laura continued to have a few dinners together, followed by surreptitious liaisons at a bit nicer motel, but they lacked the same intensity as their earlier assignations. Neither wanted to acknowledge it out loud, but an illicit relationship between two married people was almost doomed from the start. For Brian, nothing seemed to change at home, as Margaret continued to treat him as the enemy, and judging by the vodka bottle evidence, her drinking appeared to be escalating.

CHAPTER 14

It was on a dank and dismal late August day in Rhode Island that he received a call from his old friend, Jeff Price. It was Tuesday the 28th and the call would dramatically alter Brian's life. Jeff did very well in investment banking – *Didn't everyone,* Brian thought. But he had a big-time marriage problem and needed some legal advice from his friend. After a long chat, they agreed to meet for breakfast in New York City two weeks later.

The two-week hiatus gave Brian ample time to plan his future life. He could happily envision a life without Margaret, but the complications were immense. An ugly divorce would exact a terrible toll on several lives, most notably those of his stepchildren, Barry and Carol. In fact, those relationships were the only reason he could think of for not getting a divorce. Such a thing could break their hearts, and should that occur, Margaret would probably do everything in her power to limit the time he spent with them. She was the vindictive type; all that meanness and pettiness had especially manifested themselves and taken over the front stage during the past year. He could even imagine her moving away, just to put distance between Brian and the kids. Yes, his only real option was to disappear and make it look like he had been killed. New York City would give him the perfect backdrop for such an event. Having grown very close to them, they would undoubtedly take his death hard, particularly if it happened by means of a New York City mugging and robbery. Laura, he figured, would be upset as well, but his death would at least rid her of one complexity in her life. As for Margaret, would she even notice? He knew he was being a tad facetious, but she would most likely go on without missing a beat.

Now, with almost two weeks left in Rhode Island before taking the train to New York on Monday the 10th of September, he had things to do. Brian had to do everything he could to ensure that his fake death would not arouse any undue suspicion. He knew that his conduct and behavior would later be questioned by authorities. Was he of sound mind? Was he unhappy or despondent? Margaret would certainly be asked what his state of mind had been when he left for New York. Perhaps his tennis and golf buddies would be questioned too, if somehow the eventual crime scene appeared suspicious. He resolved that he would go out of his way to appear buoyant and cheerful in those final interactions during those thirteen days.

He called Laura and assured her that they would have dinner together when he returned from New York, implying as best he could that things for them would eventually work out. Through a contact from a shady lawyer acquaintance, he was able to secure a phony driver's license and birth certificate.

Brian's apparent death at the hands of a mugger in New York City was a better plan for many reasons than merely to disappear. For one, his family, friends and work colleagues would not feel that perhaps there was something they could have done to avert it, or even worse, that they might have been the reason for it. And Carol and Barry, and even Laura, must not know the truth. He really didn't give a damn, at that point, what Margaret would think. So, it was imperative that all accepted his death as another one of those unfortunate victims who happened to be in the wrong place at the wrong time.

But there was another reason as well for not merely disappearing. Brian didn't want a skip tracer looking for him the rest of his life. Skip tracers, he learned, were "professionals" who track people down for a living and uncover private information. Whatever years remaining to him might be difficult enough without having to fear that one of those skip tracers might be lurking behind the next tree. A "death" by mugging could be preferable. There not being a body would obviously raise a few questions, but that was the best he could do.

By pocketing expense account money reimbursed by his law firm, and putting away small sums from his monthly paycheck, Brian was able to accumulate almost $6000. He hoped that such a sum would keep him going until he could find another job. Just three days before his trip to the Big Apple, Brian bought and had altered a spiffy new navy-blue suit. It would be ready for pickup on the day he returned from New York. Of course, he would never wear the suit, but purchasing it made his story more plausible. Who would buy a new suit when he was planning to disappear?

In his last few days at home, Margaret seemed totally unaware of his plan. Her icy standoffishness, bordering on contempt, continued in the few interactions he had with her. He was clearly the enemy in her eyes, and it annoyed him to no end. They had enough problems without her battle against the bottle, and that was a struggle that was almost always lost. The only way to beat demon rum was to quit. There was no other positive outcome possible.

He had no idea when she began drinking, but he figured that it must have played a substantial role in her disdain for him. Maybe, maybe not, but probably. Try as he might, he couldn't pinpoint even the approximate time that she must have begun her secret drinking. And never once did she arouse his suspicion by slurring her words or acting erratically. She was too smart for that, he guessed, but something had obviously happened which triggered her response of finding a solution in the bottle. It never worked, but that was no longer his problem.

As he packed his bag on Sunday night in preparation for his late morning train ride to New York City, he felt an anxiety that threatened to overwhelm him. He worried about missing some important detail, something that would derail his plans. Brian had called Barry and Carol on Saturday night, something that he and Margaret did pretty regularly every other week. He just needed to hear their voices one final time. They were difficult calls, and he hoped that they didn't sense his uneasiness. His last words to them, as they always had been, were *I love you.*

Brian wanted to take two bags with him but thought better of it since he was ostensibly going to be gone for less than two full days. He didn't want to raise suspicion by bringing so much. He chose one fairly big bag and made sure to include his favorite pants, lots of underwear, socks and T-shirts, a pair of tennis sneakers, and a sweater. If Margaret had asked about the bag's size, he would have said that he needed stuff for working out. But she didn't care, and it never came up. He checked the pocket in the bag to be certain that he had his phony driver's license, birth certificate, some prepaid credit cards, and a burner phone. There was a reason why his new name would be Brian Miller. The shady attorney acquaintance said that it was always better to assume a new surname that was a popular name such as Jones or Miller or King. That way, the shyster explained, it would be more difficult for authorities to trace.

The following afternoon, he would become Brian Miller,

although everyone else eventually would know him as the unfortunate Brian Hart, who had been attacked, robbed, and killed in downtown New York City. Somehow his body would never be found, but that wasn't particularly unusual in NYC. He did worry somewhat about that angle. Without an actual body, would people believe that he had actually perished? Would the insurance company pay Margaret the $500,000 on his life without the evidence of a body? He couldn't think of a better way to cover his tracks, but he also worried that his wallet might never make it to a police station. In that case, he would simply be a missing person, instead of a probably dead missing person. That would really complicate things. As it turned out, his anxieties would prove unfounded.

CHAPTER 15

Brian arrived at the Providence train station forty-five minutes before his scheduled departure at 2:00 p.m. It would be about a three-and-a-half-hour trip to New York, and he was able to spend the morning in his office. One of his law firm buddies drove him the five minutes to the Amtrak station. This extra touch, he thought, would lend credence to the fact that Brian had been in an animated and jovial mood as he left for the big city. He wanted to cover every base he could think of and be extra communicative and optimistic on the ride to the station. His friend and colleague, Hal Hadley, would also pick him up the next day when he returned. Brian knew that he would not be returning but Hal didn't. That September 10th day was a warm one in Rhode Island, but it looked like rain ahead. The train was an hour late but the subway from Penn Station got him to his hotel by 7 PM. He called home but it was no surprise that Margaret must have been out and didn't answer the phone. It wasn't a law school night for her, it being a Monday, but she obviously was out doing something. Brian left her a short message letting her know that he had arrived in New York and was headed out for dinner.

He loved walking the streets of New York City, not minding the need to be always looking up and anticipating a collision with some nerd talking on their cell phone or texting. There was a certain excitement to the city that just wasn't available in Rhode Island.

Not particularly hungry, he just popped into a fast-food restaurant on Vesey and Church Streets in Lower Manhattan and sat down with a cheeseburger and fries. He had already reserved a rental car on Morton Street under the name of Brian Miller, just a few blocks from his scheduled breakfast with Jeff Price the next morning.

Originally, his plan to disappear included scheduling the breakfast with his friend, but not showing up for it. He would leave his wallet in his hotel room and knock over a few pieces of furniture in order to stage a fake robbery and killing. But there were at least two problems with that scenario. The first and most important was that Jeff Price was a dear friend and needed pertinent advice – so he needed to have the face-to-face meeting. Secondly, how would the alleged robber manage to enter the room and then make his getaway, carrying a dead body out of the hotel without being seen? That would be unlikely at best, given the probable presence of surveillance cameras. Better to have the breakfast with Jeff and then leave a wallet with ID but no money on a seedy street corner. He reasoned that a thief probably wouldn't want his Amtrak card, and hoped that the wallet would somehow find its way to a police station.

As it turned out, all that careful planning didn't really matter.

When he had stepped out of Penn Station late that afternoon and gotten on the subway, the weather had been beautiful for a mid-September day. But storm clouds quickly blew in, followed by a heavy rain. He ducked under a street store awning for refuge, but there was a brief lull in the downpour and he traversed the few blocks back to his hotel. Brian was hoping to watch the Yankee-Red Sox game on TV but it was rained out and he read a few newspapers instead. He noticed that she had left a message on his cell phone. "Sorry I missed your call, Brian," she stated coolly, "but we had a Neighborhood Watch meeting. Nothing for you to be concerned about," she added, "it was just routine." It was 10:00 when he called back, and he was almost surprised that she answered.

"If you remember," he began, "I'm meeting with Jeff for breakfast tomorrow morning." He hadn't told her about the impending divorce.

"Where are you two dining? Anywhere nice?"

"Yeah, at the Windows of the World in the North Tower of the World Trade Center."

"Wow! Pretty nice, but isn't it at the top of the building?"

"Yup, all the way up on the 107th floor."

"I don't think I would be comfortable being up that high."

"Well, Jeff says that the view of the city and the Statue of Liberty is incomparable."

"I guess I'll have to take your and Jeff's word for it," she responded.

"I should be able to make the 11:07 back to Providence and be in my office by 3:00. Hal Hadley is going to pick me up."

"Well, have fun with Jeff and make sure he sends my regards to Cindi."

"Will do." He was surprised that the call went so well and that she seemed fairly nice. In fact, it was the first decent discussion they had in months. *Probably because I'm out of town and she doesn't have to deal with me,* he thought.

Brian was so happy to be back in New York City that he didn't even mind the interminable din of the traffic noises emanating from the street below. It took a while for him to drift off to sleep.

CHAPTER 16

The hot shower felt extra good the next morning and his spirits rose even higher when he opened the window drapes. There wasn't a cloud in the bright blue sky. After checking out of the hotel, Brian stepped out into a perfectly beautiful, sunny, sixty-degree day. It was now 7:00 a.m. and he estimated that he was only two hours away from being a free man. He dropped his luggage bag at the car rental facility before going to breakfast.

When the elevator door opened at the 107th floor of the WTC North Tower, he was taken back by the sheer elegance of the restaurant and the incredible views of the city afforded the patrons. A very exotic-looking hostess named Naomi greeted him warmly and escorted him to the reserved table by the window. It was now 7:20 a.m. and Brian was ten minutes early, as was his custom. An old saying of his father's stuck with him throughout his life. "If I'm late," the elder Hart used to say, "send flowers." The old man was always punctual, and the message was clear – *if you're late, you're basically telling the other person or people that your time is more important than theirs!* The point Mr. Hart had made was well taken, and Brian Hart would never be late meeting anyone.

He gazed out the window and saw the majestic sights of the Statue of Liberty and Ellis Island. Seeing an abandoned newspaper at the empty table next to him, he grabbed it and turned to the editorial page. It was 7:50 when his cell phone rang. It was Jeff.

"I'm so sorry to be late, man," he hastily apologized. "Damn commuter train was late. I can't get there until 8:50 or even 9. Is that too late for you? We lost cell service or I would have called you earlier."

"That's okay, Jeff," he fibbed, "I'm enjoying this incredible view!" He ordered a coffee from a pert young waitress named Penny and mulled over the hour or so wait ahead of him. The coffee tasted exceptionally good and the outdoor scene was remarkably beautiful, especially the magnificent view of the iconic Statue of Liberty. Spotting another discarded paper – this time the *Wall Street Journal* – two tables from him, he grabbed it quickly and had the time to read it thoroughly. The bad news was a glance around the room that revealed no other reading material. He still had at least a half hour to kill before Jeff would arrive, so he decided to get something in the lobby. He caught Penny's attention and explained that the friend he was meeting was running late, so he would be back in about twenty minutes. Penny was fine with that, especially when she saw that he was leaving his briefcase by the table along with his cell phone. "Can you keep an eye on these things for me, Penny?" She responded that she would.

A few other patrons joined him on the elevator down to the ground floor. It was now 8:40. Brian barely had time to purchase a couple of newspapers when suddenly the entire building structure rocked as if it was hit by a bomb or an earthquake. Everyone within 50 feet of him had quizzical looks on their faces which quickly turned to stark terror. Several people raced in the door and yelled to no one in particular that a plane had hit the building. It was 8:46 a.m. on September 11.

He saw a police officer and explained that he was meeting someone at Windows of the World at 9 a.m. "You've got to be kidding, buddy!" the burly officer replied. "The only people going up there now will be firemen." When Brian stepped outside, his senses were accosted by the horrible din of screams, sirens, and debris, including shards of glass flying all over the place. He looked up and saw a huge and frightening gash in the north face of the building and was horrified to see some of the patrons of the Windows of the World restaurant waving napkins and tablecloths out of the windows of both the 107th and 106th floors. A terrible inferno was directly below them. He immediately thought of Penny, his pretty and friendly waitress who was now facing certain death. So would he, had Jeff not been late. People were streaming out of the stairwells and running out of the North Tower by the dozens, some almost hit by the flying debris. He thought again of Penny and of the attractive hostess, Naomi, who were undoubtedly still in the restaurant.

The plane seemed to have struck and entered the building about fifteen floors or so below the restaurant. A large shard of glass fell almost at his feet and seemed to explode on impact. He quickly ducked back into the lobby to assess the situation, but it was utter chaos. And then the horrible thought occurred to him – *What if Jeff passed him in the elevator? What if he made it to the restaurant at a quarter to nine? What if those unfortunate people in the restaurant cannot take an elevator down to safety?* He wondered if he would ever know the answers.

Amidst all the hysteria and confusion taking place, he tried to collect himself. *I better leave, get my rental car, and get out of the city now!* In his haste, he had forgotten to leave his wallet with his Amtrak card on the street corner as he had originally planned – a good thing, it turned out. Another thought occurred to him as he walked hurriedly east on Vesey Street while turning right on Church in search of the rental car agency. *What if Jeff didn't get there before the plane hit the building? He will think that I was up there and would die.* There was no one in line when he walked in the door. Both rental agents were totally absorbed in the TV reports of the tragic events unfolding before them. He looked at his watch. It was 8:53 a.m. One of the two male clerks seemed to be annoyed that Brian chose his station. He was the first to speak.

"How dumb can you be to fly into the World Trade Center?" he said disgustedly. Within just a few minutes, the disgruntled employee had his answer. Screams were heard not only on the television broadcast but also on Church Street. A second airplane had flown into the South Tower at precisely 9:03 a.m. Suddenly it was no longer a case of a poorly trained pilot of a small plane accidentally crashing into the WTC. Everyone knew at the same time that they were terrorist attacks. By the time the clerk, a long-haired young man with thick, bushy eyebrows, and the name of Carlos on his badge, had processed the phony driver's license and had accepted Brian's prepaid credit card payment, sirens were blaring all over the place and people were running toward the North and South Towers for a closer look. Others were running away from the buildings and the falling debris.

Brian quickly went to his rental car and carefully guided the Ford Taurus towards the Brooklyn Bridge, just a few miles to the southeast, dodging frantic pedestrians along the way. Once over the bridge, he picked up Route 278 and drove southwest to the Verrazzano-Narrows Bridge through Staten Island to New Jersey. Under normal circumstances, he would have driven north to the George Washington Bridge, but the second plane crash and resulting chaos forced him to find the fastest exit out of Manhattan before they closed all the roads and bridges. It was 11:30 by the time he arrived in Philadelphia, and he had listened intently to the radio all the way. All the stations carried the tragic and horrifying news of the terrorist attacks, and the news only got worse with each passing hour. He was barely out of New Jersey when the South Tower fell at 9:59, and within a half hour of that cataclysmic event, the North Tower followed at 10:28.

Brian didn't completely understand it when he began to cry softly, tears rolling down his cheeks. It was the convergent thoughts of the attack on America and Naomi and Penny perishing in the collapse of the building. Two innocent young women, with their lives all ahead of them, struck down in their early twenties. And what about Jeff? He probably got to the North Tower elevator too late to meet Brian in the restaurant, but he didn't know for sure. The thought finally struck him at 11:45 that Jeff would have assumed that Brian died in the North Tower. His failure to remember to place his wallet with the Amtrak card on the corner was actually a good thing – that is, for his own purposes. But it was such a bad thing for so many other people. It would be days before the total carnage would be verified. The Pentagon in D.C. had been hit by another plane at 9:45, just 14 minutes before the South Tower collapsed. And, 18 minutes later in Shanksville, Pennsylvania, the brave passengers of United flight 93 stormed the cockpit of yet another plane commandeered by terrorists, and forced the airliner down instead of the likelihood of it hitting the White House or the Capitol Building. In all, 2977 innocent people died that day from the terrorist attacks.

CHAPTER 17

Brian Hart thought that his newly found freedom would fill him with excitement and joy, but here he was driving west of Philadelphia with tears streaming down his cheeks. Originally, he planned to escape to Maine or even New Brunswick, but he feared that it might be more difficult to just blend in there with the smaller populace. He would drive instead to Pittsburgh and head west until he just felt like stopping. It was just after 6:00 p.m. when he pulled into a motel on Route 10 near Monessen, southeast of the Steel City. Endurancewise, he had the nervous energy to drive several more hours, but he was also anxious to watch the television reports of the 9/11 events. The radio coverage had been non-stop throughout his drive, but he wanted to see it for himself.

A diner was conveniently located across the road from his motel, so it was easy to find a place to eat. He always preferred diners to other types of restaurants. Perhaps it was the folksiness; maybe it was because so many "regular" people patronized them. Whatever it was, this was his kind of place. A booth was open to his left as he entered the establishment, but he opted for a seat at the counter between two elderly gentlemen. They each greeted him warmly, just as he had expected, and the three spent their dinner hour talking about the unforgettable events of the day.

While all this was going on in Pennsylvania, the telephone rang for the 6th time that day at the residence of Brian and Margaret Hart in Barrington, Rhode Island. This time, Margaret picked it up. In a calm voice, Jeff Price spoke first.

"Margaret, have you heard from Brian?"

"No," she uttered, the anxiety clear in her tone. "I thought you two were meeting for breakfast at Windows on the World."

"We were supposed to meet at 7:30 but my commuter train was running late and I told him that I wouldn't get there until nine." Now she was really getting unnerved and Jeff could sense the tension in her voice.

"Did he say he would wait for you?"

"Unfortunately, he did. I arrived in the North Tower lobby just as the first plane hit."

"So, you mean, he was caught up there?" she said resolutely, the panic evident in her voice.

"I'm so sorry, Margaret," he replied weakly with his voice shaking, "but I think so."

"Then he never got out or was rescued?"

"I don't think that anyone who was on the higher floors got out," he answered solemnly.

"I tried him on his cell phone several times," she murmured.

"I tried him when I got to the lobby and then several times later," he muttered, his voice trailing off.

He could hear her heavy breathing and sniffling. "He's dead, isn't he, Jeff?" There was an uncomfortable pause.

"I...um...think it's very possible."

"C'mon, Jeff, you know it!" She could sense the increasing shrillness in her own voice.

"Let's wait until we know for sure," he implored.

"He was in the restaurant when the plane hit," she said more calmly. "No one got out from above the crash site. He's dead. It's that simple." Her voice seemed to fade away.

Jeff could sense that it was time to get off the phone. He also thought it a good idea not to mention that it had been his idea to meet Brian that morning at Windows on the World. Jeff Price was also very grateful that his commuter train had been late that morning. But he felt guilty that he was very much alive while his good friend probably wasn't. And it didn't help either that Brian had come to New York solely to help Jeff with divorce advice.

Margaret put down the receiver and composed herself. While she no longer loved Brian, she did feel badly for him to have died in such a gruesome manner. Undoubtedly, they had been headed eventually for a divorce, but her kids loved him and would take his death hard. She poured herself a vodka, leaving the bottle on the table beside her. Margaret would probably need another drink or two before calling Carol and Barry.

Brian did not sleep well that night. Several times he teared up, thinking of Penny and Naomi, even though he had only known them for a few minutes or so. While he couldn't remember specifically any of the other patrons in the restaurant, he felt terrible for all of them, too. His heart went out to all those brave police and firefighters, and all of the others who perished on a day no living American would ever forget. Reflecting on those families destroyed was his last thought before drifting off to sleep well after 1:00 a.m.

The next morning Brian awoke as a free man but there was nothing to feel good about. The only good thing in an ocean of bad events was that his tracks were covered. He couldn't even really enjoy that. After all, his buddy Jeff would always blame himself for Brian's death, and there was nothing he could do about it. There could be no exceptions. Brian Hart had to be dead to everyone.

It was almost like being in a self-imposed witness protection program. Having no specific destination to head for, combined with very little sleep, he had slept like a baby until 10:00 a.m. He headed to the same diner for breakfast and read the newspaper accounts of the tragedy. The diner was packed, just as it had been when he had dinner the previous night. People just wanted to be with other people so they would not have to grieve alone. At least, that is what Brian attributed it to. He had always found diners to be friendly places, but in the aftermath of the World Trade Center catastrophe, now everyone seemed to be a personal friend. By this time, it was estimated that over 300 firefighters had perished along with over 20 police officers. They were all running into the Twin Towers to save people they didn't know while everyone else was running out of the two buildings to save their own lives. Such bravery only exacerbated Brian's sense of guilt, because he was only presumed dead. The many heroic first responders took their final breaths attempting to save others. Everyone in the diner, whether they were at the counter or seated at the tables, was talking about New York City, Shanksville, and the Pentagon. It was a Pearl Harbor moment or possibly even worse. Brian felt so bad that he even considered shelving his plans and driving back to Rhode Island. His biggest concern, along with the great loss of American lives, was his friend Jeff Price. Knowing him as well as he did, he knew full well that Jeff would blame himself for Brian's demise – and he would undoubtedly carry that guilt to his grave. Obviously, he couldn't contact his friend, but not to would constitute a great sin and he wondered if that act alone would bar him from Heaven when that moment arrived.

It was almost noon by the time he guided the Ford Taurus out of the diner's parking lot toward Highway 70W. He had no idea where he was going, but he was now accountable to no one. It felt good despite the horrible events of the previous day. It still weighed heavily on his psyche what toll his disappearance might exact on Jeff.

When he first thought about his vanishing act, he considered settling in South Dakota or even Montana. If he was serious about either, he would have to make up his mind by the time he got to Indianapolis, some 360 miles west of his present location. It would be about a five-and-a-half-hour drive, and if he remained on Route 70, he would head south toward St. Louis. His best bet for South Dakota and/or Montana would be to begin a northerly trek out of Indiana's capital city and hook up eventually on Route 90 West. That route would take him directly to Rapid City, South Dakota, which happened to be the site of the iconic landmark, Mount Rushmore. It was a place he always wanted to visit.

There were only a few patrons sitting at the counter when he entered a charming little diner near Brookside Park, just south of Indianapolis. He had already checked into a motel across the street. When he was alone, Brian usually preferred sitting at the counter rather than a lonely booth. It was easier to converse with people. A tall and very attractive waitress came over as soon as he sat down and instinctively placed a cup of coffee in front of him.

"How did you know?" he asked with a smile.

"You had that look, handsome," she replied softly. "Not a lot of smiles since 9/11," she added demurely.

"Wasn't that awful?" he concurred, thrilled that she had referred to him as "handsome." Her badge declared that her name was Donna, and she seemed eager to talk about the recent tragedy. But then again, didn't everybody? There was something about the incomparable national disaster that shook all Americans. One didn't need to lose a friend or relative in that horrendous chaos in order to feel personally violated.

As she topped off his coffee a few minutes later, she asked him a question. "Where were you on that awful day?"

Not feeling any need to lie to her, he explained that he was near the Trade Center when the first plane hit. The emotions of that fateful day flashed by, and he was gripped again with that unmistakable pang of guilt. She saw the pain on his face and asked him if he had lost a dear one that day. He tried to change the subject.

"What do you recommend for a hungry dude?"

"Well," she answered fully recognizing his discomfort, "the hot beef sandwich and mashed potatoes are the best in town!"

"You sold me," he said while looking just a little too long at her expressive deep blue eyes. "But then again," he added, "you could probably sell me on anything." He felt foolish as soon as he uttered the words. She passed over it as if she had heard that line many times before.

"Want some green beans or salad with it?"

"The beans, please." She disappeared to take care of the only other person left at the counter. He began to admonish himself. *That is something that Harold Stapleton would have said,* he thought, *but then again, she did call me handsome!*

When Donna returned with his dinner five minutes later, she apologized to him. "Sorry I asked you about 9/11," she tried to explain. "I know that the horrible event opened up a lot of wounds."

"My name is Brian," he said, "and no need for an apology." He paused for a moment. "Actually, I was meeting a guy for breakfast at the restaurant on top of the North Tower that morning." She leaned over, exposing her voluptuous cleavage in the process, and put her hands on the counter to indicate her interest. By then, the other patrons at the counter had left, leaving the two alone except for the elderly couple sitting in a booth by the window.

"He was already late and it was almost 8:00 when he called me to say that his train was late, and he probably couldn't make it until 9. I had another coffee and read a discarded newspaper until about 8:30. Then I got bored and went down to the lobby to get another newspaper or magazine. A few minutes later, the first plane hit the North Tower before I could get back to the elevator...thank God!" She gasped and held on to his hand.

"What happened to your friend?"

"Fortunately, he hadn't entered the building yet," he answered evasively. He wondered if he should have said anything at all, and worried that he might have exposed himself and his story of deceit to a stranger.

"Oh, thank goodness." She breathed a loud sigh of relief. Her reaction only made him feel worse about lying, because he had no idea about Jeff's well-being.

Brian wasn't that hungry, but he ordered a piece of apple pie for dessert. He liked talking with Donna and really felt comfortable for the first time since the unbelievable disaster of 9/11. Besides, the two almost had the restaurant to themselves. The elderly couple was preparing to leave. When they finally did, Donna came over from behind the counter and sat on the empty stool next to him. That move, while it pleased him, made him fear that she might get in trouble leaving her post that way. She sensed his uneasiness.

"Don't worry, darlin'" she reassured him, "my boss loves me." With that and a wink, she suggested they move to a booth near the window. "Sounds like you got a big 'Godwink' on 9/11," she exclaimed with a big smile.

"Not sure I follow you," he inquired with a quizzical expression.

"Oh, sorry," she said. "There's a new book out called *When God Winks at You*, by a very interesting writer named Squire Rushnell. The premise of the book is that there is a lot more to the so-called coincidences in our lives than first meets the eye. For example," she went on, "you may have thought that going for a newspaper that horrible morning was merely a lucky coincidence. Squire Rushnell would say that it was not a coincidence, but an event or experience so astonishing that it must be of divine origin."

"Wow," he exclaimed, "I had never even thought of such a possibility."

"The book," she continued, "made me reflect on my life and realize that many positive coincidences that happened to me probably weren't coincidences at all. They were Godwinks. Just like you leaving the North Tower to get a newspaper that day. Your life would have probably ended right then and there if you hadn't."

"You might just be right, Donna," he agreed. "My need for another paper surely saved my life."

"If you think about your life and how certain people and events intersected it," she affirmed, "Godwinks are more likely the cause than coincidences!"

As he pondered that scenario, she gave him another example. "Sometimes the Godwinks work in a different way. When I was eleven years old," she went on, "I missed a trip to the movies with my friends because I had an upset stomach, and I was so bummed out. It turned out that they were in a serious auto accident and three of the girls were badly hurt. Was that a coincidence, or did I benefit from a Godwink?"

Just then, two elderly gentlemen entered the diner and went to the counter seats. "Hey, Donna," one of them declared with a big smile, "what does it take to get some service over here?"

"Hold your horses, Clem, I'll be right there!" Her leaving for a few minutes gave Brian a chance to reflect more about what she had said regarding those Godwinks. *Was it a Godwink that I went for a newspaper? Was it a Godwink when I was high-sticked by the Clarkson goalie that left a wound directly between my eyes rather than one that would have blinded me? It was literally a chance in a million that the stick's blade didn't take out at least one of my eyes. Was it a coincidence that my out-of-control auto, skidding on that cold icy day so many years ago, barely avoided three young children and went harmlessly into a snowbank?*

"Miss me?" she asked while sliding rather energetically back into the booth.

"Hope that Clem and his buddy aren't mad at you," he snickered.

"No, they're like grandfathers to me."

"Wow," he said. "While you were gone, I've been thinking of some possible Godwinks in my life. That must be what they are." His enthusiasm was palpable. "What time do you close?" he asked.

"Midnight, or shortly before, if no one's around."

"Good," was his unintentionally terse response, because he wanted to ask her if she would entertain the idea of coming back to his room at the motel across the street. He chickened out, and "good" was the only word he could muster at the time.

It was almost 10:30 and they continued talking. She grew up on a farm in Iowa City, Iowa, along with her two sisters. Donna had spent one year at the University of Iowa but was forced to give up her college dreams when her mother suddenly died. She was needed back at the farm to help her father and look after her younger sisters. Marriage wasn't in the cards for her, inasmuch as her duties to her father and family precluded any such opportunity. Donna had moved on her own to the Indianapolis area some years before after her father had died. Her two sisters had moved to California. Despite something of a hardscrabble life, Donna exhibited no sense of bitterness or disappointment.

Brian described for her an abbreviated version of his life. Born in Buffalo, went to Cornell, had been a lawyer in Rhode Island, endured a bad marriage, but was moving west in search of a new life. It probably sounded a little fishy and it certainly was, but Donna didn't push him for details. They sat and talked for another hour, and it was getting close to the bewitching closing time. It was almost midnight and she went about the business of closing the diner. He helped her with a few minor tasks and wanted to ask her to stay the night with him. But the words didn't come so easily to him. She spoke first as they left the premises.

"Are you staying near here?" she asked casually.

"Yes, just across the street. Would you think about, um, I mean could you possibly…"

"I'd love to," she said matter-of-factly with an ear-to-ear grin. His key opened room 124, and the couple stepped inside the modest room. "I've always wondered what the rooms looked like," she pretended to gush.

"Well, it's definitely not the Presidential Suite," he observed with a chuckle. There was a small table and a lamp, two chairs, and a double bed. Nervously, he led her to one of the chairs. "Would you like a Crown Royal?" he offered.

"Sure, but where are you going to get it at this hour?"

"I've got two miniatures in my suitcase. Want some tap water with it?" He winked and she winked back.

"I'll pass, thanks." He poured them into two cellophane wrapped plastic glasses and they sat in the uncomfortable chairs. "So, tell me about your less than happy marriage."

As he started his tale, he looked across the tiny table at her. He wanted to jump her bones big time! From her raven hair to her voluptuous red lips, she was gorgeous. Her flashing eyes were cerulean blue, and her small pert nose was perfect for her face. When Donna smiled, as she did most of the time, her perfectly aligned teeth gleamed. Add to that a knockout figure, a magnificent personality, and a good sense of humor, and Brian was totally smitten. He wanted desperately to hold her in his arms, deposit her on the elephant in the room, sitting so conveniently and so invitingly just several feet away, and ravish her. She seemed to sense his longing, and she got up from her seat and moved seductively toward him. The rest would be up to him. He stood up to meet her and placed his hands over the back of her head and drew her closer. They locked in an embrace and both inched their feet toward the bed. Tumbling awkwardly on it, they laughed and began feverishly kissing each other. Soon their clothes were cast to the floor, but not before removing the well-worn and slightly stained bedspread. They made feverish love for a long time before coming up for air.

"Wow! It's been so long," he murmured, "but so worth the wait!"

"Took the words right out of my mouth," she cooed. They finished their drinks in bed and she asked him again about his failed marriage. He mentioned a litany of events and other obstacles that had led to the end of their union, but there was one thing in particular that he emphasized.

"You know, it isn't the worst thing to be ignored and treated with indifference. It isn't even the worst thing to expect to be treated that way. The worst thing of all is to come to believe that you deserve to be treated that way. And that is how," he concluded,

"I felt after all those years. I needed to leave." His sadness seemed to strike a responsive chord in her, and she reached over and held him tightly.

"Will you stay the night with me?" he almost begged her.

"Yes, Brian. I'm here for you. I don't work until noon tomorrow and can run over in the morning and change at my place." This time, they made love more leisurely and she eventually fell asleep in his arms.

Sleep didn't come as easily for him, however. His mind was occupied by two major thoughts. The first was whether he should ask her to accompany him on his trip west. He thought she might say yes. She was the kind of woman that he could love. Donna was everything that Margaret wasn't − loving, caring, and nurturing, and she loved to laugh and had a great sense of humor. There was no doubt about Donna Foster being a spectacular woman, but his inner sense told him to go it alone. When he first met her, he was feeling very down, almost depressed. The past eight hours or so were among the happiest that he had ever known. Was he making a mistake not asking her to come with him? If so, it certainly wouldn't be his first, but something told him that it was best for him, and perhaps for her, that he complete his journey to find himself without her. One thing was for certain − he would never forget Donna Foster, nor the night they spent together. She had helped to instill in him a new confidence.

The other thought that contributed to him having such a difficult time falling asleep was about Godwinks. He thought about his early life and how what he had originally deemed as coincidences were probably Godwinks. Finally, sleep came to Brian. Upon wakening, they made love one final time as the sun rose and then fell back to sleep. She left him before noon and they kissed and held each other one final time.

"Good luck to you in your travels, Brian."

"Will you still be here if I come back?" he seemed to plead.

"Maybe," was her response.

CHAPTER 18

It would be about a sixteen-hour drive and almost 1200 miles to get to Rapid City, just a little too ambitious for him to accomplish in one day. It was time to unload his rental car and secure a new vehicle. He was able to get another Taurus, although it was four years old and had 70,000 miles on it. Driving northwest, Brian went around Chicago and across Illinois to La Crosse on the Wisconsin – Minnesota border. When he had already driven seven hours, dinner time beckoned. It would be another nine-hour trip west to Rapid City from La Crosse, but it would be on super highway 90. Again, he chose a motel near the road.

He was in the mood for a cold beer after a long drive. He learned from the front desk attendant at the motel about a local watering hole called Sammy's. He decided to walk the half-mile to get there, and it felt good to stretch his legs. Several stools were open at the bar, so he took one on the end and ordered a cheeseburger and a beer. He was talking about the weather with an old geezer two seats away from him, when a young, blonde woman, probably in her early twenties or so, ran up to him appearing to be in some kind of distress.

"Make him stop, mister!" she cried out to him anxiously. Brian didn't have any idea what she was talking about until a young tough followed directly behind her and grabbed her hair. As he yanked her toward him, she shrieked again. No one in the bar made any effort

Tim Norbeck

to help her and some patrons pretended not to notice. The pretty young woman reached out in a failed attempt to grab Brian's arm, and the bully looked him squarely in the eye and said, "This don't concern you, buddy!" Brian sized him up quickly. He appeared to be in his late twenties, about six feet tall and a skinny 165 pounds or so. Dressed totally in black, from his jeans right up to his baseball cap, he looked ominous but not overwhelmingly so.

"Don't grab her by the hair," Brian warned.

"What did you say, mister?"

"I said don't treat her that way!"

The punk in black spat out his cigarette, let the woman rush away, and swaggered over to confront Brian. "I told you, mister, that this don't concern you. What part of that don't you understand?" The agitation in his voice was obvious. One could have heard a pin drop, such was the level of tension in the bar. The oppressor was now inches away so that Brian could smell his tobacco breath. He had a Fu Manchu moustache and his face was pock-marked. His nose was crooked and looked like he had been on the wrong side of a punch or two. Hooded black eyes and a nasty scar across his left cheek completed the sinister look. The man suddenly gave Brian a hard shove on his shoulder with the palms of his hands, but he had expected such a tactic. His knees were bent with his right leg extended back a few inches in order to absorb the push. He countered it in the only way he knew. Lashing out with a karate chop to his adversary's Adam's apple, he then brought his other hand down hard in another chop on the bridge of the punk's nose. Instantly rendered helpless by these two blows, the man in black staggered back, choking and temporarily unable to see. Brian moved forward to finish him. An uppercut sent the tough sprawling against the bar stools, and a right cross sent him crashing to the floor. To his credit, he tried to get to his feet, but Brian hit him hard with his knuckles on his left temple. The man was down and out cold. Some people in the bar yelled their approval and others clapped, signifying their delight in seeing the town bully get a very severe and emphatic comeuppance. Brian sat down again on his bar stool to finish his burger and the bartender brought him another beer. An avuncular man of about sixty, and with a ruddy complexion, he smiled while placing it next to Brian's almost finished cheeseburger.

"One on the house," he said with a wink. "I'm betting that this fracas wasn't the first time for you!"

"Sorry if I disrupted things a bit," Brian apologized.

"Not at all," the bartender replied, "Todd has started more than a few fights in here. But," he added, "this was a much different ending for him."

After a few more minutes and when Brian had finished his dinner and was ready to depart Sammy's, the man he had knocked out struggled to get back on his feet. The victor got up from his stool and readied himself for round two. But the young tough, still a little unsteady, was not looking for a rematch and stumbled his way out of the bar. A few locals came up to shake Brian's hand and to buy him another beer, but he declined, saying that he had been driving all day and was very tired. As he left Sammy's, it was dark, and he was wary and cautious when he stepped outside. Half expecting Todd to appear with a few buddies to exact some revenge, he looked left and right but the coast seemed to be clear.

Back in his motel room, Brian watched a little TV and ruminated a little about the earlier events at Sammy's bar. A Marine friend of his, and a member of the boxing team, had given him a few pointers on how to deal with aggressive tough guys. In addition to his boxing experience, he was also a street-smart guy from South Boston and had a lot of fights in his childhood. From them, he gleaned a number of maneuvers which he was more than happy to share with Brian. Ted Lewis was his name, and what he told Brian about fighting stuck!

"Avoid the fight if you can," Ted had said, "but if it's inevitable, you want to get in the first punch. Not a shove, not a push," his friend exhorted, "but a real hard and effective punch. Then you move forward into him and finish it. Don't give him a moment to breathe or collect himself. Go after him and pummel him until he is done." *All good advice*, Brian had agreed. Ted had also given him some sound advice when dealing with a guy who was physically much larger and stronger.

"Say some guy who is six inches taller than you and fifty pounds heavier wants a piece of you. Stick your fingers into his eyes and then karate chop him in the throat. Then step in while he is disabled," Ted added, "and don't hold back. Clobber him with your fist in his temple and even a real big tough guy will go down. And Brian," he cautioned him, "don't let up until he is knocked out cold." *Good old Ted,* Brian thought, *he would have been proud of me tonight.*

The next morning, he was excited by the thought of visiting the famous Mount Rushmore National Monument. He realized that it was a little risky visiting such a public place, inasmuch as he would have to spend the rest of his life avoiding people he knew. Brian didn't bother shaving since he had left Rhode Island on Monday, so there were visible signs of a mustache and beard. He would also wear a hat, just in case he encountered someone from his past life. It was 7:00 p.m. when he arrived in Rapid City. The traffic hadn't been heavy, but the glare of an all-day sun served to enervate him. A shower, more fast food, and a good night's sleep prepared him for the coming adventure the next day.

CHAPTER 19

This was the closest he had ever been to Mount Rushmore, not counting the epic 1959 film *North by Northwest* starring Cary Grant and Eva Marie Saint. Perhaps one of the more interesting tidbits about the movie was that Director Alfred Hitchcock reputedly wanted Cary Grant to play the Roger Thornhill role, but Jimmy Stewart assumed that after having done *Vertigo* the year before, that surely it would be his – and he was eager to do it. Supposedly, Hitchcock didn't want to hurt his feelings and waited until Stewart was already committed to doing *Anatomy of a Murder* before offering the role. Of course, he couldn't accept it. A few other interesting anecdotes endure from the popular film. In order to satisfy the censors, Eva Marie Saint was forced to change her original line: "I never make love on an empty stomach" to "I never discuss love on an empty stomach." Censors today wouldn't bat an eyelash! When villain Martin Landau first encounters Cary Grant, he declares: "He's a well-tailored one," when in fact, all of Landau's suits for the movie were made by Grant's personal tailor. Thinking *North by Northwest* would be a disaster at the box office, Cary Grant was shocked at its premiere, where it was wildly popular with the viewers.

After a good night's sleep and a big breakfast, he drove from his motel to the Mount Rushmore site. From the observation deck, the view was utterly breathtaking, and the day presented him with a bright, beautiful blue sky. There, before him, were the four U.S.

Presidents: Washington, Jefferson, Teddy Roosevelt, and Lincoln – so huge and lifelike, in stark contrast to the hills and granite surrounding them. He made his way down to the Avenue of Flags, opened in 1976, which proudly displayed fifty-six flags. The flags represented all fifty states, the District of Columbia, the three territories of Guam, American Samoa, and the Virgin Islands, and the Commonwealth of Puerto Rico and the Mariana Islands. It was a beautiful walk through all of the flags. Now strolling down the avenue, he gazed up again at the sculptures where Gutzon Borghum had worked his wonders so many years ago for fourteen long years, and accompanied by four hundred men and huge amounts of dynamite. Local legend insisted that an important American tradition actually began during the carving of Mount Rushmore. Allegedly during one cold morning, the granite carvers were attempting to warm themselves with hot coffee when the sculptor Borghum happened upon them and instructed the foreman to have donuts and coffee ready for everyone the next morning at 10 a.m. Supposedly that was the genesis of America's coffee break!

Of course, Brian was not part of any organized group, so he hung around a small gathering of people who were in the presence of a park ranger. Mount Rushmore cost nearly one million dollars to construct, and despite harrowing conditions during those years (1927-1941), nary a single worker was killed. According to the ranger, the story of Mount Rushmore began in 1923 when South Dakota historian Doane Robinson envisioned a project which would attract people from all over the world. Originally his plan involved the carving of Wild West heroes into the stone, and he invited Gutzon Borghum, the American artist and sculptor, to come and visit the area and put his dream to work. Upon viewing the site, Borghum had his own vision. It was far more grandiose than Robinson's. "Why not a 'Shrine of Democracy,'" he asked, "which would include gigantic carvings of U.S. Presidents out of stone?" Robinson agreed but wondered how they would ever find the federal funding to do the project. South Dakota U.S. Senator Peter Norbeck came to the rescue. Somehow, they needed to enlist the help of President John Calvin Coolidge, but how? Silent Cal, the only U.S. President born on July 4th, had become the American leader in 1923 when the 29th president, Warren Harding, had died unexpectedly. The new president had lost one of his two sons, Calvin Jr., in a tragic accident that would never occur today. Young Calvin was sixteen years old and had incurred a blister on a toe of his right foot while playing tennis in 1924 with his brother John. A septic infection spread to his bloodstream. With no infection-fighting drugs like penicillin available back then, the boy died.

In 1927, his last full year as president, Coolidge expressed an interest in spending a summer away from the oppressive heat, bugs, and a White House renovation. His bronchitis didn't help either. Norbeck and Robinson worked diligently to have the president vacation in the Black Hills of South Dakota. On June 13th, Coolidge along with his spouse, Grace, arrived in Rapid City. Intending to stay just a few weeks, the Coolidges remained there for two months, probably due to a little chicanery on the part of Senator Norbeck and Mr. Robinson. Knowing that the president enjoyed fishing, especially fly fishing for trout, workers stocked the stream outside his room at the state game lodge where he and Mrs. Coolidge stayed. He barely needed to make a cast before the trout responded! He was so happy with his success, they extended that two-week vacation to two months. That time period gave Norbeck and Robinson all the time they needed to convince the willing president to fund the almost $1 million needed for the carving of Mount Rushmore.

Coolidge officially dedicated the project in August of 1927.

In addition to his fishing success, the president also went horse-back riding and attended rodeos. It was, in fact, during that vacation in the Black Hills of South Dakota where he uttered the famous state-ment: "I do not choose to run for president in 1928." As famous as that saying was, it was probably his second most famous comment. As Governor of Massachusetts in 1919, he declared in response to three-quarters of the policemen in Boston going on strike: "There is no right to strike against public safety by anyone, anywhere, any time." That show of decisive leadership certainly helped to catapult Coolidge into the public conscience and contributed to his being elected as Warren Harding's vice-president in 1920.

Brian felt lucky to have joined the organized group where they learned about the "inside" history of Mount Rushmore from the ranger. They digested one other interesting fact about the proj-ect before breaking for lunch. Apparently Borghum attempted to carve Thomas Jefferson's likeness first, and to the left of George Washington. But the granite proved too brittle, and that carving had to be destroyed in mid-project.

Now hungry from wandering around the premises and absorb-ing so much captivating information, Brian settled in his seat in the memorial's cafeteria and dined on soup, a BLT, and iced tea. It had been an exhausting day so far but a very fascinating one. It was intriguing to learn that a US President had played such a major role in the creation of Mount Rushmore. Although he hadn't planned to, since it was still early afternoon and he was only about 20 miles away from the Crazy Horse Memorial, he decided to take a ride a little further southwest before heading back to his motel. He had heard that Crazy Horse was an interesting character, having been a war chief of the Lakota Sioux. He was not disappointed in his decision to visit the memorial.

The Crazy Horse Memorial was the world's largest mountain carving in progress. Chief Henry Standing Bear was an Oglala Lakota Chief who invited New England sculptor Korczak Ziolkowski to carve a memorial honoring North American Indians. In 1939, Ziolkowski first came to the Black Hills to help Borghum on Mount Rushmore. That same year he also won first prize for his Carrara marble portrait, *"PADEREWSKI, Study of an Immortal,"* at the New York World's Fair. Chief Standing Bear read the news of Ziolkowski's achievements and invited him to create a mountainous tribute to the North American Indians. The sculptor returned to the Black Hills in 1947 to begin the project with the first blast taking place in June of 1948, and it is still far from completion. Five Indian survivors of the Battle of Little Big Horn had attended the event. When completed, the head of Crazy Horse will be 87 feet high compared to just 60 feet for the Mount Rushmore presidents.

While at the monument, Brian took advantage of the educational video showing in the visitor's center. He learned that this project was not government funded but made possible by donations from individuals, quite different from the Mount Rushmore project. After learning that fact, it was obvious to him why the project was still a work in "progress." He learned that the mission of the Crazy Horse Memorial Foundation was to protect the culture, tradition, and living heritage of the North American Indians. And they were doing this by having a repository of American Indian artifacts and arts and crafts through a museum, and by providing educational and cultural programming through a cultural center. Brian then took a short bus ride to the base of the monument and was overwhelmed and awestruck by the size and magnificence of the edifice.

CHAPTER 20

Visiting Mount Rushmore and the Crazy Horse Memorial was fun and he thoroughly enjoyed the leisure time, but now it was time to think about his future and where he would be spending it.

Meanwhile, some 1900 miles due east, chaos reigned in Barrington, Rhode Island. Upon learning of their father's "death" at the World Trade Center, Carol and Barry drove home immediately to comfort their mom. Margaret was conflicted. She no longer loved her husband, but he was a good stepfather to her children and he certainly didn't deserve to die. Especially that way. Members of Brian's law firm were shocked. Two of them had relatives who perished in the South Tower, so it was a double whammy for them. His friends in his hometown took his death very hard. Their distress and grief were profound, added to the pain all Americans felt over the terrorist attacks on America. But, without question, there was no one who quite matched the level of misery and agony felt by Jeff Price. In his mind, he was the reason his friend had died. Had he not been so late, he and Brian probably would have finished their breakfast and left the restaurant and building before the plane hit. But not only did Brian lose his life, Jeff was spared his own. That combination was devastating to Jeff and with a possible divorce looming, his sense of heartache had no bounds. It would not have been possible to overestimate his feeling of guilt. Of course, Jeff never had figured in the original scheme. The two friends would have breakfast, talk business, and depart and only later on would Brian suffer his phantom mugging and disappear. Everyone would have been better off had he stuck to the original script. But the terrible terrorist events had occurred and gave him the perfect opportunity to disappear. Unfortunately, his disappearance came at a considerable personal cost for Jeff as well as countless others.

Brian needed to move on, establish himself somewhere, and get a job. If he drove five hours on 90 W, he could easily get to Billings, Montana by dinner time. It might possibly be a suitable place for him to settle down and spend his future. It was the largest city in Montana, but that wasn't saying a whole lot. Heck, the population of the entire state wasn't much over a million. He had taken his family to the Northwest U.S. a few years before and they had spent a night in Billings. The people were nice and he enjoyed the town during their brief visit. He remembered it as a growing area nicknamed the "Magic City," and it was a successful trade and distribution center for the state. It had one other very good thing going for it – he didn't know anyone in Billings, or even in all of Montana for that matter. He would spend a few nights there and get a feel for the place. If he wasn't comfortable there, he could always drive south to Denver or Colorado Springs, which were just eight or nine hours away, respectively.

After checking into a motel on that Friday, he headed for an establishment that could serve him a sandwich and a real drink. Brian also wanted to see the local color and get a feel for the community, and what better way than to visit a bar? Harry's looked the part and was only a five-minute walk from where he was spending the night. It was a little on the dark side when he entered the place, but he liked the overall ambiance. The bar accommodated about fifteen stools and most were occupied. There were six small tables along the large window facing the street. Four of them were full of patrons seemingly engrossed in deep conversations. As he ambled up to the bar, he noticed a somewhat wizened elderly gentleman sitting next to an empty seat toward its end. The old man appeared to be engaged in some unfriendly banter with the fellow to the left of him, who was no spring chicken himself.

"Is this seat saved?" Brian addressed them as he sidled up to the last stool.

"No," the first man replied without even glancing at him, and continued his lively conversation. "Look, if you don't like it, too fuckin' bad!" With that exchange, the object of his derision got up, gave the old man the finger, called him an old bastard, and abruptly left the premises.

Brian turned to look at his seatmate. The man had to be over eighty and looked his age, he thought, as he quickly examined his countenance. He had deep creases in his face especially near his eyes, and a thatch of unkempt gray hair running from the top of his forehead all the way down to his tensely arched bushy dark eyebrows. His deep-set eyes were remarkably clear blue but the rings under them had their own rings. A ruddy complexion, a wide craggy face, and ears too big for his head completed the picture. Brian held out his hand and said, "I'm Brian."

"Charlie," the old man returned the salutation as he took Brian's hand.

"Too bad about your buddy."

"Oh, him. He's a real asshole."

"Hopefully you guys can make up and be friends."

"Who gives a shit?" his new acquaintance replied acidly. "You know the trouble with you young fellas?" Charlie didn't wait for a response and he continued on. "One of the good things about being over eighty is that you don't give a shit anymore. I don't feel the need to be liked by everyone. Either you like me or you don't. Either way, I don't really give a shit."

I like this guy, Brian thought to himself.

"Yeah," his new friend went on unabated, "young people today care too much about being liked by everyone. People aren't honest with people anymore."

"You know," his younger new friend pondered, "I think you are absolutely right. And, I confess to being one of them." The old man sat back and laughed.

"What are you drinking?" Brian asked.

"I started with a whiskey ditch, but I'm going to change to a shot and a beer."

"What's a whiskey ditch?"

The old fellow threw back his head and laughed. "It's Montanan for whiskey cut with a little water – a Montana favorite," he added.

Catching the eye of the bartender, Brian shouted out: "Two boilermakers please."

"Thanks," Charlie said with a nod. "Where ya from, Brian?"

"Buffalo, Charlie, before moving to New England."

It turned out that Charlie had been born in Anaconda, about 250 miles due west, and had moved with his family to Billings when he was seven years old. He had two brothers, and with his father, the four of them had been in the logging business. His wife had died from breast cancer back in 1980 and their three children lived in Chicago, Rochester, New York and Naples, Florida. He was obviously lonely and was enjoying the conversation with his new confidant. They drank and had cheeseburgers together and conversed for almost two hours. Brian picked up the tab despite the old man's protestations. Before he left, he needed to ask a few more questions.

"You must like Billings, since you never left it."

"Yeah."

"Why?"

"The people are great, and there is no better trout fishing anywhere!"

Brian was intrigued. "Near here?"

"Yeah, the Bighorn River comes up north from Wyoming. You can wade fish in spring and late summer. I'll take you sometime if you want." By now Brian was really warming up to this spunky graybeard. Then Charlie really came out of left field.

"Ever read *Paradise Lost*, Brian?"

"Are you shitting me?" Brian responded. "Nobody has read it! I'd rather go to the dentist!"

"I read it," the old man asserted. "Probably the most famous line in the twelve books is where Satan says, "It is better to reign in Hell than to serve in Heaven."

"I must admit," Brian confessed. "I never read a page."

"Well, you missed a lot, young fella."

"What else from *Paradise Lost*?" he asked with a slight smile of condescension. The old man noticed it but didn't let it bother him.

"Just the greatest explanation of human behavior, that's all," he responded in kind. By now Brian fully realized that he had short-changed Charlie. This guy was really worth listening to. Without waiting for any further prompting, the oldster spoke again.

"Milton said that the mind is its own place, and in and of itself can make a heaven of hell or a hell of heaven. That explains as well as anyone ever did why people who have nothing can be happy while millionaires can be despondent."

The younger of the two pondered that statement for a moment before replying. "You're absolutely right Charlie, that is brilliant!"

The old man's face lit up like a Christmas tree. "My father wasn't an erudite man, nor am I, but he showed my brothers and me how important it was to read. My youngest brother, Norm, never bought into it, but my other brother, John, and I did."

"Charlie, did you ever go to college?"

"Not a chance, Brian, we were all trying too hard just to survive. Our logging put food on the table but little else."

"Sorry about that, but I've received a pretty good education in the short time I've known you."

"Good to meet you," the old man replied as he slid off his bar stool. "I've got to go now, but I come here every Friday night at six. Hope I'll run into you again. Thanks again for the drinks."

As he left the bar, Brian noticed that his new friend had a considerable limp. The old man had practically dragged his left leg across the room, aided by a cane. *I will make certain to ask him when we run into each other again*, Brian declared to himself. *What a neat guy!*

CHAPTER 21

The following week, Brian worked as a grocery store clerk and did odd jobs at Carl's Auto Body Shop just to provide himself with a little extra cash and give him something to do while he was "feeling out" Billings. He knew that he would have to find a full-time job in the next month. The money was running low, and he hoped that somehow a lawyer opportunity would pop up. But how? It was now Friday afternoon and he cleaned up back at his motel after spending the afternoon doing oil changes. The clock said 6:00 p.m. when he left his room and began the short walk to Harry's. Sure enough, his friend was already seated at the bar with an empty stool next to him.

"Howdy, Charlie!"

"Oh, hi Brian," the old-timer retorted, a bright smile on his face. "I was hoping you'd make it."

"You kidding, Charlie? I'm always game for a free education."

The senior citizen beamed hearing that and those blue eyes began dancing. Brian wanted to ask about Charlie's limp but didn't feel he knew him well enough to delve into it at that particular time.

"Got time for dinner?" he asked the venerable old man.

"Yup, but let me buy."

"Next time, Charlie, this one is on me." They managed to get through their BLTs, fries, and a boilermaker before a question was put to Brian.

"What are the two most important days of your life?"

He weighed those words for more than a moment, and then suggested that one of them had to be the day he was born. "But I'll be damned if I know what the other is."

"You're right on the first, Brian. According to Mark Twain, the second most important day in your life is the day you find out why."

Man, he thought to himself, *this guy is really something. I thought I was reasonably well-educated, but clearly not.* "Mark Twain wouldn't think much of me," Brian conceded, "because I have never even given it any thought. How about you, Charlie? Why were you born?"

"I didn't find out until about ten years ago," he allowed. "My calling, I think, is to care for some of my old friends, several of them who are dying. I try to be there for them and make their difficult lives a little easier."

"That's very noble of you, my friend," countered Brian, who by this time was convinced that before him was a special man. "Are you religious, Charlie?"

The old man downed his second shot of bourbon and paused before the beer chaser. "I believe in Jesus Christ and that he is my personal Savior, if that is what you mean. I go to church occasionally. I don't wear it on my sleeve, but yes, I'm religious. How about you, Brian?"

"Well, I'm not there yet," he replied, "and I have a few things to work through."

Charlie wasn't going to go there at this point, even though it was his young friend who had initiated the subject. "Well, let me know if I can ever be of help to you," was as far as he went. It was time for Charlie to leave, and he slipped off the stool while grabbing his cane. "Hope to see you next Friday," were his parting words.

"You can bet on it," Brian replied with a big grin. He stayed for another drink while mulling over the words of his friend.

This guy is really something, he thought. "You can bet your sweet ass I'll be back, Charlie," he muttered out loud to himself as he left the bar.

By this time, Carl Lombardi, the owner of Carl's Auto Body Shop, had taken a shine to Brian and used him in different capacities. A legal matter had arisen and Brian assured Carl that he could handle it. So, his duties increased, as did his paycheck. But he knew that it wouldn't last and that soon he would have to find a full-time job that satisfied him.

The following week, Brian found himself thinking about meeting up with Charlie on Friday. The old man's wisdom had made a deep impression on him. He was the perfect example of why one should never judge a book by its cover. Brian missed the old geezer, especially since he and Carl were the only people he really knew in Billings. *Charlie said that he went to Harry's every Friday at 6:00,* he thought. *I wonder if he might be there tonight?* He wasn't, so he had a Crown Royal over ice. The shot and a beer scenario was a special thing he only enjoyed with Charlie.

Just as he was asking for a check, he noticed a man three or four stools down staring at him.

Oh, my God, he realized, *it's Pete Norman.* Although not close friends, they had served together on the Cancer Society board back in Rhode Island. *What the hell is he doing in Billings?* was his second thought. His third, and far more important than the others, was – *Does he recognize me?* He soon had his answer. Just as he was paying his bill and preparing to slip away from the bar as unobtrusively as possible, he felt a hand grab on to his arm.

"Brian Hart. Is that you? How in the hell did you ever survive 9/11?" Norman added almost stridently, "It's your buddy, Pete Norman!" Brian was forced to think very quickly.

"Not sure who you've confused me with sir, but my name isn't Brian Hart."

One look at the man along with the unwanted whiff of his breath told him that he was clearly intoxicated. He was slurring his words, and he seemed shaky on his feet. Pete Norman was a big man who stood well over six feet. His substantial paunch had not receded in the past three years since they had last seen each other. He possessed a very ruddy complexion, a large, almost bulbous nose, and hooded black eyes which gave him an ominous and sinister look. His neatly combed black hair resembled a wig, but who cared? The plentiful hair growing out of his nose and ears seemed enough to house a bird's nest. Brian figured that it was unlikely that there was a Mrs. Norman, because who would let their husband go out in public looking like that?

Pete briefly considered Brian's denial before launching into a diatribe. "Don't shit an old friend," he said adamantly, "you have to be Brian Hart!"

"My name is Ralph Kennedy," Brian insisted.

"No freaking way, Brian," Pete pursued it.

"I was born Ralph Kennedy and remain so," he continued to lie. "But, no harm, no foul. Let me buy you a drink." With that said, he signaled to the bartender that the two would like refills. Brian's mind was going a hundred miles an hour, but not so fast that he would be fooled enough to use his true first name. Something immediately had told him that his acknowledgement of "Brian" as his first name might help trigger Pete's memory of the encounter the next morning. Hence the use of "Ralph." Sizing up Pete

Norman's obvious state of inebriation, he decided that one or more additional drinks would probably put him over the top, and the big fellow would never even remember their meeting from the night before. Norman didn't seem to mind the extra libation at all, and Brian gambled that the additional beverages would only serve to increase the haze and confusion that Pete was already feeling. If Brian had merely walked away instead of engaging him, his "friend" would undoubtedly surface again at Harry's or inquire about him. Either option was not acceptable and could pose a serious challenge to his need for anonymity.

The two men remained anchored to their stools while Brian, aka Ralph, continued to humor him.

"Where you from, Pete, and what brings you to Billings?" As he spoke, he attempted to use a lower voice than usual to try and disguise it. Pete answered that he was originally from Rhode Island but had moved a few years ago to Sheriden, Wyoming – about two hours away. "Every year I come up here with two of my buddies to fly fish for trout." Upon hearing that, Brian began to breathe easier.

"Where are your friends now?" he asked casually.

"They both got drunk and are sleeping it off." *Just like you should be doing, you big oaf!* Brian thought.

"So, Pete, when are you guys heading for home?" Again, he tried hard to sound like it really didn't matter to him.

"Tomorrow morning, Stan – I'm sorry, what was your name again?" he stammered. The extra drink was clearly having its desired effect. His response was music to Brian's ears.

"It's Ralph," he responded, almost forgetting the fake moniker. They had one more drink together and it was obvious that Pete was fading fast. Brian had watered down his own last two drinks unbeknownst to his bar mate.

"I still think you look an awful lot like my friend Brian Hart," but now he wasn't so sure. The extra alcohol had just about done the trick.

"Hey," he replied, "I saw a guy about two weeks ago who looked just like my brother," he lied. Of course, Pete didn't know that he didn't even have a brother. They both laughed at the comment, and Brian finally sensed, with great relief, that he had successfully managed to dodge a potentially perilous bullet. He knew that he was unlikely to even remember being at Harry's that night, much less recall running into one Brian Hart. After Pete left the premises, "Ralph" walked to his motel with a little extra bounce in his step.

The motel charged him only 40% of the daily rate for a monthly stay, so the cost was not exorbitant, but he knew that the time was coming soon when he would have to secure a more permanent lodging if he were to remain in Billings. As of now, he liked the community, but it was a must to expand his number of contacts and friends. By 5:45 p.m. on Friday, Brian was already comfortably settled on his bar stool waiting for Charlie's arrival. Sure enough, at 6:00 sharp, there he was. A wide grin broke out on his craggy old face as he spotted his friend and he ambled over to the bar. They exchanged a hearty handshake and half a hug.

"You know, Charlie," Brian began, "we don't even know each other's last name."

The older man smiled and nodded. "Moore. Charlie Moore."

"Hey Charlie Moore, good to see you. My last name is Miller."

"I guess it's Miller time," the old timer joked, "but remember, this time it's on me." Over their boilermakers, they talked about family.

"Tell me, Charlie," Brian began, "about those three kids of yours.

Are they humble like their old man?"

"Yes, I'm happy to say they are," he responded. "Do you know what true humility is?" Brian shook his head, indicating that he didn't.

"I think that true humility is not thinking less of yourself, but thinking about yourself less."

"Wow, that is really profound."

"Wish I could take credit for it," Charlie smiled, "but that belongs to C.S. Lewis."

"Who the hell is C.S. Lewis?"

"He was a British writer and theologian. That great quote came from his book, *Mere Christianity.*"

"Man, you are really well-read."

"Thanks Brian, not sure about that, but appreciate it. You know something interesting?" the old man continued. His younger companion leaned forward to hear. "C.S. Lewis died on the same day and year that JFK was assassinated in Dallas."

"November 22, 1963?"

"Yup, that very same day."

Brian didn't allow that he had two stepchildren, although he felt very comfortable with Charlie and trusted him implicitly. He just couldn't afford to open up about his life to anyone, not even this charming and very bright senior citizen. At least not yet. They parted ways and Brian felt that he had received another free education. By this time, however, he was in the mood for a little female companionship. He had noticed a number of attractive women in his three trips to Harry's, but they all appeared to be attached to someone. He would have to develop some type of strategy, and that clearly was not in his wheelhouse or comfort zone.

There was a Presbyterian church within walking distance of his motel, and Brian decided that it was time to pay it a visit. Besides, he was feeling grateful to the good Lord for having had the good fortune to meet one Charlie Moore. It was a Godwink. If he had made the mistake of casting judgment on the old man simply by his wizened features and chiseled face, he might never have had the opportunity to meet him, much less engage the fascinating man in meaningful conversation.

Brian grew up as a Presbyterian, but he did not deem a particular denomination to be an important factor. What was important was to worship in the House of God, and according to Brian that meant any church. He didn't think that God cared, just as long as people went to a church or synagogue. Attending the 10:00 a.m. service, he chose an end seat in the last pew. The sermon was on service to others, and he couldn't help thinking about Charlie and what he had learned from him. What was the second most important day in Brian's life? He didn't yet know but was determined to find out. Perhaps the church might help him on that journey.

There was a mixer for the parishioners after the service, and he almost slipped out of the church without attending. Something inside of him suggested that he at least make an appearance. He was glad he did. While sipping some punch and clutching on to a donut at a side table, he sensed a figure next to him. She was tall and very attractive. Her stick-on name tag indicated that she was "Kate." He hadn't bothered to get one.

"Hi," she said, "I'm Kate Harper."

"Sorry, I don't have one of those." Brian pointed to her name tag.

"But you do have a name...right?" she responded with a big smile.

4

"Oh, yes, I'm Brian Miller," he replied, noting to himself that he had almost forgotten his name.

"Well Brian Miller, I'm happy to meet you. I don't come every Sunday, but most of them, and I don't remember ever seeing you."

He looked her up and down without being too obvious about it. She was drop-dead gorgeous. Kate had long black hair, perfect white teeth, and flashing green eyes. Her skin seemed to be without imperfection and her mouth seemed fixed in a continuous smile. Her nose and ears were on the small side but appeared just right for her face. In short, he was quickly taken by Kate Harper. That did not portend well for him, particularly since he was often tongue-tied in the company of beautiful women. And she was a beautiful woman.

"I, ah, um, I'm new to town and this is my first visit to this church." She signaled that there was a small table available just off to their right.

"Want to sit down?" she invited him.

"Sure," he replied as he followed her to the table and pulled out the chair for her.

"I see that chivalry is not dead," she exclaimed with a broad grin. His old Rhode Island friends would have had a clever retort, but sadly, he didn't. He merely smiled and then sat down face-to-face. Those enchanting green eyes immediately drew him in. *She may be the most beautiful woman I've ever seen,* he thought to himself.

"Where are you from, Brian?"

"Buffalo, New York," he responded after thinking for a moment. "How about you?"

"I'm a Billings, Montana girl through and through!"

He was very hesitant to talk about himself, which she sensed. Brian admitted to having gone to Cornell, both undergrad and law school, and playing hockey and football there. That was about the extent of it. To avoid talking about himself and answering questions about a past he wished he could forget, he continued to throw questions her way. She, too, was a lawyer, having graduated from the University of Montana and its law school.

"Ever hear of Montana's Jeannette Rankin?" she asked.

"Sure. She was the woman's rights activist and the first woman, I believe, who held federal office in the United States."

"Wow, I'm really impressed."

"And, she was the first woman member of Congress," he said emphatically, now suddenly proud of himself. Kate began to speak, but he held his hand up with its palm towards her, indicating that he wasn't finished. "She voted against declaring war against Germany in World War I, and was the only member of Congress to vote in opposition to declaring war against Japan after Pearl Harbor."

"Now you have really impressed me. Did you know that she went to the University of Montana?"

"That, I didn't know."

"She was a pacifist, of course," she continued, "and I don't think anyone in Montana was particularly proud of her vote against declaring war on Japan." He nodded.

"So, Brian, what brings you to Montana?" He thought for a moment to collect himself. The answer to her question had to be a plausible one.

"Well, frankly, I was getting tired of my law practice and had just been divorced. My father had been born in Montana," he lied, "and I had never been out here before."

"Where?"

"Where what?"

"Where in Montana was he born?"

"Oh, Anaconda," he continued the falsehood.

"That's about 250 miles due west from here," she noted.

"I've been in Billings for less than a week," he declared, "and I really like it." Looking at her, he added with a smile, "I like it even more today!" He was surprised by his boldness, but he had already passed the infatuation stage by the time he had first sat down with her. Her face turned crimson, and he smiled back at her.

"Are you practicing law here in Billings?" he asked.

"Short answer – yes," she replied, "long answer – no."

He raised a quizzical eyebrow. She noticed it and tossed her head back in laughter.

"What I mean," she went on, "is that I had originally planned to go to a big city like LA or San Francisco and work for a large law firm."

"What happened?"

"My mother happened," she responded. "My mom got very sick during my last year of law school and my dad needed some help. I am without siblings, so he didn't have anyone else to turn to. I was very close to my mother and wanted to comfort her. I was at her bedside when she passed, and that was such a blessing."

He reached across the table and boldly took her hand in his, and then realized that she might interpret it as a rather brazen move for a stranger. But she didn't make any effort to remove it. Then he saw tears forming in her eyes. "It must have been tough for you," he empathized.

"Thanks, Brian. The cancer moved rapidly through her body, and she lasted only eight months." He didn't ask what type of cancer, nor did she reveal it. "My father really took it hard, and it was then that I decided that I should join his law firm, which he had founded, and remain in Billings at least for a few more years. And that was," she continued, "nine years ago. Enough about me," she gushed, "I want to learn more about you!"

Not wanting to go there, he had other questions to ask her. "Have you ever been married?"

"No, I haven't."

"Why not?"

"Never had the time."

"Did you ever get serious with anyone?"

"Not really, but kind of," she hedged.

"How so?"

"Well, during law school I met this guy. He seemed interested, but Mom was sick and I never had any real time to give the relationship. It stalled out in my last year of law school, and I never heard from him again."

"What a fool he must have been," Brian opined.

Kate blushed and smiled.

"I wouldn't have let you get away," he said adamantly.

"Okay," she interrupted, "that truly is enough about me. I want to learn something about Brian Miller!"

He allowed to having one brother who was an architect in New York City, and immediately was in wonder as to how he pulled that lie out of the bag. It was all lies. He worked for a Boston law firm – and, he just felt the need for a new start. They talked for a while about the tragic events of the past week at the World Trade Center, the Pentagon, and in Shanksville. Fortunately, neither of them knew anyone who had perished. But Jeff Price would always be on his mind.

"My goodness," she observed while looking at her watch. "We've been here for a full hour and I think they want us to leave." He knew that he had to make a move.

"Do you think you might be up to having lunch or dinner – or even a cup of coffee?"

"I'd love to, Brian. Any one of the three would be fine."

"Let's make it dinner then," he said enthusiastically. As they said goodbye and began going their separate ways, she stopped suddenly and took a step toward him.

"Do you want to know how to reach me?" she asked with a beaming smile.

"Oh, gosh, I'm sorry. I'm not very good at this." She gave him her office, home, and cell phone numbers, while he was limited to only one number, and he didn't even know what it was.

"Sorry, I'm in Room 207 at the Track Motel. I lost my cell phone and need to get another."

She thought that strange but didn't say anything. He wanted to call her the next day, which was Monday, but he thought he might sound desperate. He waited until the next day and they agreed to meet on Thursday night at Barton's Steakhouse in the center of Billings.

He was captivated by her; she was interested but somewhat reserved about him. Dinner at Barton's would be an important engagement for both, but for different reasons. Tuesday went terribly slowly for Brian as he sifted through some legal papers for Carl Lombardi before doing a few oil changes in the afternoon. It was going to be an interminable wait for him until Thursday. He asked himself repeatedly the same inevitable questions all guys ask when they are interested in a woman. *Does she like me? If so, how much? Was I too shy or too brazen? Is she seeing anyone else? Is she being nice to me because I am new? Will this be one date and I'm out? Is she going on a mercy date?* Of course, if he had any real experience with women, or several successful relationships, he wouldn't have so many doubts. His total female relationship experience, he reminded himself, was one wife, one brief affair, and a childhood romance with a young woman who became a nun. And none of them had worked out that well. So going into the main event at Barton's, here was a man with precious little confidence, swagger, or bravado, but he did have plenty of doubts, apprehension, and uncertainty. Not a good trifecta if a man is attempting to impress a woman.

Thursday evening finally came, and they met at Barton's at 6:00 p.m. She wore jeans and a black turtleneck; he, brown corduroys, and a matching long-sleeved shirt which he had purchased at Adams Department Store on Wednesday.

"You look beautiful," he stammered.

"You're not so bad yourself," she countered with a grin.

During their conversation about her childhood and her hometown of Billings, it was obvious to him that she was extremely fond of her father.

"How is it, working with him?"

"Well, we don't really see that much of each other," she explained, "especially since his firm has grown and we added two more lawyers last year. Did I mention that Dad had been a prosecutor for the county before he put together his small law firm?"

"No, you didn't. That's interesting."

"About thirteen years ago, he prosecuted two brothers for murdering a rancher on the county line. It was a tough case. It got complicated, and in fact, the case helped him to decide to go into private practice. He had been thinking about transitioning out for personal reasons, but the Taylor case was the catalyst for him."

"It must have been quite a case, for him to make that decision," he opined.

"There were indirect threats to our lives, and my father was livid. He could never directly connect them to the threats and that really frustrated him."

Brian was intrigued by the whole case. "So, how did the Taylor brothers kill the rancher?"

"They just murdered him in cold blood, chopped him up and buried him. It was so grisly." She winced as she described the deed.

"Please tell me that your father got a conviction for those two thugs."

"There was a secret eyewitness who is now somewhere in the Witness Protection Program."

"I hope they at least got life sentences," Brian opined.

"No, that was another bad thing about it. Rufus Taylor got life with no parole, but his younger brother, Jed, got only fifteen years. He was the driver and supposedly only helped to bury the victim's body. Both guys resembled Charles Manson when they were arrested," she went on, "but the defense lawyer had them looking like choirboys at the trial."

"Is the younger brother, Jed, out of prison yet?"

"Yup, it was about a year ago, I'm not sure. I think that he got three years taken off his sentence for good behavior, so he only served twelve. The rancher's family wasn't happy about that, for sure." With that said, Brian thought it best not to pursue the subject any further.

"So, what about you, Brian?" she asked. "How long are you going to hole up at the Track?"

He smiled. "Well, as nice as it is," he said with a twinkle in his eye, "I should be looking for an apartment."

"So then, you've decided to stay?"

"I think that attending the after-church social had a lot to do with it." He winked at her and shrugged his shoulders. She blushed and her face turned that shade of crimson again.

They were off to a great start. They both ordered their steaks medium rare, baked potatoes, and a salad. His steak came back a lot more medium than rare, but there was no way he was going to send it back.

"Are you going to look for a position in a law firm?" she phrased her question delicately.

"It's what I know best, Kate," he responded emphatically, "but I just don't know for sure."

He was really pleased to hear that she liked to play tennis and she also liked to jog, but that didn't elicit any interest on his part. Throughout the dinner, he did everything he could to avoid talking much about himself, an evasion she noted. *He is so secretive,* she thought. *I wonder if he is hiding something.* But she fancied him nevertheless and liked the way he carried himself.

After dinner, he walked Kate to her car and had a decision to make – kiss her or not kiss her. As they approached her vehicle, he decided that his best and safest course of action was to give her a peck on the cheek. During that awkward moment, they agreed to meet for a tennis date on Saturday morning.

Brian looked forward to the following evening because he would see his buddy Charlie Moore at the bar. He was there in his usual spot and had been saving the end seat for his younger, new-found friend. They greeted each other warmly and spent almost their entire time together talking about baseball. The old man loved the game and had played it as a boy. The Colorado Rockies was his favorite team— mainly, as he explained it, because they were the closest major league team to Montana. Brian had grown up in Buffalo and then moved to New England and fittingly, he was a Red Sox fan.

Kate met him for breakfast on Saturday morning before their tennis outing. He had one too many pancakes and felt bloated. They found a hard court available at a public park that she recommended. Her game was much better than he expected, and she lobbed him until his tongue was hanging out. Needless to say, he felt that extra pancake. They played for over an hour and a half before calling it quits.

"Wow, that was quite the workout!" she declared.

"I'll say," Brian returned the thought. "Let's rest a bit and if you'd like, we can at least grab a cold drink."

"Sounds like a plan!" she quipped while grinning. They walked to a nearby concession in the park and had hamburgers and iced teas, and enjoyed many laughs together. Kate really liked a man with a sense of humor, and he did make her laugh.

At the end of their late lunch, he suggested having dinner together the following Friday at Harry's. *Somehow,* she thought, *I'm going to have to figure out how to get my father to meet Brian.* He called her several times the next week and their relationship seemed to blossom. Brian planned a surprise for her at Harry's on Friday night. Little did he know that she had one in store for him as well. This time, he picked her up at the house she shared with her father and they headed out to the restaurant. Charlie was sitting on his regular perch when they entered the bar. Before he could introduce her to his new buddy, she rushed over to the old man and gave him a big hug.

"Charlie," she gushed, "it's been a while. So nice to see you again."

"I see that the two of you have met," Brian chirped, with a look of surprise on his face.

"You're in good company, Brian, if you're with Kate Harper!"

"I was going to surprise you by introducing you to my best friend in Billings," he declared, "but I see that the surprise is on me!"

"I'm probably his only friend in Billings," Charlie added with a wink towards Kate.

The three moved from the bar stools over to a table by the window and ordered a pitcher of beer and dinner. It wasn't as sumptuous as their dinner the week before at Barton's, inasmuch as Harry's was more of a burgers, sandwiches, and brews kind of place. Halfway through their meal, a large and imposing figure appeared next to Charlie.

"Hey you, old man," the apparition bellowed while bending over and giving him a hug. "Don't get up," he commanded, and then stuck out his hand for a vigorous handshake. Brian had no clue as to this man's identity.

"Brian," Kate said with a smile enveloping her face, "this is my dad, Hank Harper."

Brian immediately jumped to his feet. "How do you do, Mr. Harper?" he said while extending his hand in a firm handshake.

"You must be a city boy," Hank replied. "But he has a great handshake and looked me in the eye, so he can't be all bad!" All four of them laughed.

"Come join us for dinner, Mr. Harper," Brian beseeched him.

"It's Hank, Brian. My father, Mr. Harper, died many years ago." Hank was a big man, probably six feet four with massive forearms, a wide chest, and broad shoulders. He had a full head of salt and pepper hair which was graying at the temples. His eyebrows jutted over deep-set black eyes, and while his nose was prominent, it was not too big for his chiseled face. A square and firm jaw housed a full set of teeth, somewhat discolored, probably by a nicotine habit. In short, he was formidable looking and certainly one to avoid in a fight. Brian took an instantaneous liking to the big man and pulled up a chair for him.

"I can't join you because I'm meeting some of the guys here, but I will definitely take a rain check. It was nice to see you, Charlie, and nice to meet you, Brian." And just like that, he was abruptly gone just as suddenly as he had first appeared.

"Your dad sure seems like a great guy, Kate." Brian broke the silence.

"You never want to fool with him," offered Charlie Moore.

"He looks tough," Kate added, "but he really is a lovable guy."

When the three broke up after dinner, Brian drove her home. On the way Kate explained that Charlie and Hank were old friends. This time he was determined to kiss her. At the front door, he paused a moment and told her how much he enjoyed their dinner and meeting Hank.

"Do you want to come in for coffee?" she invited him.

He froze. "Um, I ah, think maybe not tonight. I'm kind of tired." She seemed disappointed but said nothing. Realizing the gravity of his stupid mistake, he attempted to cover for his foolishness. "I'd love a rain check," he offered weakly.

"Sure," she said unenthusiastically. He didn't get that good night kiss.

He called her on Saturday morning, feeling as much embarrassment as he did remorse. *I handled that like a real seventh-grader,* he admonished himself. As soon as she answered, he began his apology. She set aside her disappointment and pretended that she hardly noticed the slight.

"How about dinner on Tuesday?" he asked hopefully.

"Sorry Brian, but I can't," she replied. His heart sank and he assumed the worst for his blunder. "But I could on Wednesday,"

Kate broke the momentary silence.

"That's great," he sounded relieved. "Do you want to pick out the place?"

"Sure. How about Guliani's for some great pasta?"

"Perfect. Sounds great to me. I'll pick you up at seven." He felt like he had dodged a bullet. *I won't pass up the opportunity again,* he vowed to himself.

Wednesday evening finally arrived and she greeted him at her door wearing blue slacks and a ruffled white blouse. He wanted to take her in his arms and sweep her off her feet right then and there. But, of course, he didn't act on that impulse. "You look terrific," he stated emphatically as they descended the porch stairs. She merely smiled.

At Guliani's while having their first glass of wine, he leaned forward as if he were telling a secret. "I never had much confidence with girls and women," he earnestly confessed. "I don't know if it was because they could sense that I wasn't very comfortable around them or something else."

She listened intently.

"When I was a young kid, the older ladies really seemed to like me, but not so much the girls my age. When I got older, little girls and elderly women were super friendly to me, but not those in my age group."

She focused on his every word, but said nothing and let him continue.

"I married the first woman that I really had a relationship with," he lamented, "that's how inexperienced I am." Kate winced as he mocked himself. "Go on," she urged him.

"I wanted so much to kiss you the other night," he continued, "but I was afraid."

"Afraid of what?"

"Afraid you would rebuff me."

"Has anyone ever rebuffed you?"

"No, not really. But I was afraid that you would."

"Well, Brian, I'll tell you what. Why don't you get up and come over here and kiss me right now?" His face turned red.

"You mean right now?"

"That's what I said...right now!"

"You mean right here in the restaurant?"

"Yes, right here in the restaurant. I don't see any sign anywhere that says 'no kissing in this restaurant,' do you?"

"But in public?"

"Yes, in public!" He got up from his seat, moved around the table, and gave her a peck on the cheek. "Not on the cheek, Brian, on my lips!" He kissed her fully on the lips but was aware that patrons from other tables were looking at him.

"Now that wasn't so bad, was it?" she said smiling broadly.

"I'll say," he agreed and then he sheepishly returned to his seat. It was probably one of the oddest first kisses in the annals of couples' first kisses. Somehow, he felt like a huge burden had been lifted off him. The tension he felt getting through that first kiss now totally eradicated, he could be himself. He felt a new assured-ness take over his being, and he loved his new freedom. They even ordered a third glass of wine and were at the table for almost three hours of frivolity and laughter. It was almost like he was a new man.

Kate pointed to the table next to them where an elderly couple was engaged in a game of chess while enjoying a glass of wine.

"Aren't they cute," he observed. "I remember seeing people play in coffee houses in Rhode Island more than a few times."

"You mean Massachusetts?"

"Yeah," he replied, "how foolish of me. I meant Massachusetts!" *Careful, fella! No more wine for you,* he reprimanded himself for the blunder, hoping she didn't notice any discernible uncertainty in his reply.

"Do you play?" she asked.

"A little, but I'm not very good."

"We'll have to play sometime."

"Sounds good to me," he chuckled. "I can't remember the last time I had three glasses of wine," he remarked as they left the restaurant. When they reached her door, he did not hesitate to take her in his arms and plant a very affectionate and amorous kiss on her lips.

"It's getting late now Brian, but I do want you to come in after our next dinner."

"How about tomorrow?" he laughed with a new surge of confidence.

"Silly man," she responded as she returned his passionate kiss.

When he returned home and went to bed, all he could think of was her. He was now totally smitten. Before he had left her, they agreed on the following Wednesday for dinner.

But it wouldn't happen.

CHAPTER 22

Brian looked especially forward to his dinner on Friday with Charlie. The two no longer had to formally agree to meet; it was now taken for granted that the two new fast friends would meet up every Friday at six. They talked for a while about Charlie's long friendship with the Harpers.

"I'll tell you something Brian," the old man said emphatically, "you can do worse than Kate Harper. She is the real deal and I hope that you two will be a couple."

"If I have anything to say about it, Charlie, we will!" That pleased the old man and they drank to it. "And if we were to make it to the altar, I'd be pleased to have you as my best man." Their glasses clanked again. After their second boilermaker, Brian posed a question.

"I hope I know you well enough to ask this question, Charlie."

"Of course, you do, my friend," he responded with eyes slightly arched in a curious expression.

"Well, I just wondered why you have that limp?"

"Believe it or not, Brian, I was a pretty good sprinter in my high school days. This old guy ran the hundred in just over ten seconds, which was pretty darn good in my day. And then I went to Iwo Jima. I was in a foxhole with a fellow Marine, about one week later, when a Japanese sniper got me twice in my left knee. My buddies got me out of there and on a hospital ship. The war was over for me. The battle lasted more than a month, although a lot of people think it was over in a week."

Charlie Moore was feeling it. Sensing the old man's emotion, Brian mistook it for uneasiness.

"You don't need to tell me anymore if you don't want to, Charlie."

"Not a problem, my friend, I'm just starting. I didn't talk much about it when I first returned home, but I don't mind now."

"Are you sure?"

"Absolutely! Do you remember the famous Joe Rosenthal photo of the six flag-raisers?"

"I sure do; it's probably the most well-known and iconic war photo of all time."

"I was almost in it," he said with a proud smile.

"No shit, Charlie! What happened?"

"The invasion began on February 19, 1945 and the fighting was fierce. The Japanese, of course, were well-fortified and hidden away in Mount Suribachi. Joe Rosenthal was just one of several cameramen that day on February 23, a few days after the battle began. A Marine sergeant photographer, Louis Lowery, actually was the first on the summit snapping photos of Marines proudly raising the American flag. Rosenthal heard the commotion and decided to ascend the summit himself. Then a firefight with some Japanese began and Lowery tried to take cover and fell, destroying his camera in the process. Are you still with me, Brian?"

"You bet, Charlie, keep going."

"Well, Lowery went back down the mountain to retrieve a new camera. Apparently on the way down, he met Rosenthal and a couple of other photographers going up. 'You're too late, guys,' Lowery allegedly said, 'there's already a flag up there.' But at the same time, Lowery urged them to continue their ascent in order to see the breathtaking view. Now, this is the really interesting part, Brian. Once they reached the top, they spotted a few Marines holding a second flag. They told the photographers that they had been instructed to replace the first one with a larger one so it would be more visible to those below. Acting on that comment, Rosenthal realized that he had a second chance to photograph an important moment in the battle. His timing was perfect, and he took the shot just as the flag was being raised. The photo made the front page of almost every newspaper in the world. Unfortunately for Rosenthal," Charlie went on to say, "there was always a suspicion that his photo had been staged. It wasn't, but there were many who thought it was."

"How did you almost get into the photo?" Brian asked.

"Well," the old-timer continued, clearly enjoying the telling of his story, "I was deployed at the summit and some captain came up to me and said that they might need another Marine for the photo. By the time I arrived, he told me that they already had enough guys. I was kind of disappointed at the time, but I really regretted it when the photo made all the papers! It was just two days later after I had been redeployed when the sniper got me. The good thing about being shot," Charlie quipped, "is that I always get an early warning before it rains!"

"Man," Brian exclaimed, "I marvel at how you don't let things get you down."

"Brian, it is what it is and there is no changing it. There's a great quote," he continued, "that I always try to keep in mind." The old man paused for a moment to take a swig of his beer chaser. "Anyway," Charlie began where he left off, "the quote was originated by an author and motivational speaker by the name of Sonia tti. Everyone should live by it; I sure do. She said, 'Accept what is, let go of what was and have faith in what will be.'"

"Boy, that is really cogent, Charlie!"

"See what I mean?" Charlie said triumphantly.

Kate and Brian couldn't play tennis the next day since she and Hank were visiting a family friend in nearby Laurel, just west of Billings. He spent most of the day looking at a few apartments and a condominium. The charm of Kate Harper was proving to be very magnetic. It rained heavily that night and he spent almost all of it at the Track Motel, except for the fifteen minutes he spent locating some fast food for dinner. Kate called him when she returned, and they talked about their next scheduled dinner for the following Wednesday night.

"I might even summon the courage to kiss you," he teased.

"I would certainly hope so," she encouraged him. Their relationship seemed to be on sound ground and was progressing. But a challenge loomed imminently ahead.

Brian arose Sunday morning to a beautiful sunny day and decided to go to church after breakfast. He also needed to restock his small refrigerator at the motel. Entering the grocery store, the first thing he noticed was a small group of people congregated together to his left before he felt the cold steel barrel of a pistol held behind his right ear.

"Don't move or say a word, motherfucker," commanded the shadowy figure standing behind him.

"Take it easy," Brian assured him

"You shut your mouth or I will splatter your brain on the floor."

Brian turned around slowly to assess the situation and to size up his adversary. He was dressed in black pants and a matching tee shirt and face mask. His tensely arched bushy black eyebrows were hard to miss. The gunman's bulging eyes were a foreboding coal black and his tousled, unkempt hair of the same color splashed over his ears. He was skinny and seemed nervous.

"Who said you could turn around?" he spat out while simultaneously lunging forward to pistol whip Brian across the cheek. "Do what you're told and shut up," ordered the thug, who left little doubt that he meant business. Slowly the two ambled over to join the others, who were huddled together on the floor. The store manager for that day and his fellow workers had been herded together, along with the shoppers who had been unlucky enough to pick that particular time to shop at that specific store. Had Brian been alone with the assailant, he might have comported himself differently, but there were twelve other hostages, including two young children. Their mothers were in the group, and two men, one of whom looked to be in his eighties. The other man appeared to be in his seventies but looked very frail. By now the two kids were whimpering, something that was clearly aggravating the other gunman, who was pacing impatiently. Sensing his ire, the two mothers worked earnestly to calm them down by stroking their hair. Meanwhile, the thug who had assaulted Brian had moved back near the front of the store to position himself for any incoming shoppers.

Brian scrutinized the remaining shooter, who was holding what appeared to be an AR-15 assault rifle along with a Glock 9-millimeter pistol in his belt. He also wore a black mask and was wearing tattered blue jeans and a faded green tee shirt. Looking not at all like his cohort, he had a husky build, was totally bald with protruding ears and bulging, uneasy brown eyes. Of the two, he seemed to be the one in charge and exuded a quiet but ominous presence as if to say that this was not his first attempt at robbery or hostage-taking

– whatever his motive. Brian's left cheek was throbbing and dripping blood, but he was oblivious to it.

"What do you want?" he asked the gunman, who was just a few feet away and who probably considered him to be the only real threat among the hostages.

"Do you want your other cheek smashed?" he said threateningly.

Brian measured his words carefully. "Of course not." He tried to sound meek and nervous. "But maybe I can help you get what you want." Then Brian felt the butt of the assault rifle strike his forehead. He staggered backwards and sat down with the others.

"Are you with the police?" the bald tough asked.

"No, I'm just a regular citizen, just like these good people. Do you intend to keep us hostage?" For a moment it looked like the thug was going to lash out against him again, but if that was his intention, he decided against it. "Hear me out," Brian said softly.

The gunman raised the AR-15 as if to shoot. "You want to get shot, wiseass?"

"You would have shot me already if that was your intention."

"Don't be so sure, smart guy."

"The last thing you want is to shoot anyone," Brian said assertively. "You would have snipers and the SWAT team all over your ass. I can help you!"

"If we are going to take you as hostages, how the hell can you help us?"

"It's simple," Brian opined, "just take me as your hostage and let the others go."

"No, they give us more leverage."

"They also add to your problems."

"How the hell is that?"

"Do you really want to deal with two crying young kids and their mothers? They will have to be fed and go to the bathroom."

"Yeah, so?"

"And do you want to be held responsible for the two old guys? What if one of them has a heart attack? If he does, it will be a murder charge for you, even if you don't lay a hand on him. You and your partner certainly don't want to face a murder charge, do you?"

"I'm listening."

"Let these good people go and just keep me as your hostage. You both can watch me better than you can watch thirteen people. And you can find sympathy – at least leniency with the press, especially if you let the children go." Brian could feel the sweat trickling down his back.

"Keep talking, fella."

"Tell the police that you don't want the kids, their mothers, or the elderly gentlemen to get hurt, and that you'll let the six grocery workers go when you see the money. That you are going to hold me as your only hostage. It will simplify your endgame, whatever it is, and make your exit here easier. By the way, what is your endgame? Is it money?"

"One million dollars in small, unmarked bills."

"Billings, Montana is not exactly New York City—this is not a bank, and today is Sunday," Brian ventured.

"Well, $500,000 dollars should be doable," the gunman conceded. "And we want a Gulfstream jet."

"Just like D.B. Cooper!"

"One more crack out of you, smart ass, and we'll have one less hostage!"

"Let the other hostages go," Brian pleaded again, "and I will stay with you and help get what you want. If you don't do it this way, the police will come in and you'll have a shoot 'em up – and everyone dies, including you two."

By now the gunman's accomplice had rejoined the group and seemed to agree with Brian's assessment. "C'mon Lester," he said, "this guy's right. The ones we let go can tell the police what our demands are. Otherwise, how are they going to know?"

Mr. AR-15 pondered the points and advice for a moment. "Maybe you're right, Marvin."

Capitalizing on the momentum, Brian urged them on. "Let the two kids and their mothers leave first. Less trouble for you, and they can explain your demands to the police."

The plan made sense, and the mothers were almost frantic by now. Someone else had to stand up and be another leader. The grocery store manager, whose name was Will, stepped forward and declared, "I can do it." Will appeared to be a thirty-something, forty-pounds-overweight, timid, and non-threatening fellow. In short, he had the perfect personality to serve as the go-between messenger.

"Ok, buddy," the ringleader agreed, "here's what you say. We are nice enough to let the women and children go free, but we want $500,000 dollars in small bills and a Gulfstream jet fueled and ready to go. If we don't have both of those things in two hours, we'll shoot one of the nine men. Tell them that we'll shoot some-one every fifteen minutes after that, and that we mean business!" Once we have the money and the jet, we will release the two old guys. Smart ass here – what is your name, smart ass?"

"Are you talking to me?" Brian brazenly responded clearly in jest.

"Yeah, you."

"Brian."

"Brian what?"

"Brian Miller."

The front door had been locked early on and several would-be shoppers congregated there for a few moments before dispersing. By now, however, there were several policemen and a gathering, inquisitive crowd near the front door. The thug named Lester held his assault rifle in plain view as the women and children and Will filed out of the store. Then the freed hostages explained the situation to the police.

"I hope one of you guys can fly a Gulfstream," Brian muttered, apparently not so softly.

"You know," Lester said in exasperation, "I've had just about enough out of you!"

The two older men and six store workers sat huddled with Brian on crates while they all began to wait.

"Where you from?" Brian turned to the ringleader.

"What the hell do you care?" he replied acidly. "What do you think this is, smart ass?" he added, *"This Is Your Life?"*

The other assailant accompanied the hostages, one by one, to the vacant deli department to get something to eat and they all sat down near the front of the store with their sandwiches, water, and chips. None of them felt like eating, but they did anyway so as not to anger their captors.

It was now 2:10 p.m. and the women and children had been gone for over an hour, and Mr. AR-15 was getting anxious, and his nervous state was perceived by everyone. Although he had a burner phone on him, he didn't see any need to communicate with the police. Lester had seen enough crime shows to know that communicating back and forth usually didn't end well for the bad guys. A few more policemen and SWAT team members joined their other colleagues outside. The curious bystanders had been told to get back from the immediate area, although a television station reporter and cameraman had joined the group. All of that seemed to be fine with the thug, but he was growing impatient. It was clear to Brian that both Lester and Marvin were rank amateurs; who else would use their names during such an event? But Brian also knew that they could be even more dangerous because of their inexperience. He didn't dare make a stand because of the other eight male hostages. Based on their behavior, he was almost certain that Marvin didn't have it in him to kill anyone, but he wasn't so sure about Lester. If anything went wrong, the two hostage-taking dilettantes were capable, probably, of shooting anybody by accident.

The time was ticking by slowly. At 3 p.m., Lester was already edgy. He sent the senior member of the hostage group out the front door to talk with the police. The thug made sure he didn't venture very far, and everyone could see the assault weapon trained on him.

"The money will be here in another ten minutes," the old man said as he slid back inside the door. "And the jet is at the airport being fueled right now." This information calmed Lester down considerably and he sensed a positive outcome. At 3:20, the police indicated that the money had been raised and it sat in a very large knapsack outside of the door. Lester ordered Marvin to go out and verify that the money was all there. He wasn't happy with that assignment, but, with a little glare from Lester, he stepped gingerly outside the door and picked up the knapsack. After looking at the packaged money, he revealed a thumbs-up to his partner in crime and crept back inside the store.

"I didn't count it all, Lester," he proclaimed proudly, "but it appears to be 500 grand!" Lester allowed himself a slight smile.

"Okay," he bellowed out to the hostages. "Eight of you line up here. Smartass will go to the car with us." Marvin had parked their getaway car in the first spot marked "disabled." As the hostages filed out of the grocery store, Marvin followed behind them while carrying the large stash of money. Lester had told him to place it in the car and get the motor running before coming back, and then they would both emerge from the building with their guns fixed on the remaining hostage. He thought it would look more threatening if both criminals accompanied their hostage to the car without the encumbrance of the satchel.

"Here they come," someone yelled out as the door opened. The TV anchorwoman instructed the cameraman to start filming, and the police and SWAT team members inched closer. The drama was ready to play out. Lester stood to the left of Brian with his AR-15 pointed directly at his head. Marvin was behind Brian, applying a headlock so he wouldn't break free. After the first step, however, Brian said a short prayer to himself and made his move. Suddenly he stopped, threw his arms straight up, and sat down. There was a brief moment when Lester and Marvin were exposed, and the SWAT team took quick action. They fired at Lester first because he was the most dangerous one, brandishing the assault rifle. His partner, who had held Brian in a headlock, was momentarily distracted from his 9mm Glock pistol and was able to fire only one round as he fell in a hail of bullets. Unfortunately for Brian, his right shoulder was the recipient of the lone round. Lester was cut down just as quickly in a salvo of savage firepower. One of the SWAT team members, acting immediately with little room for error, mistakenly shot Brian once in the left thigh while he was firing at Marvin. Both hostage-takers were killed almost instantly and tumbled to the ground. Their hostage was alive but bleeding profusely from his two wounds and was draped across the store's doorway. An ambulance had been called to the site before the shooting thanks to the quick-thinking police chief. Brian was hustled into the ambulance and hastily given oxygen while two paramedics applied compresses to the bullet torn areas. During the confusion, another TV anchor and a newspaper reporter, who had just arrived at the scene, were yelling out if anyone knew the identity of the wounded hostage. No one did.

Brian struggled to get his breathing under control but the oxygen did the trick and he remained conscious. He knew he was in trouble because of the blood loss, but blind faith gave him the confidence that he would not bleed out and could survive the ordeal. The paramedics worked feverishly on him, knowing that his body probably contained about five to six quarts of blood. If he lost forty percent or about three quarts of the vital fluid, he was in danger of dying. The two working in tandem estimated that he had probably lost one quart already, but they had nearly contained the bleeding. At the hospital he was quickly moved into the emergency department's intensive care unit, where he would receive a red blood cell transfusion. Soon the peril had passed, and after receiving additional IV medications and being cleansed of the blood and grime, he rested comfortably. His forehead and cheek received six stitches each, although everyone was puzzled about how that could have happened in the shoot-out. They checked out his wallet and found that his name was Brian Miller, but there was no address or next of kin. He also didn't seem to carry any health or hospital insurance, at least not from any cards they found in his billfold. His reputation as a hero preceded him, and the hospital would treat him pro-bono as they did other such patients.

Meanwhile at 4:00 that Sunday afternoon, the phone rang at the Harper household. Kate was the first to answer.

"Turn on the TV right now," Charlie Moore commanded. "Brian

was involved in a hostage-taking at the grocery store and was almost killed!" With desperation in his voice, he continued. "Apparently he was shot twice and is in the hospital's ICU." Stunned by the news, Kate just stood there helplessly. "Kate," Charlie shouted, "Brian is a hero! I'll meet you at the hospital." And then he hung up the phone.

"Dad," Kate yelled, "we've got to go to the hospital now! I'll explain in the car." Fifteen minutes later, Hank dropped off his daughter at the Emergency entrance and parked the car. Charlie arrived at the same time. The intensive care unit did not allow visitors, but after a half-hour wait, Brian had been moved to a private room and they could see him. Kate went in and immediately dissolved into tears when she saw his bandaged face. Charlie and Hank followed her in. Strangely, the patient had a big smile on his face. The look of horror was obvious on Kate's countenance and Brian tried to lighten the moment.

"You should see the other guys," Brian chirped with as much enthusiasm as his aching and sore body could muster.

"They're both dead," Charlie countered.

"I figured they would be," he said approvingly and with a wince.

"Does it hurt bad?" Kate asked.

"That's 'hurt badly,'" he corrected her with a wink. "They've given me some pretty good stuff to control the pain." The stitches on his cheek tugged when he smiled, so he kept that to a minimum.

"I guess he's feeling better," Hank chimed in.

Brian was tired but told them everything he knew and could remember about the chaotic situation.

"The TV reporter said you must have had some military training," Charlie weighed in, "to have the wherewithal to escape the headlock the way you did." Brian broke out in a slight smile and laughed, feeling the stitches in his cheek.

"That's a load of crap," he exclaimed. "Every eighth-grade kid in the United States learned that maneuver. Head locks were popular when we were kids, and it was a foolproof escape by throwing your arms straight up and then sitting down. That's all I did," he added modestly.

"Did you know that the SWAT team would shoot them?" Hank asked.

"I didn't know for sure, Hank, but I was hoping they would!" Since his face was hurting from his injuries, he only managed a slight chuckle.

"Well, the media is acting like you were the second coming," Charlie noted.

"Charlie, you and I know that there is only one second coming, and it sure isn't me!"

"We should probably let you rest now," Kate interjected while stroking his hand. Everyone agreed except Brian.

"Kate, would you mind staying with me for just a while longer?"

"Of course, Brian," she replied. "Charlie won't mind driving Dad home, would you, Charlie?"

Once the two men were gone, Kate asked, "Why did you do it? Why did you have to be a hero? You could have been killed!" She continued to stroke and caress his hand.

"I'm not the hero type, but I kept thinking about the two little kids. These guys were stupid enough to kill everyone. I knew that if they let everyone else go," he continued, "I would have a chance to get away. But I couldn't jeopardize the safety of the kids or the others to do it."

"But what if the SWAT guys didn't shoot them, and those thugs ended up shooting you?"

"I thought about that, but I was confident that they would do their job. What I didn't figure on was that someone would miss and hit me!"

"There wasn't much time, from what I've been told, and you are pretty lucky to be alive."

"Lucky, yes, but I'm alive. I'm still ticked off that the shaggy-haired punk named Marvin got me on his way down."

"Thank goodness it wasn't worse!"

"You know what I feel really lucky about?" he said earnestly.

"What?"

"That you're here with me right now." She squeezed his hand and began to cry softly. Brian's eyes were slightly hooded and he was ready to get some rest.

At that point, there was a knock on the door and a nurse peeked in. "There are two members of the press who would like to talk with Mr. Miller," she announced. Before Kate could even react to the request, Brian held his other hand up to indicate an emphatic "no."

"Please tell them that I'm sleeping," he lied. "No media, absolutely no media," he repeated. She didn't understand the urgency behind his demand. Brian certainly did and decided that he would not shave anymore and hopefully could grow a beard to complement his moustache. *I won't be able to avoid the camera forever,* he feared.

Some of the painkillers were wearing off, and Monday was a tough day. In late morning, Charlie wandered in and sat down at his bedside. He had his scruffy looking baseball cap on his head.

"How's it going?" the old man asked.

"Hanging in there," Brian responded.

"There are media-types hanging around the lobby and a few

made it all the way to the nurses' station before being turned away. Are you up to an interview?"

"I don't want any publicity, Charlie. I was just doing what anyone else would do."

"That's bullshit, Brian. Very few would have done what you did. But they're being relentless. You're going to have to talk with them sooner or later."

"Any suggestions? I just don't want any hoopla."

"Hoopla you're stuck with, but you can manage it. Let's face it," the old-timer continued, "you're a huge story, and it will probably go national."

"Geez, I sure don't want that! What do you mean by managing it?"

"Well, you could agree to seeing them from your bed. If there is a question you don't like, you can feign pain or exhaustion and put an end to it. Just give me a look."

"I'm not real comfortable about talking with a lot of people I don't know. Can I borrow whatever the hell you have on your head?"

"Oh, this?" Charlie said chuckling, as he took off the cap. "Why the hell would you want to wear this piece of shit?"

"I just like it."

"I'll get you a better one in the gift shop."

"No, I'd like that one if you don't mind."

"Sure," he muttered as he handed it to his friend, "but it will show everyone that you don't have any class!" They both laughed at that utterance as Brian slipped on the cap.

"It will make me more comfortable. Would you mind setting up a brief meeting with them for me? And I do mean brief."

"No, not at all. When do you want to do it?"

"I don't want to do it at all, but if I have to, how about something this afternoon? Would you stay with me during it?"

"Sure, buddy."

Just then, Kate arrived by his bedside. "How are you guys doing?" she asked.

"The patient is doing pretty well," Charlie responded, "but I'm not so sure about me." Kate smiled.

"Kate, Charlie thinks I ought to have a short meeting with the media people. What do you think?"

"What do you think?"

"Well, I sure don't want to, but I think he's probably right. Otherwise," he continued, "they'll continue to swarm all over this place and there will be no peace."

"I agree with Charlie. I just passed a lot of them in the lobby and the hallway."

"Charlie says that I could do it from my bed and that I can always end it if I'm tired or in pain."

"Wise man, that Charlie," she nodded her head in agreement. "But you have to lose that grungy hat!" Both men laughed vigorously, although Brian winced and held back somewhat.

"Apparently you two old reprobates have already had this conversation," she pouted in mock derision.

"How about at 2:00 this afternoon?" Charlie suggested.

"That would be okay, I guess," the patient replied. "Kate, would you mind being here with us?"

"Of course not," she said decidedly.

Word went out quickly that the wounded patient and hero, Brian Miller, would visit with the media from his bedside at 2:00 that afternoon. His physicians believed that he was well enough for such a task, and doing so was actually a relief to them. The hospital administration, his two physicians, and numerous nurses responsible for his care had been inundated with inquiries about an interview since he had first arrived as a patient. Hospital security had been put on alert to manage the group. This was big news almost anywhere and certainly for Billings, Montana. And the media axiom: "If it bleeds, it leads," was especially relevant in this case.

With a haggard-looking face, a ratty hat on his head, bandages on his cheek and forehead, a moustache, and a developing scruffy beard, Brian was confident that no one could possibly recognize him – even if there were photos carried in some newspapers. In fact, he was counting on that. Throw in the large bandages covering his left thigh and right shoulder, and he almost looked like a mummy.

By 1:50 p.m., the reporters were plentiful and both Charlie and Kate could hardly move. The old man decided to start the proceedings despite the presence of one of the physicians. "Hi, I'm Charlie Moore. Some of you know me. I am a close friend of Brian's, and I just want to caution you as to his willingness to appear and talk with you. As you know," he went on, "he was shot twice just a day ago and is exhausted and in pain and on painkillers. He may have to stop the interview sooner than you would like, but he knows that you wanted to speak with him. With that said, who has the first question?"

There were six newspaper reporters in the room, some from as far away as Bozeman, about 140 miles west, and two Billings television anchors. The hospital had approved the use of their auditorium for the press interview, but Brian had respectfully rejected the offer. Only he really knew why. The group of reporters assembled seemed to defer to the senior reporter among them.

"How are you feeling, Mr. Miller?" Max Kallas, the dean of the local newspaper reporters began the questioning.

"I'm doing okay, thanks, but a little tired and quite sore."

"You are a hero," Max followed up. "How does it feel to know that you saved twelve other people?"

"I don't consider myself a hero, Mr. Kallas. I did what anyone would have done." There was muffled laughter in the hospital room. A thirty-something woman from the *Billings Herald* added, "But someone else didn't do it," she insisted. "You did, and you risked your life. I was actually there and everyone seemed to marvel at how you escaped the headlock."

Brian attempted a laugh but winced in his effort. "Actually, that was a maneuver I learned in eighth grade," he chuckled, "along with probably every other eighth-grader in the country!" Everyone in the room snickered.

"What exactly are your wounds?" one of the two TV anchors asked.

"I took a bullet in my upper left thigh and one in my right shoulder. And I got pistol whipped on my cheek and forehead," he added. "I'm not very pretty anyway, so maybe they helped!" The room erupted in laughter hearing him make light of it. Fortunately for Brian, the softball questions continued.

"Do you intend to stay here in Billings, or do you plan to move?"

"I've only been here for a couple of weeks, made some nice friends and the people are great, so I think I would like to settle here." Both Kate and Charlie smiled.

"Is there a Mrs. Miller?" one pert young reporter asked.

"No there isn't," he declared.

"Where did you live before coming to Billings?" one of the reporters inquired. Brian could sense that the questions were beginning to reach the probing level, and he signaled as surreptitiously as he could to Charlie that he would like to end the interview.

Charlie picked up on the look Brian had given him and announced that this would be the last question. "I know that you're disappointed, but this man has been through an incredible amount of trauma and is suffering considerable pain right now. I'm sure you understand." Heads all nodded.

"I lived in the Boston area," he responded to the question. "Sorry, but I'm just feeling pretty groggy right now," he added. When the group of reporters were gone, Brian breathed a little easier and thanked Charlie for his help. Kate moved over to him, sat down, and held his hand. The encounter with the media surprisingly had not enervated him further but actually had the opposite effect. He felt a surge of energy but didn't let on to Kate or Charlie.

"You must be tired, Brian," she said softly. "Are you in pain?"

"It comes and goes," he explained. "Right now, it's coming."

"We should leave you alone," Charlie suggested. "I'll be back to see you after dinner."

"Thanks for coming, both of you," he said genuinely. When the room was clear of everybody, Brian reviewed in his mind what had just transpired. He felt confident that he had done an adequate job in responding to the questions, but was clearly on dangerous terrain if he talked much more about his past. All his disappearance plans would be shot to hell or go up in smoke if an enterprising reporter learned too much. And yet, he knew that he would be hounded by the media as long as he was practically held hostage in the hospital.

When his attending physician came to check on him in late afternoon, Brian asked him about how long he would have to remain in the hospital.

"Normally," he replied, "in a situation like yours, it would require almost a full week. But you've snapped back very well. I may be able to discharge you on Friday," he added. While this was good news, the patient was expecting something a little sooner. His shoulder and thigh throbbed when the meds wore off, but he could handle it. They acted up on occasion, but he had been fortunate that neither wound was too deep. He felt that his head hurt worse than did the damage inflicted by the bullets.

On Tuesday afternoon the bandages were removed from his head, revealing two nasty purple welts. "Oooh, ouch," Kate winced, as she saw the finished product. "It must be painful if they feel as bad as they look."

"You mean I'm not so pretty anymore?" he pretended to pout. "It's just twelve more stitches added to the hundred already there!" Charlie had arrived by the time of the unveiling, and he made a big production out of flinching and then recoiling away from Brian.

"Man, you are flat-out ugly!" he declared. The nurse who had removed the bandages didn't seem to have a sense of humor and looked at the two visitors with disdain.

"I'm still prettier than you, Charlie," Brian quipped.

"In your dreams!" the old man retorted.

Kate had to leave for a meeting, but his venerable old friend remained. "Am I going to have to hold another press conference, interview, or whatever the hell you want to call it?"

The local newspaper had carried a huge article about the hostage situation and its resolution, including a photo of Brian in his hospital bed. With his baseball cap and facial hair, it didn't look much like him. His first thought upon seeing it was fear. But then he felt a sense of relief and recognized that it was not an accurate likeness of him.

"You probably should, Brian. Do you want to?"

"No frigging way. I'm not a real media-type kind of guy," he went on to explain. "But I wonder if I have to."

"You don't have to do anything, Brian. You don't owe anyone anything. But if you think it would look good to schedule one, I have an idea." Brian leaned forward in his bed to indicate that he was very interested in what Charlie was proffering. "Why don't we have a press conference on Thursday afternoon? That will satisfy the reporters who have been congregating around here today and who, no doubt, would be back here tomorrow. That would buy you two days."

"That's nice, Charlie," Brian interjected, "but I really don't want to meet with them again."

"Cool your jets, Brian, we won't have it! Late on Thursday morning," the old man continued with those deep-set cerulean blue eyes now flashing, "I simply cancel it."

"How the heck are you going to do that without arousing suspicion?"

"Simple. I just tell the press that you've taken a slight turn for the worse – nothing life threatening – but that you're in pain and were unable to sleep Wednesday night. What can they say?" Charlie finished with a flourish and a big grin. "Who can question it?"

"I like it, Charlie! It's perfect – I hope!"

Things did go just as planned on Thursday afternoon, and Brian could even hear the groans of disappointment emanating from the reporters in the hallway outside of his room. He felt guilty at first but then very much relieved. The improving patient thought that he wouldn't have to deal with them again.

But he was mistaken about that.

CHAPTER 23

B rian was discharged from the hospital on Friday, late morning, just as his physician said was likely. Hank and Kate insisted
that he spend at least a week with them in their guest room. He
offered no resistance whatsoever. Members of the media didn't
know where to track him down, so he rested comfortably with the
Harpers while he regained his strength and mobility.

Each evening Hank, Kate and Brian discussed law cases they
had handled over the years, and he could feel himself growing ever
closer to both of them. He was sorely tempted to sneak into Kate's
room late at night when Hank was sleeping, but he didn't want to
anger or insult his host. Kate would not have needed any coaxing
and even invited him in one night, but Brian had steadfastly refused,
citing concerns about her father. Occasionally Charlie came over to
visit him and ended up staying for dinner.

On the next Friday evening following his hospital discharge,
Brian was determined to meet up with his old friend for conversation and a few boilermakers. Fortunately, he no longer needed
the heavy painkillers and was able to get by with over-the-counter
meds. They sat together at the end of the bar, just like old times.
Charlie sat there beaming.

"My friend," Brian broke the silence, "how do you always manage to be in a good mood?"

The old man shifted for a moment on his bar stool and said, "It's

---

simple. Voltaire said that the most important decision you make every day is to be in a good mood. He was definitely on to something, and I have tried to follow his advice every single day. But," he added with a grin, "some days are easier than others!"

As they dug into their cheeseburgers and ordered their second round of drinks, Brian posed a very serious question. "Charlie, you told me that you had three kids, but you didn't tell me anything about them." As he awaited a response, he noticed a small tear welling up in the old man's right eye.

"I'm ashamed to admit it, Brian, but I haven't been the best father. In fact, I haven't even been close to being a good father."

"Aren't you being a little hard on yourself?"

"Thanks, but no. I began drinking too much," the old man continued, "when the kids were young. My wife and I had our problems and I found solace in the bottle." Brian could see that he was struggling to get the words out.

"We don't have to talk about it, my friend, if you don't want to."

"Yeah, Brian, maybe some other time."

"Mind if I ask you something else, Charlie?"

"Nah, of course not."

"You've had more than your share of bad luck, it seems, and yet you manage to always project a positive persona. Except, of course, when I first met you and you were arguing with that guy!"

"Well, Brian, thanks for the kind words. No one wants to be around a grouch," he added. "It's a few things, actually. Remember that quote I gave you about accepting what is, letting go of what was, and having faith in what will be?" His younger friend nodded. "That's part of it. I also learned how to take pleasure in the simple things. You'd be surprised how much I enjoy reading the newspaper while sipping a cup of coffee in the morning, or almost seeing the face of God on Beartooth Mountain while I'm fishing for trout. I love taking a walk on a crisp morning or having a chat with you at Harry's over a shot and a beer. I have a lot of faith in God and Jesus Christ," he continued, "and if I died tomorrow, mine would have been a happy life."

Brian could only marvel at the old man's wisdom and resiliency.

"Oh, one more thing," Charlie said while holding his hand up. "Avoid grouches, because they will only pull you down with them, and don't take guilt trips!"

"That's two, Charlie," his grinning friend gently admonished him.

"Don't be an asshole, Brian," was his riposte.

CHAPTER 24

The next three weeks almost flew by for Brian as he continued to see Kate and would, on occasion, talk with her father about the law. He had become a local celebrity by now, and it was not unusual for him to get meals gratis from the restaurants he frequented. Brian would try to make up for the generosity in the tip amounts he left, but he always appreciated the gestures.

It was nearing November, and the cold air in Montana confirmed it. He was a cold weather guy anyway, and he loved to don the flannel shirts which were so popular in that part of the country and the almost obligatory fur-lined jacket to complement it. Even as a small boy in Buffalo, he loved to see his own breath. New York winters, even in his hometown, probably never reached the severity of those in Big Sky Country, but they were cold nevertheless!

Brian was contemplating the purchase of his own condo when at dinner one night, Hank and Kate suggested that he move in permanently with them.

"I don't want to compromise our friendship," he insisted. But by dessert, they had him convinced.

It was a large, sprawling house with five bedrooms, which he already knew since staying there while recuperating from his wounds. The relationship with Kate had escalated to the point that she often shared her bed with him, but it was comforting to know that he had his own room and privacy. Hank was fully aware of the arrangement and had no problem with it.

Brian continued to perform legal work at the Body Shop and assisted sometimes with oil changes and other minor tasks. One night Kate had a girls' night out with three of her closest friends, so Hank suggested that the boys go out to dinner. Over a bottle of cabernet and their huge Montana-sized steaks, baked potatoes, and salad, Hank began talking about his law firm.

"Did you meet Spencer Dixon when you came over to the office that time for lunch?"

"Yes, he seemed to be a very nice guy."

"Well, he's leaving the firm to join his father's practice in Los Angeles."

"That's certainly nice for him," Brian nodded.

"What I'm leading up to, Brian...is would you like to take his place and work with Kate and me?"

"Wow, I wasn't expecting that, Hank."

"Give it some thought, Brian. We could really use you! Of course, it would mean your passing the Montana bar, but that won't be a problem for you."

You have no idea, Hank...he thought.

He knew it represented a great opportunity for him, but he worried about his credentials regarding his new name. In short, he would not be able to produce his Cornell law degree. *Is there a way around it? That is the question.* Hank was secretary of the state bar association, and combined with Brian's local and now state celebrity status, it might just be possible. If Hank sponsored him, perhaps he would have the opportunity to take the bar exam. And that was precisely what happened. The combination of Brian's heroism and celebrity, along with Hank's position with the bar and his willingness to sponsor Brian, were enough. But he still had to pass the bar by himself.

He boned up on Montana law with lots of reading and intense sessions with Kate at night, sometimes going until 1:00 a.m. Attendance at a Montana Law Seminar was required and he had to wait until early December for one to be held in Billings. The requirement for state residency was met, thanks to Hank and Kate. Now all that awaited him was the almost four-hour trek to Helena. The next bar exam was scheduled for February 21, which left him plenty of time for preparation. He continued his friendship with Charlie, the two faithfully meeting every Friday night at 6:00 at Harry's. Thanks to periodic legal discussions with Hank, and Kate's solid support and help studying, Brian felt equal to the task before him.

He took to the road on Wednesday, February 20, arriving at his motel in Helena by 4:00. After checking in and a satisfying dinner at a nearby diner, he holed up in his room for one last review of the material. The exam started at 9:00 the following morning. After a good night's sleep and a hearty breakfast, Brian was more than ready for the next step of his journey. The Montana Bar Exam was a two-day process. Day 1 consisted of six 30-minute Multistate Essay Exam questions and two 90-minute Multistate Performance Test questions. Day 2 was the Multistate Bar Exam, a 200-question, multiple-choice exam.

On his way home Friday afternoon, he felt elated. He needed at least 266 points out of 400 to pass the exam and after the two-day grueling event, while maybe he didn't ace it, he was confident that he would achieve more than the minimum required. Kate had dinner waiting for him, and she and Hank wanted to be filled in on his experiences. They had invited Charlie to join them, too.

"I had to have gotten at least 300 points," he said hopefully, "but I guess you never know for sure!"

While it usually takes about eight weeks to get the exam scores,

Hank, due to his position as Secretary of the state bar, was able to fast-track getting Brian's results. Brian scored 311 points, which was pretty good for a newly minted Montana lawyer. Now he could officially measure for drapes for his new office at the Harper Law Firm.

It was a cold and windy March 11, and that by itself did not make for a particularly noteworthy day. But it was for Brian Miller. As he looked at the date at the top of that morning's edition of the *Billings Herald,* it hit him. *My God,* he muttered to himself, *this is the six-month anniversary of 9/11.* It was also exactly six months ago when he disappeared.

His thoughts immediately went to the brave firefighters and police who died in New York City that day, along with more than 2300 other very unfortunate people. And that didn't even include the forty lost in Shanksville, Pennsylvania and the one hundred eighty-four at the Pentagon. He had read somewhere that the average age of those lost in New York City was between thirty-five and thirty-nine. His eyes misted as he thought of the needless carnage. Then Brian's attention shifted to his friend Jeff Price. He was almost certain that Jeff was safe and hadn't gotten to the Windows on the World restaurant just as he left it. But he was worried that Jeff would have blamed himself and felt overwhelmed by guilt, thinking his being late led to his friend's death. What probably made it even more difficult for Jeff was that Brian had only come to the city in order to help him. He recalled what the crime writer, Robert E. Dunn, noted: "Guilt is one of those emotions that feeds on itself. With every bite, it gets a little heavier."

Brian Hart could relate to those words. He tried to imagine what he would feel if the situation were in reverse. The tears formed quickly. And, of course, Carol and Barry were often on his mind.

Margaret – not so much. *Did his stepchildren miss him? Were they truly sorry when he supposedly perished? Was Laura sorry? How about his law associates, friends, and neighbors? Was he really missed?* He wished that he could have been a fly on the wall when they spoke of him.

CHAPTER 25

It was early April. Hank and Kate were visiting old family friends for dinner in Columbus, less than an hour away due west from Billings. Brian was working on legal papers, had secured a tasty take-out dinner, and was seated comfortably at the kitchen table. He easily recognized that it was going to be too difficult eating messy ribs while juggling important documents, so he put the papers aside and turned to the sports pages.

Meanwhile, it was dark outside as Hank guided his F-150 black Ford pickup truck onto super highway 90 East. As they neared Park City, he sensed another vehicle speeding up behind him. He slowed down a little because of a curve in the road. Suddenly the truck at his rear appeared at the side but then swerved directly into the F-150 and tried to run it off the road.

"What the hell!" Hank yelled while Kate steadied herself in the passenger's seat. Hank valiantly attempted to keep his truck on the highway, but it was a losing battle. The aggressor next to him was bigger and heavier and had the advantage of the element of surprise. The F-150 strafed through a rather flimsy guardrail and plummeted down a slight embankment, rolling over in the process. A group of large bushes helped to cushion the fall and avert another roll. The vehicle that caused the accident paused for a moment at the site of the collision, and then the sound of its screeching tires filled the night air.

Brian picked up the phone immediately when it first rang. "We were in an accident, but we're okay," a shaky Kate explained. "Thank God we were wearing our seatbelts. Can you call the police and send a tow truck, and meet Dad and me? We're slightly south of Park City, and just off on Route 90 on the south side of the road. Please make those calls, Brian, and I'll fill you in when you call back." Although she sounded very matter-of-fact and in control, Brian could sense a tone of near panic in her voice.

"Are you sure you and Hank are okay?"

"Yeah. We're a little banged up but fine. Please make those calls, Brian," she pleaded as she hung up. He was amazed at her calmness under such duress.

Brian made the calls and rushed to his own car. On the way, he called Kate back and she explained that the long trail of ravaged guardrail would give him their exact location. Two police cars, an ambulance, fire truck and a tow truck all preceded him to the accident scene. Except it really didn't appear to be an accident. Hank and Kate knew, and the police suspected, that the incident was definitely intentional. It was egregious enough to ram a car off the road, but to hover over the area without offering help was proof of intent. The problem was that neither Hank nor Kate had even gotten a glimpse of the perpetrator. Both victims of the vicious broadsiding were not badly injured, save for a few bumps and bruises. The seat belts, with a little help from a grove of thick bushes, prevented serious injuries or worse. Park City police detained the two passengers, along with Brian, for another hour to take an official statement. The bottom line for the injured duo was that while they didn't know for sure who did it, they had a good idea who it might have been. After the visit to the police station, the trio made it home without further incident. This was the first strike, but Hank feared there would be more to come.

As they approached the Harper driveway, Brian pleaded once again with his passengers. "Let me take you to the hospital, so they can have a good look just in case there's something we can't see." Both father and daughter were adamant in their refusal. They weren't worried because neither had struck their head. If they had, they insisted, they wouldn't argue with him about it. The first thing Hank did when he entered the house was to pour a drink for the three of them.

"We dodged a bullet tonight," he exclaimed, but then he added, "for now."

"It had to be Jed Taylor," Kate said, certain that it must have been one of the two brothers her father had prosecuted.

"Well, it was intentional, that's for sure," Hank affirmed. "I thought he was in California."

"Now what?" Brian interjected. "You two need to be protected."

"I will be damned if I'm going to change my life for that piece of shit lowlife!" Hank shouted.

"Dad, we do have to be careful," Kate admonished him.

"The local police will take a few runs through our neighbor-hood," he responded, "but only for a while."

"Unfortunately," Kate added, "Jed is a sick man, and a very angry one."

The next day, Hank had an alarm system and surveillance cam-eras installed. "One of the great things about living in Montana," he muttered aloud, "is that we don't normally need alarms and cameras."

"One thing is for sure," Kate weighed in, "and that is...he'll be back."

"I'd give anything to get my hands on the son-of-a-bitch just for a minute," Hank uttered.

The next morning, their neighbors, the Rosens, appeared at the front door. Steve and Sally had been old friends of Hank and Kate and were concerned for their welfare after hearing about the accident. After being convinced and satisfied that they were doing fine, the Rosens left to take their son, Jimmy, who was ten, to a soccer game. Their fourteen-year-old daughter, Stephanie, reluctantly joined them although she would rather have gone to the mall with her school friends.

The last three weeks in April were like waiting for the other shoe to drop. Hank and Kate had filled Brian in on the Taylor boys' prosecution. All three strongly believed that Jed would strike again. They just didn't know how or when. Law enforcement friends of Hank, and he had many of them, tried to locate the whereabouts of one Jed Taylor, but to no avail. No one had any idea where the man lived, or even if he was still alive. But at least two people in Billings were absolutely certain that the bastard was still kicking.

Hank had previously prosecuted several ticklish and tricky cases, and some of the defendants went to prison, but the Taylors were a different sort. They had spat out their defiance at being arrested and sentenced for a heinous murder, and they promised retribution to those involved. They reserved a special hostility for Hank because he had the audacity to try them and seek a death penalty for the elder Taylor. Rufus died in a prison fight and his loss only served to intensify the enmity and deep hatred that Jed felt toward Hank. Since the younger brother had only been the getaway driver and helped to bury the victim, and supposedly had not been involved in the actual killing, he only got a fifteen-year sentence with the possibility for parole. With time off for good behavior, he apparently was out of prison. At any rate, he had now become a major threat for the Harpers.

Late April soon turned into May, and spring, it seemed, finally caught up with Montana. Everything was good with Charlie Moore, Brian Miller, and the two Harpers. That is, until Hank went out to dinner with some lawyer and rancher friends.

They were coming out of Barton's Steakhouse at about 9:30 p.m. It was Thursday, May 9, and the eight close dinner buddies shuffled out of the restaurant one by one. Hank was last and clearly visible from the black pickup truck, motor idling and parked directly across the street. One loud and very well-placed rifle shot rang out, disturbing the quiet which had previously existed in the cool night air. The 44-caliber slug caught Hank Harper just below his heart. To compound matters for the victim, the gunman had used a hollow-point round, which caused the bullet to expand on impact, acting like a mushroom when it hit him. The medics were well aware of the catastrophic damage hollow-point bullets could inflict and worked feverishly on Hank as he went into cardiac arrest. His heart stopped and the bullet expansion damaged too much of it to save him.

The official time of death was 9:47 p.m.

No one of the seven witnesses could identify anything more than a nondescript dark pickup truck. They didn't even know if the truck bore a Montana license plate. Montana plates were very distinctive, unlike some states, in that the word Montana clearly stood out in dark letters at the top of the plate on a pure white background. It happened too fast. No one got more than a glimpse. And at 9:30 on a Thursday night, the streets were deserted.

In the hospital, Kate was sobbing frantically and almost out of control. Heavy-hearted himself, Brian found it difficult to console her. Everybody's friend, and father non-pareil, it was difficult to fathom how such a wonderful man could be struck down like that in cold blood. An all-points bulletin was issued immediately by local police to locate Jed Taylor. That issuance was based on Hank's last words, faint as they were, while he was in the ambulance. Both medics believed that they had heard the name Jed Taylor emanate from the dying man's lips. There was no proof, of course, but he was the only possible suspect, in the minds of many. Hank had mumbled his name, clearly implicating him. Taylor's photo appeared on television the next day and for a solid week along with the caveat that he was wanted for questioning regarding the murder—and to call the authorities if he was spotted. A warning was also included that stated that the suspect was "armed and dangerous."

It was difficult for Kate to function. The doctor had given her a prescription for anxiety, which she was reluctant to use, but succumbed at Brian's urging. She had a tight bond with her father, it was true, but it was the brutality of his death that angered her so. The use of a hollow-point was over the top and inexcusable. Her father never had a chance. She knew that the killer had to be Jed Taylor, and she promised herself that she would bring him to justice. For Brian, the big question was his concern for Kate's safety. Would the bastard strike again? If he did, there was little question about his intended target. Jed Taylor would have to go through Brian in order to get to Kate. And that wasn't going to happen. Or would it? Despite many efforts to locate the whereabouts of Taylor, no one had a clue. Some speculated that he could be in South America, or California, or even New York City. In other words, no one had any idea. Surely, he would never show his face again in Billings. Brian wasn't so sure and deep down he knew that they probably had not seen the end of him.

By the end of May, both almost wanted him to make his move. It was like the Sword of Damocles hanging over them. They didn't feel comfortable going out at night and felt compelled to leave by the back door if at a restaurant for dinner. Jed Taylor was holding them hostage without, possibly, even being in the State of Montana. He owned their psyches and they just couldn't do anything about it. The no-good murdering bastard was going to strike again, no doubt about it, but when? And where? And how?

Their relationship began to unravel, but what human connection wouldn't under the circumstances? Brian had never seen Jed Taylor in person, but now he saw him behind every tree. He couldn't walk down the street and see a pickup truck without fearing that Jed was behind the wheel. Things weren't much better for Kate. Combined with the hatred that she felt for him, the fear factor loomed large. She thought she spotted him at the grocery store or even in church. And that was the most unlikely place that he would ever be. He was in her head, and she was powerless to do anything about it. Brian did everything he could to support and comfort her and to let her vent her frustrations and anger.

It was early June, and the couple had spent every day since Hank's murder thinking about the cruel and sadistic assassin who had such a deep and profound hold on them. By this time, police surveillance of their neighborhood and around the law office had lessened considerably. Most in law enforcement were convinced that Taylor would never be found or be foolish enough to show his face again in Montana, much less Billings. But Brian and Kate were not so sure. It got to the point where they could barely wait to encounter this man who had exacted such a terrible toll on them. Each night when they retired, Brian made sure to have a loaded revolver on the bedside table and a baseball bat under the bed. He would be ready should the maniacal bastard choose to attack them in that venue. Several times, Brian woke up in a cold sweat, thinking mistakenly that he had heard an intruder. Sometimes, he would just go downstairs and read until 3:00 or so because sleep was so elusive. Both he and Kate, bereft of any meaningful sleep, and their dispositions so compromised, would argue over nothing. Their relationship was in peril, and both recognized that ugly fact. While they still loved each other, their anxiety had become almost insurmountable. Employees in Hank Harper's law firm understood as best they could the trauma that the couple was going through, but many of them were losing patience with Kate and Brian nevertheless. The couple even thought about leaving Montana and moving practically anywhere else, merely to avoid the clutches of Jed Taylor. Brian was the first to fight off that impulse, but she soon followed. No man, no matter how evil, would force them to live in seclusion in some place they didn't want to be. Billings was their home, damn it, and it would remain so.

CHAPTER 26

It was a humid Thursday evening in July, the fourth to be exact, and Kate and Brian returned from the fireworks display just outside of the Billings' city limits. It was almost nine and the locals, probably kids, were still at it with cherry bombs and other assorted fireworks.

By 10:00, they lay exhausted in bed. It was probably 10:30 or so when Brian finally drifted off to sleep, despite the occasional fire crackers going off somewhere on his block. One of them woke him up and he saw a figure hovering over Kate. He leapt at the sinister form and took him to the floor. As he went down on top of the person, he felt a searing pain in his left side. Brian reached wildly with his left hand in search of his assailant's hand brandishing the weapon. The blade pierced his knuckles, but he grasped the attacker's wrist. Unfortunately, the baseball bat was under the other side of the bed, so it was of no use to him. Kate woke up just then but was in a daze and didn't know what was happening. Brian was in great pain but knew that he would die if he released his grip on the man's wrist. They rolled over to the edge of the bedroom wall, and he could see in a brief glimpse of moonlight that the assailant was wearing a mask. Brian thrust the fingers of his right hand into the man's eyes but was only half successful. His adversary groaned but used his freed left hand to lash out at his victim's throat. Brian was reeling now from the pain in his neck, allowing his opponent the leverage to climb on top of him. He could just make out in the moonlight his opponent's hand coming down on him with the knife. In that moment, he envisioned his past life floating by. Then he saw a light and heard a crack which was accompanied by a thud. His attacker toppled directly on top of him, but the knife fell harmlessly out of his grasp. Above the two fighters stood Kate, holding a baseball bat. During the scuffle, she had the wherewithal to grab the bat from under his side of the bed, return to the death struggle, turn on the light at her bedside and clobber the assailant over the head. A lot of pent-up rage had gone into her swing.

"Oh my God, Brian, what should we do now, call the police? Are you okay?" She was nearly on the verge of hysteria.

"No!" he urgently commanded her. He reached down to check his attacker's pulse and yanked off the mask. To no one's surprise, it was indeed Jed Taylor, stretched out on his stomach, and he was still breathing.

"Kate," he implored, "I want you to do something for me but not to phone anyone yet! Will you do that for me?" She stood there shaking like a leaf, stammering something unintelligible. "Did you hear me, Kate?" he said with frustration building in his voice.

"Yes, yes," she replied still quivering. He stood up and steadied her and held her by each shoulder.

"I need for you to go in the other room for a moment. Can you do that for me?"

"But, but you're bleeding pretty badly, Brian. Please let me call the ambulance."

"Go to the other room, Kate. Grab a towel and give me a minute. Then you can call 911 and the police. Okay?"

"Okay," she finally relented but grudgingly, still somewhat in shock.

As soon as she left, Brian rolled Jed over on his back. He thought for a moment, grabbed the errant knife which was within reach under the bed and placed it in the assailant's right hand. Despite his searing pain and being in a dazed state, he had used part of the sheet hanging over the bed to wipe his fingerprints from the weapon. Then he maneuvered the knife deep into Jed's heart and fell on him with his torso in order to get a lot of blood on himself. It looked like the two had a life and death struggle and that during the ferocious fight, Jed's knife had turned and gone into his own heart. At that moment, Kate appeared with the towel.

"You can make that call now, Kate. I think he's dead."

"What happened?" she asked frantically.

"After you hit him, he woke up and came at me again with his knife. We rolled over a few times," he lied, "and my weight must have caused his knife to go into his heart. It happened so fast, and it's just a blur!"

She reached for the phone and called 911 first and then the police. Then she applied compresses to Brian's left side which was covered in blood and bleeding profusely. Kate was concerned about the amount of blood all over his chest, but he told her that almost all of it came from Jed.

"Lie down on the bed," she commanded him.

"Naw, I'll get blood on the bed."

"Get on the bed NOW! You've probably lost at least a pint of blood."

"I think I can lose at least two quarts before it's a problem," he quipped. And then he felt a little dizzy and staggered over to the bed with her help.

The ambulance arrived within about twelve minutes and the attendants brought the stretcher up the stairs to stabilize Brian and bring him to the waiting vehicle. After calling 911 and the police, Kate had called Charlie and he arrived just as the police pulled up to the crime scene. Against her better judgment, she did remain at the house to await Charlie and the police. The EMTs assured her that Brian was out of danger and should be fine. She could follow him to the hospital when she was done with the police.

Charlie hugged Kate, and then Captain Baker and Sargeant Bell accompanied the duo into the house. She knew both men well, having first met them with her father and then again during Brian's ordeal with the hostage crisis. John Baker was tall and muscular and presented a figure who definitely was in command. A little over six feet, he had a craggy face and broad shoulders, and ears that pro-truded just a little too much from his head. His jaw was strong and square-shaped. He had thinning brown hair above piercing blue eyes and tensely arched eyebrows. He was in a friendly but pensive mood. Sargeant Ray Bell was short and stocky with a full head of blond hair and brooding hazel eyes. His teeth needed some work and he appeared humorless but was known to be a keen observer of crime scenes.

The first thing he noticed during a quick inspection of the scene was that the Harper alarm system hadn't been used.

"Captain," he yelled out, "their alarm system wasn't activated."

"Thanks Ray," Captain Baker answered. "Kate, do you remem-ber whether you turned it on?"

"I always do it, but must have forgotten in the July 4th fireworks excitement. Believe me," she continued, "I have taken extra pains ever since Dad's death, to be sure it's on. But somehow, I forgot. I really was tired," she added.

"Kate, are you sure you're up to this now?" Captain Baker asked as they mounted the stairs to the bedroom. She was obviously still very rattled by the fierce ordeal that she had just endured, but she nodded her head.

"Thanks, John, for your concern," she replied, "but I might as well do it now." As they entered the crime scene, she shuddered. Charlie held her hand tightly as they ambled over close to the bed. By then, several forensic detectives had arrived and were gathering evidence. They were now looking down at Jed Taylor. His mouth was open but still had a threatening look. His coal-black eyes, dead and lifeless, still managed to look evil. The mask he had worn lay at his side.

"How did he lose the mask, Kate? Do you remember?"

"I can't remember if he lost it while he and Brian tussled," she responded, "or whether Brian yanked it off. Does it matter?"

"No, I don't think so," Captain Baker remarked.

"Tell us what you remember, Kate," the police veteran began.

"Well, I was sleeping, and then all of a sudden I woke up to grunts and noises next to me on the floor, and there was a loud thrashing. I rolled over to Brian's side of the bed and reached under it to get his bat. Then I rolled back over to my side, stood up and turned on the light. I saw Brian fighting with this man on the floor and the man had a knife and was just about to kill Brian when I hit him over the head with the bat."

"Then what?" Baker asked.

"He seemed to be unconscious, but we weren't sure. Then apparently the man, I mean that Jed scumbag Taylor, woke up and they began fighting again. When I came back, Brian was sprawled over him."

"Where were you, Kate?"

"I went into the other room."

"Why?"

"Brian asked me to."

"Why did he ask you to leave the room? To get something?"

"Maybe a towel, yes, he asked me to get a towel. He was bleeding pretty badly. And, he probably didn't want me to see the bloody scene."

"That makes sense," the captain seemed to agree. "Anything else you can think of?"

"No," she replied. She began shaking uncontrollably.

"We can talk again tomorrow or even Monday, Kate. This has been very trying for you, to say the least." The captain continued, "It appears to be an open and shut case. Let's go over to the hospital and see how Brian is doing, okay?" She nodded and reached for Charlie. She began sobbing and he wrapped his arm around her shoulder and steered her downstairs.

Charlie drove her to the same Community Hospital that had treated Brian ten months before during the hostage crisis. Since it was a holiday night, most of the regular hospital personnel were not there. But one nurse who was there remembered him. By the time Kate and Charlie arrived, Brian was resting comfortably in his hospital room. The wound to his side had required forty-seven stitches to close and the fingers on his left hand were badly lacerated and needed a total of nineteen stitches. Fortunately, there was nothing life-threatening and he would probably be able to go home on Saturday.

Soon after Kate and Charlie seated themselves at Brian's bedside, Captain Baker arrived by himself. "Feel like talking about it now, Brian?" he asked, "or do you want to wait until tomorrow?" It was now 1:15 a.m. and the answer was pretty obvious. "Let's do it tomorrow," Baker decided. There was no disagreement from those in the room. "Sleep in if you can," he added, "and I'll drop by in the late morning."

Charlie and Kate remained for another fifteen minutes before departing for his residence. Kate would stay the night there. The clean-up effort at the Harper home would take quite a while and the forensics people had their job to do. Besides, Kate was in no emotional state to stay overnight there regardless of the company.

After the blood transfusion of almost one quart of new plasma, the elaborate stitchwork, and a reasonably restful night, Brian actually felt pretty good by noon. His left side ached and the fingers on his left hand stung, but he knew that he was a very lucky man. Kate had saved his life, but of course, he had saved hers as well. Jed Taylor probably spent a moment figuring out in the darkness who was positioned on the left side of the bed. He had definitely made a mistake in choosing to strike her first. But then again, he may have thought in the pitch black of the room that it was Brian lying there. No one would ever know who was the first intended target. But it didn't really matter. The world now had one less living degenerate in its midst.

At 11:00 a.m. there was a gentle knock on Brian's hospital room door. It was Captain Baker and he was accompanied by officers Hooker and Cairns. Jack Hooker was a large man, probably twenty pounds too heavy, with a rather generous nose on his broad face. His grey eyes bulged a tad just below his tufted brown eyebrows and matching crew cut. He was not an attractive fellow but seemed very amiable. Tanya Cairns, on the other hand, was a tall and striking woman with flashing, deep set brown eyes, a narrow nose, and gleaming white teeth. She wore her sleek black hair in a low-slung bun. The three were there to interrogate Brian, and Captain Baker gently asked Kate if she would mind leaving the four of them alone. At first, she was offended, but then realized that they were only doing their job. Baker just wanted to see if their stories of the grim episode matched. Brian recited the events of the struggle and included everything that he could remember.

"What happened right after Kate struck Jed Taylor over the head?" Baker asked.

"He toppled over on top of me and was clearly groggy and dazed, but he was very much alive."

"What then?"

"He began struggling and I was afraid that he might still have the knife. But the light was on and he was reaching for it under the bed."

"Did you tell Kate to leave the room?"

"Yes."

"Why?"

"Because I didn't want her to see any more of the violence, and I needed a towel. I was losing blood fast."

"You said that to her," Captain Baker noted, "even though you were in the middle of a death struggle? That sounds a little strange, unless you had an incredible amount of composure."

"Well," Brian hedged a tad, "he was wobbly and almost unconscious. I felt confident by then that I could defend myself, and I didn't want Kate to see any more of the bloodshed. Plus, I was bleeding big time."

"Then what?" the captain pushed on.

"He reached for his knife, but I grabbed his wrist with my hand. Then we rolled over and as I fell on him, the knife must have gone into his chest."

"It went deep into his heart," Officer Hooker interjected. "How come there was so much force?" He sounded skeptical.

"I fell on him hard; my hand was still grabbing his wrist. It must have turned as I fell," Brian responded.

"Tell us again why you asked Kate Harper to leave the room," Officer Cairns importuned. "It doesn't seem to make sense."

By now, Brian was clearly annoyed, but he recognized that they were merely doing their jobs. He knew that he held the upper hand – he had been there and they hadn't. And the scenario was on his side as well. A murderer invaded the house with the intention of murdering them both. The question was being raised as to whether Brian killed Jed in self-defense.

I probably shouldn't have told Kate to leave the room like I did, he thought, *but how else could I justify to her that I basically killed a defenseless man?* But during those brief moments when Kate had left the room, all Brian could see was a long, emotionally painful trial for the two of them. Undoubtedly, Jed Taylor would get a life sentence, but he would be breathing the air that Hank Harper no longer could. And there was also the possibility, scant as it might be, that the bastard could break out of prison and terrorize them again. Brian had his chance to end all those possible scenarios in one simple act. Stick a knife in his heart, and it would all be over.

"I guess you had to be there, Officer Cairns," he replied. Everything happened so quickly. I wanted her out of there. I wanted her safe. I didn't want her to see any more bloodshed and I knew I was bleeding profusely. I probably made a mistake by doing so," he continued, "because he still could have killed me. I was lucky to turn the tables on him."

The police officers could suspect all they wanted, but it wasn't going to make any difference. A craven murderer was now dead as a doornail, as William Shakespeare had first employed the term in Henry IV but more popularly used by Charles Dickens in *A Christmas Carol*. Any benefit of the doubt would go to the surviving Brian Miller, and there was nothing law enforcement could do about it. His ordering Kate out of the room may have sounded a little too contrived for the police officers, but the story was indeed plausible. And the intended victims' versions of what transpired that gruesome night were almost identical and panned out. As the officers left his room and the hospital, Jack Hooker offered his opinion.

"You know what I think?" Without waiting for a response from Captain Baker or Officer Cairns, he finished his thought. "I think that Brian Miller needlessly killed Jed Taylor and covered his tracks by having his girlfriend leave the room. I doubt if Taylor offered any resistance once she hit him over the head with the bat. Miller saw an opportunity to end it all without a trial, and he took it."

Captain Baker thought for a moment and responded. "You know, Jack, I think that we would have done the same thing given the same circumstances. The bastard killed Hank Harper and was ready to brutally murder them as well. He saved the state an expensive trial, as far as I'm concerned."

"Count me in, Captain," Tanya Cairns said enthusiastically. "I would have killed the bastard any chance I got," she added.

"Just sayin', that's all," Hooker murmured weakly. The case was basically closed and that was the end of it.

It took almost two months for Brian to completely heal. He had no nightmares about the grisly night of July 4. As far as he was concerned, he had performed a public service in ridding society of a menace, and he avenged the killing of Hank Harper.

Kate, on the other hand, had several recurrences of upsetting dreams and nightmares, and woke up in a sweat more than a few times. But she had no problem whatsoever that the monster killer of her father was probably dodging the flames in hell. That was fine with her! Now totally free of the Sword of Damocles that Jed Taylor had presented, the couple resumed their amicable ways, and those who knew and worked with them sensed, with relief, the difference.

CHAPTER 27

America was close to reaching the first anniversary of its own hell on 9/11, and Brian's head was full of thoughts about it. None of them were good. It was also, of course, the same first anniversary for his own personal freedom. His mind was soon full of the brave firefighters and policemen and women who died that day, the unfortunate passengers and the crews on the four airplanes, those who died at the World Trade Centers, Pentagon and Shanksville, and all the families who lost sons and daughters, fathers and mothers, husbands and wives, brothers and sisters, grandmothers and grandfathers, aunts and uncles. The list seemed to be endless. But also foremost in his memories were Jeff Price, Carol, and Barry. The greatest guilt he reserved for his friend, Jeff, who never learned that Brian had survived. Carol and Barry were loved by him but had probably moved on with their lives, something he would have wanted them to do. As for Margaret, he was surprised that thoughts of her never entered his mind.

It was August 29, a Thursday, which meant that Charlie Moore and Brian would be drinking boilermakers together the next evening. His old friend hadn't been feeling well of late and was forced to miss the past two Fridays. Charlie's eighty-fifth birthday was coming up soon – September 10, and he planned to take him out for a special dinner that night.

Fully recovered from his wounds, and in a jovial mood, Brian swung open the door to Harry's and saw his esteemed friend sitting at the bar. He headed directly over to the old man and gave him a hug.

"Easy, buddy," Charlie cautioned him, "I don't want anyone to think we're that friendly!"

"I don't think that's a problem, old buddy," he laughed. "How's the ticker doing?"

"Doing okay," he replied. "I got a pacemaker last week and I feel a whole lot better."

"Why did you need a pacemaker?"

"I was getting light-headed, was short of breath several times, and had a little chest pain. Doing great now, though!"

"Good to hear, Charlie. I missed you!"

"And how are you doing, young fella? You had your own share of trouble, that's for sure. Glad you killed that Taylor son-of-a-bitch!"

"Oh, fine now, Charlie. I'll tell you something that even Kate doesn't know." With that comment, the old-timer leaned over with his good ear, closer to Brian.

"I really didn't have to kill him, Charlie. He was practically coma-tose after Kate nailed him with the bat. But I hated him so much, and he was going to continue to stalk us," he continued, "that I sent Kate out of the room so she wouldn't have to see. Then I put the knife back in his hand, guided it toward his heart, and fell on him so it sank in."

"Did you leave any prints, Brian?"

"Naw, I used part of the sheet to put his hand on it."

"I would have done the same thing, Brian. He needed to die and he ran into the wrong guy."

"Kate sure helped on that score."

"Thank God that you jumped him before he could get you both."

"Yes. I think the police suspect that I killed him unnecessarily, but they can't prove it."

"Hell, there's not a police officer living who wouldn't have done what you did, given the same circumstances. And Brian, there's not a jury in North America that would find you guilty of killing that slimebag." Brian smiled upon hearing his passionate friend's comments.

"I'm not worried, and besides, you're the only one who will ever know the truth."

"What truth? It goes to my grave, buddy!"

"I know it does, Charlie. So, let's talk about your big birthday coming up!"

"Nothing special, Brian, just a trip to Paris," he said with a broad smile.

"You old goat, you wouldn't go if I flew us first class!"

"You're right. Just too old to travel, buddy, and getting older."

"I know you don't like to talk about it," Brian shifted into a more serious mode, "but tell me something about your kids—that is, if you are up to it."

The old man hemmed and hawed for a moment and then, surprisingly, spoke earnestly about them. Maybe it was his age, perhaps it was his mood, possibly even the boilermakers – but he was finally ready to talk about them.

"Charlie Junior was born in 1950 and has a construction firm in Chicago. Jimmy, my second, was born in 1952 and lives in Rochester, New York, where he is in the food and beverage business. My third, Jenny, and my only daughter, teaches high school in Naples, Florida, and she was born in 1954."

"How long has It been since you've seen them?"

"My wife's funeral was in 1980, but I saw very little of them after 1974. She died of breast cancer," he added.

"What happened in 1974, if you don't mind me asking, Charlie?"

"I found out that my wife had been having an affair with my best friend for three years. It absolutely crushed me and I wanted nothing to do with her or him after that. I moved out of the house, and she begged me not to tell the kids why. Biggest mistake of my life. I honored my pledge to her, liar and cheater that she was, and my three children blamed me for the divorce. Of course, the kids were grown by then, but they shunned me from that time on. I called them a few times, but they never answered or got back to me."

"Well, what about your supposed best friend?" Brian inquired.

"I hope he's pushing up daisies, if you know what I mean!"

"I know exactly what you mean, buddy!"

By this time, the old-timer had to wipe his eyes a few times with a Kleenex that Brian provided him, but it was almost as if he needed this conversation. Brian could sense the old man's pain and consternation, but something told him to plod on despite the difficulty.

"Charlie, what does Jenny teach?"

"History, which we both loved when she was a little girl." His face lit up as he talked of her.

"Do you know where she teaches? Is she married? What is her married name?"

"Sure, or at least," he hedged, "she used to teach at Lincoln Academy, and her married name is Hardy. What...are you writing a book?" he added.

"So, you hadn't seen them since 1974 until 1980 when your wife died?" Brian ignored the old man's sarcasm.

"Yeah, that's pretty much it."

"Was it awkward at the funeral?" his friend asked.

"Of course it was. They didn't even want to speak to me. I went to them and said how sorry I was about everything, but they turned and walked away."

"And you still didn't tell them about her cheating?"

"My word is my bond, Brian."

"I'm so sorry, Charlie; you didn't deserve that."

"In all fairness to the kids, Brian, I must admit that when I discovered the chicanery and moved out of the house, I began drinking heavily. Even though they were gone by that time," he went on, "they called me a few times and I was either too drunk to answer or so upset I didn't want to. It wasn't their fault," he added, "it was mine."

"No, Charlie, it was hers. It was her fault," he repeated.

The old man wiped his eyes a final time and arched those bushy dark eyebrows as if to say: *That's the way it goes.* The two men then shifted their conversation to happier things, like college football. The season was about to begin.

CHAPTER 28

It was a cool Tuesday evening in Billings when Kate joined Brian to celebrate Charlie Moore's eighty-fifth birthday at Barton's Steakhouse. The old-timer was in a pretty jovial mood when they greeted him at their table.

"Good evening, old man!" Brian laughed with a wink as he hugged his friend.

"I'd much rather hug Kate, to be perfectly honest with you," he chuckled.

They toasted him, his birthday, and his life with a bottle of champagne and ordered steaks with all the fixings. Kate had brought a few balloons to add to the festivities and gave him a high-powered flashlight. Brian presented him with a flannel shirt and new fishing chest waders. The waiters and waitresses brought Charlie a piece of carrot cake with a lit candle and they all sang "Happy Birthday" to him. They all laughed and shared jokes about the wonders and challenges of aging. Charlie seemed to be in high spirits when they parted ways at 9:15 p.m.

On the way home, Brian relayed to Kate his recent conversation with Charlie. "I feel so badly for him," he declared. "Can you just imagine it, Kate? Here he was a total victim of his wife having a long affair with his best friend, and her treachery cost him his kids. It's so unfair." Kate reached across the front seat of the car and took his hand in hers and gave it a squeeze.

"I wouldn't have been as kind as he was, that's for sure," she said matter-of-factly.

"Don't get any ideas, Kate!" She laughed. As they entered the Harper house together, she asked, "So, do you want to play some chess?"

That wasn't his first choice, as he had something more intimate in mind. "Sure," he responded without much enthusiasm.

"Wine?"

"You mean like those old geezers we saw in the restaurant?" She laughed and brought over a bottle and two glasses. Then she placed the chess set on the table by the couch where he was seated.

"White or black?" she invited him to make a choice.

"It doesn't really matter," he replied.

"In that case, I'll take white."

"Then, I'll start," Brian asserted.

"Oh, no you won't Mr. Miller," she admonished him, "white always goes first!"

"That's right, oh great chess master," he chuckled. "I forgot." They played for thirty minutes or so before he was checkmated while she smiled demurely. "Are you that good," he asked, "or am I that bad?"

"Could be a little of both," she teased. "By the way, it does make a difference whether you choose black or white," she added. He looked a tad befuddled. Sensing his confusion, she continued. "What I mean is that the player with the white pieces wins 52 to 56 percent of the time."

"You've got to be kidding, right?"

"No, really—studies have shown that the person who plays with the white pieces wins that often. In fact," she rambled on, "in tournament games, the winning percentage is even higher, at about 60 percent."

"Wow," he exclaimed. "That's really interesting stuff."

"Supposedly," she explained, "going first helps one control the game from the start."

"And the better you are," he interrupted, "the more likely you are to take advantage of that."

"Right you are, Brian, although these are just studies."

"I'll have to remember that tidbit," he said with a huge grin, "the next time I play Boris Spassky in a tournament!" The reward for his humor was a full kiss on the mouth, something he was more than happy to reciprocate.

"By the way," he added, "since this is apparently an educational moment, I have one for you." He smiled broadly.

"Let's hear it," she challenged him.

"What is so unique about this sentence? The quick brown fox jumped over the lazy dog."

"It sounds like a *Dick and Jane* sentence from when we were in kindergarten."

"Does that mean you have no clue?"

"Yup, it sure does," she smirked at him.

"The sentence uses every letter of the alphabet!"

"Wow, I'm impressed," she admitted. No doubt about it, she loved this man.

CHAPTER 29

The next day was a day of mourning over the entire United States. It was Wednesday, September 11, 2002. An unsubstantiated comment revealed that one out of every five Americans knew someone hurt or killed in the attacks. The age group of the greatest number of those who died was between thirty-five and thirty-nine. And the terrible toll included 115 nations who lost at least one citizen. All of the numbers were sobering and sad, and the country would never again be the same. Brian had other reasons for mourning that day and his mind kept coming back to one Jeff Price. He wondered if he ever got that divorce, or had the events of that fateful day brought them back together?

Brian recognized how lucky he was to have Kate in his life. Their relationship had only grown stronger since Jed Taylor had paid them that final visit, and he suspected that she wondered why he never mentioned the possibility of marriage. They had not declared their love for each other, yet, it was time. It was obvious to everyone that they enjoyed a very special bond.

"You're a damn fool if you don't marry her," Charlie had admonished him at their last Friday night dinner together.

He didn't really need any prodding from his friend. Brian knew that he loved her and that she was the woman of his dreams. There was only one problem. Marrying her would make him a bigamist. But after what he had been through during the past year, what did it matter? Nobody would know except the good Lord, and that part did bother him. But not enough not to go forward with his plans.

Two days after his dinner with Charlie, Brian insisted that he and Kate go to a quaint and quiet Italian restaurant named Luigi's. They arrived at 7:00 p.m. and were seated at an isolated table all by itself in the corner. After a glass of wine, Kate excused herself to visit the ladies' room, something she almost always did. Brian had the waiter clear her dishes and replace them with a small dark blue saucer. In the middle of the saucer, he put a gleaming diamond engagement ring. She couldn't possibly fail to see it when she returned. Kate got to the table and looked down. The tears ran down her cheeks as she brought her right hand up to her mouth in surprise.

"Oh Brian," she exclaimed, "is this what I think it is?"

"It is indeed," were his words as he stood there smiling broadly.

"Yes, definitely yes!" she repeated.

Several tables in their vicinity recognized what was happening and began applauding. He walked around the table and over to Kate, hugged her and placed a kiss on her mouth. By this time, more patrons became aware of the scene and joined in the applause. On the way home that night, she posed a question.

"How did you know I would say yes?"

"I didn't."

"Would you have been embarrassed if I said no?"

"Yup."

"Well, that was never going to happen," she said emphatically. That night they made love under the light of a flickering candle that Kate had put on her bedside table. All seemed good for them.

Over breakfast the next morning, they decided to get married on Saturday, September 28 in a simple ceremony at the Harper home. Why wait longer, they both agreed. Charlie Moore would, of course, be the best man and Kate chose a lawyer colleague, Amanda Paquette, to be her matron of honor. It was now the middle of September, so Kate had less than two weeks to plan for the event.

For a honeymoon, they chose the Broadmoor Resort in Colorado Springs. It wasn't exactly a hop, skip, and a jump away from Billings. The trip south would take at least nine hours by car to cover a little over 620 miles. Kate had been there once as a child with her parents, and Brian had always wanted to visit the beautiful resort since he was an adult. On the way, they could stop and watch a rodeo in Cheyenne, Wyoming.

Brian's first move once he reached his office that morning was to ask his secretary to check on a few personal things for him. He was also preparing to arbitrate a divorce settlement between two people he had come to know since his arrival in Billings just twelve months earlier. Brian wasn't keen on doing it, but the couple felt comfortable in his presence and trusted him. They insisted, and who was he to resist?

In addition to his law practice, he played some tennis but longed to make a difference in the community. He had helped to serve meals in a Providence soup kitchen during his "prior" life, and he liked the feeling it gave him. One kitchen about five miles away needed a server on Saturday mornings and someone to help clean up. He volunteered and did both.

Then, a law firm friend told him about a new baseball league for those with special needs that had been established five years before in Georgia. Called "Miracle" baseball, the idea spread throughout the country and several had caught on in Montana, including one in Billings. The game was designed for individuals with physical and/or cognitive challenges. And the game was not limited just to children; adults could play, too. Unfortunately, the season had just ended in late July and wouldn't begin again until the coming April. Nevertheless, Brian contacted the Billings leader, had lunch with him, and offered his services to manage a team. The leader was a tall, middle-aged man and Notre Dame graduate by the name of Red Cooney. He was an energetic and passionate fellow with red hair, flashing green eyes, and wore a broad, warm smile as the men greeted each other. Red was also a lawyer with a rival local firm and had moved to Montana from New Jersey. By the time lunch was over, Brian was totally sold on participating in the Billings Miracle baseball program.

Each team played two games per week, and Cooney needed another manager. There was something special about this man, Brian thought, and Red Cooney's enthusiasm for helping disadvantaged people was infectious. He seemed totally committed to providing fun for the players, along with a sense of achievement.

"I'm in!" Brian declared toward the end of lunch.

"That's great, Brian! You'll really help us," Red exclaimed enthusiastically. "Welcome to the team!"

As he walked to his car, he shook his head in disbelief. Red Cooney's warmth and sincerity, dedication, and faith in the cause of Miracle baseball totally captivated him. *He could probably sell ice to Eskimos.* Brian smiled at the thought. As he drove away from the restaurant, he couldn't help thinking that he had just met one of the finest people he would ever know in his entire lifetime. That was the effect Red Cooney had on him, and undoubtedly others as well.

At dinner that night, Brian was excited to share with Kate the details of his lunch with Red Cooney. "The league sounds like great fun for all," he exulted, "and Red Cooney is definitely someone I would like to have as a friend. I think you would really like him, Kate." Brian was going to have to wait until April for the Miracle baseball season to start. Until then, he would be there on Saturdays for his duties at the soup kitchen. In the meantime, Kate sought some therapy to help her through her most recent ordeal on the night of July 4, but she also needed help in finding and accepting closure regarding the traumatic death of her father.

Both Kate and Brian were in good places by the time their wedding date of September 28 arrived. It was a beautiful, sunny, but chilly day in Billings, Montana. Reverend Merritt performed the short, personal ceremony at 717 Pine Hollow Drive, the Harper house, with Amanda Paquette and Charlie Moore serving as the official witnesses. Kate had arranged for dozens of pink and white roses and other flowers to be placed in front of the fireplace and on its mantel and throughout the house. The home looked very festive and inviting for the happy occasion. A caterer had prepared amazing appetizers and finger foods for the few guests that had been invited, mostly from the law firm and a few friends from the community. Brian had also invited Red Cooney and his wife and was pleased that they had accepted on such short notice. Kate looked radiant in her simple cream-colored sheath which showed off her long legs and stunning figure. Brian wore a tan suit with a light-blue shirt and looked quite dapper in his attire. He would later admit that she had taken his breath away when he saw her ready to be his wife. It was a much-needed happy day for the bride and groom!

It was the day after their wedding when Charlie had a heart attack. Based on all the tests and findings, his cardiologist was worried that the old-timer didn't have much time left. Brian knew there was something he must do. The old man was in his hospital bed with his friend by his side. A day passed.

"It's been a good life, Brian," he said, "but I definitely have some regrets."

"What regrets, Charlie?"

"I didn't want to die with some music still left in me." He could see by Brian's expression that he didn't grasp what the old man was saying, so he elaborated. "Oliver Wendell Holmes, Sr. was a great man," he began, "a physician, a poet, and a polymath. He once said something so cogent that it has always stayed with me."

"I feel another interesting lesson coming on," Brian suggested.

"Holmes said that 'Many people die with their music still in them.' He meant that so many of us don't live up to our potential and that we die without fulfilling it." Charlie then finished the quote. "Too often it is because they are always getting ready to live and before they know it, time runs out."

"That quote certainly doesn't apply to you, Charlie!"

"Oh, but it does," the old-timer averred. "I could have done so much more with my life. I should have been a better father to my children. I dearly loved them," he went on, "but I never really told them how much." Then the tears started falling down both cheeks. Brian tried to assuage him but to no avail. "I failed them and now I must die alone," he continued, as the tears glistened on both cheeks. There was nothing Brian could do to ease his friend's anguish. At that moment, there was a knock on Charlie's hospital room door. The door opened slightly and in came three people whom Brian had never seen. One of them stepped forward and introduced himself.

"Hello," he said softly, "I'm Charlie Moore, Junior, and this is my brother Jimmy and sister Jenny. Are you Mr. Miller?" he asked, looking directly at Brian.

"Yes, I am, Charlie, and it is so good to meet the three of you."

"Thank you, Mr. Miller," Jenny interrupted the banter, "for calling us and telling us about Dad. The old man looked up from his bed, recognized his children, and began to cry. Jimmy was the first to reach his father's bedside.

"It's okay, Dad, we know. Mr. Miller filled us in about Mom and we wondered about it for so long. We just didn't know anything for sure. We were puzzled why your best friend never came by the house to see you after Mom died. Several times, one of us saw him visiting Mom, but we never really connected the dots." Charlie looked up; his eyes filled with tears. "It's okay, Dad, we know. Mr. Miller told us about Mom's affair with him."

"I drank too much, Jimmy, and I wasn't there for you."

"We understand, Dad," Jenny chimed in. "We weren't exactly there for you either."

"But we're together now, Dad," Charlie Junior said, "and that's what counts."

Charlie Senior couldn't stop crying. This tough old buzzard was really a softie! Jenny sat there calmly applying a cold washcloth to her father's forehead, and the old man clearly had never known such happiness before. "This is the happiest day of my life," he exclaimed to everyone. "I've never stopped thinking about or loving you three. Never!"

"We know, Dad," they all said in unison. "The same for us."

And then he addressed his friend, Brian. "Do you remember when we first met and talked about the two most important days of our lives?"

"I sure do, Charlie. My first was the day I was born, and the second, you said, would be the day I found out why. I told you that I didn't know why, and you said that I would learn."

"Precisely," the old man affirmed, his voice getting weaker.

"What about it?" Brian asked. Charlie grabbed his hand.

"Well, Brian, today shows me that you are on the way to finding out why." Brian looked at his friend quizzically, with his eyebrows arched as if to say *How so?*

"This is the kindest thing anyone has ever done for me in my eighty-five years. You brought my dear children to me. Now I feel like I can die a happy man." With his children gathered around his bed, and everyone with tears of happiness and sadness running down their cheeks, that is exactly what he did. He was gone, but his children would always remember that special moment.

Sad as he was to lose his best friend, Brian's heart had rarely felt so full. He sensed that he had done something important and significant. Charlie's children got real and needed closure and a final understanding of their father. And the old man had died happy. Brian felt a sense of great satisfaction that he was able to help a wonderful, although previously estranged family. *Thank goodness I acted as soon as I did,* he thought. *Now everyone is happy and complete.*

He had only known the old man for a little over a year, and yet he learned so much from him – life lessons and some very cogent quotes. Charlie, the old wizened geezer, was the smartest man he had ever known. Brian would miss him dearly.

CHAPTER 30

Two days after Charlie's memorial service, Brian and Kate left Billings for Cheyenne, Wyoming, the first leg on their way to Colorado Springs. The trip was well over 400 miles and took them a little over six hours, including two short stops. They checked into a hotel, had dinner, and since they were still mourning the death of their very special friend, they went to bed early.

The next day they wanted to experience some of the local culture and attended a rodeo, and Brian was particularly impressed by the bull riders.

"Man," he declared after watching several cowboys fall on their keisters, "they must be tough dudes!"

Kate, on the other hand, seemed to like the chaps that they wore. "Why don't you get a pair of those, Brian? I think you would look cute in them!" She winked coyly and blew her new husband a kiss.

Since it was only another 170 miles to the Broadmoor, they left in mid-afternoon and covered the distance in less than three hours. They were able to arrive at their destination just before dinner. After checking into their suite, they sat outside the main building at a small table and enjoyed a glass of wine. A beautiful pond lay just forty feet in front of the terrace. From the sidewalk, large stones sloped down to the water's edge completely around the pond. It was a heavenly night in an angelic setting and the couple, although nearly exhausted, was reluctant to leave it all and return to their room. After taking a warm bubble bath, they made slow, comforting love and slept soundly that night.

Much of the next day was spent walking through the beautiful grounds of the magnificent resort property. To the left of their building was a walkway to the tennis facility, which boasted three hard and two Har-Tru clay courts. Near them was the huge putting green. Lush green grass appeared everywhere. Two beautiful golf courses on the property, built in the foothills of Cheyenne Mountain, were quite a sight. Brian walked over near the 18th hole of the East Course to look at a small statue of the great Jack Nicklaus, signifying his triumph there in the 1959 US Amateur tournament.

After a leisurely lunch, the newly married couple walked around the perimeter of the large pond, which took patrons past several buildings which housed the guest rooms and some restaurants. Despite the early October date, a bevy of white swans was floating majestically on the water, catching the last warm rays of the sun that day.

On their third evening at the Broadmoor, they were enjoying a drink again on that same lovely outdoor terrace. Kate excused herself to go to the ladies' room. Brian sat there absorbed in thought when a figure emerged from the darkness and sat down at the table.

"Brian Hart, you son-of-a-bitch!" He sat up abruptly to see his old friend, Jeff Price. "If you only knew how much I blamed myself for your death on 9/11, and you didn't even have the decency to tell me you were okay? What the hell? I'm really glad you survived, but you ruined my life with the guilt I've felt."

Brian drew a deep breath, swallowed hard, and got ready to respond. "Look," he replied, attempting to use a deeper voice, "I don't know who you think I am, but you're mistaken. I am Brian Miller from Billings, Montana and I don't know who you are." He tried to be emphatic but sensed that he didn't quite pull it off.

"That's absolute bullshit, Brian," Jeff spat out the words. Seeing Kate approach the table, Jeff made one final comment. "This isn't over, asshole. If you don't admit who you are, I'll call the police. There's a bench across the pond. If you're not there precisely at 9:00 tomorrow night," he threatened, "I will call the police right then and there!" With that said, he disappeared into the darkness as Kate sat down.

"What was that all about, Brian?" she asked.

"Oh, nothing much," he replied as casually as he could. "Just a case of mistaken identity."

Needless to say, he didn't sleep well at all that night, pondering all that Jeff had said – especially the "call the police" part. He would have to meet Jeff at 9:00, that's all there was to it. Otherwise, he would be hunted down and eventually caught. Prison time could ensue because of insurance fraud—that is, if the insurer had paid off on his life insurance policy with Margaret as the beneficiary. There would be no getting around that. And what about the bigamy?

Why in the hell did I have to tell Jeff that I was from Billings? That was really dumb, he admonished himself. He would have to meet Jeff and try to convince him that his one-time friend had indeed expired in the Windows on the World restaurant that September 11th day. Failing that, he would have to prevail on him to forgive him and beg him to be silent about it. Jeff was very worked-up about it, so that scenario seemed unlikely. He also wondered about the 9:00 meeting and the location. Perhaps Jeff was at a meeting and didn't want to cause a scene. These were all things that he couldn't settle in his mind. Jeff held all the cards, he conceded, and he couldn't even talk to Kate about it – that was obvious. Brian would have to develop a viable plan, that was for sure. His life as he knew it, was at stake and very much on the line.

Morning came and with it a very drowsy Brian Miller. It had to be Brian Miller and a mistaken identity for Jeff Price. Could he pull it off?

The day was inexorably long for the man who was expected to meet Jeff Price at 9:00. Brian strolled into the hotel lobby to check on the daily activities. He noted that there was some kind of financial summit or conference scheduled. *That must be it,* he guessed, *that's why Jeff is here.* Cocktails and dinner hour was listed on the program, beginning at 6:00. *That's why the 9:00 meeting with me,* he figured, *and he doesn't want a scene. At least that's in my favor.*

He and Kate had a tasty Italian dinner that night and then repaired to the tranquility of their suite for some serious reading. Their balcony looked out over the golf course and garden area and they liked leaving the sliding door open to let the fresh night air in. *Thank goodness our room doesn't overlook the pond,* Brian thought. *That would not be good, especially tonight.*

Kate was quickly and deeply engrossed in her mystery novel, while Brian was just thumbing through a sports magazine, his thoughts elsewhere. By 8:30, he was getting agitated and growing anxious. It was difficult for him to relax. Finally, by 8:45, he popped out of his chair.

"I've got the heebie-jeebies," he announced. "I think I'll go out for a jog."

"Do you want me to join you?" she asked unenthusiastically.

"No, you're reading a good book. I won't be very long." He leaned over and gave her a kiss on her forehead. She continued to read without looking up at him.

Thank goodness, he thought, *she would suspect something if she wanted to come along and I had said no.* He changed into shorts, put on his sneakers, and pulled on a sweatshirt over his tee-shirt. He gave Kate a final affectionate kiss on the lips before leaving and couldn't help wondering if Jeff was already there. As he pushed the down button on the elevator, his body was gripped with a tension that he had never experienced before. *How long can I get away with this charade? Should I refuse to admit who I am? But if I do, Jeff said that he would bring in the police, and that won't end well for me. I'll go to prison for bigamy and insurance fraud. My life will be over as I know it! Shit, shit, shit,* he chided himself.

He exited the building and hit the pavement, looking slightly to his right and across the pond. In the darkness, it was difficult to see anything but the reflection of the lights on the water. It was a beautiful scene with them so strategically placed every fifty feet or so on the beveled stones surrounding the entire circumference of the pond. Unfortunately, he wasn't exactly in the mood to admire its luminescence, lovely as it might be. He began to traverse the short journey before him, heart pounding like never before. Would Jeff want to fight him? Would the old friends duke it out? *Will he understand if I explain it all to him? Will I go to prison? Will Kate leave me*? All these questions and many other thoughts completely overwhelmed him. He would find out soon enough. Too soon.

As he negotiated his way around the end of the pond, he could barely make out the bench and a lonely figure in the distance. Jeff was there. It had to be him. When he was within ten feet of him, Jeff spoke first.

"Brian, is that you?"

"Yes," he answered. Immediately he could sense that Jeff was more than half in the bag. He could smell the alcohol on his breath. They shook hands and it appeared to Brian that Jeff was much less hostile and confrontational than at their unexpected meeting the previous night. He seemed quite mellow.

"Brian," Jeff began, "let's have an honest talk like we used to. Don't give me the bullshit about being someone else. I know it and you know it. Let's talk like real men." Brian had a decision to make, and he had to make it on the spot – keep playing the Brian Miller masquerade or be straight with him. Honesty won out.

"Jeff, I'm so sorry that I let you down. Please hear me out. I have not lived a day since 9/11 that I haven't deeply regretted what I did to you."

"Brian, by the time I got to the North Tower, it had been hit by the jet. I could see the big gash in the side of the building just below the Windows on the World. All I could think of," Jeff continued, "was that I had killed my friend who was doing me a favor being there. I threw up, right then and there. No garbage can. Just let it go by the curb when I looked at the burning building. It was bad enough...all that carnage, but I thought you were going to die." He was overcome by his emotions. Instinctively, Brian reached over and gave him a hug. He wasn't sure if he did the right thing.

"But don't misunderstand me. I'm still pissed as hell at you."

"I can't blame you, Jeff, but please hear me out."

"I'm listening, but I don't know if there's anything you can possibly say to get me to forgive you. Seriously? What the hell were you thinking?"

"Hear me out, Jeff, that's all I ask. If you want to sic the police on me after that, so be it. I've been feeling so guilty about you, I don't really care." He did care, but the words slipped out. Jeff seemed willing to hear his story.

"Before you begin, Brian, there's something I need to tell you." Brian leaned closer to his tipsy friend. "Margaret is dead," Jeff declared. That was stunning news, even if his feelings for her had dampened considerably during their last year or so together.

"What? I don't know what to say," he stammered in response. "What happened to her?"

"She developed a form of brain cancer, in January, or was it February?" he asked himself. "Sorry, Brian, I'm a little woozy. Had too much to drink during the cocktail hour and then downed a martini at dinner. I guess I was nervous about our confrontation." Brian patted his friend on the shoulder solicitously.

"It was February, Brian," he remembered through his personal fog, "it was definitely February."

"When did she die?"

"Just two weeks ago." Suddenly Brian shifted his thoughts to his recent marriage.

"Do you remember which day?"

"Yeah, I think it was September 21."

Brian felt guilty for his next thought. *My god, that means I'm not a bigamist.* "You think or you know?"

"Yes, it was a Thursday when I heard. It was definitely the 21st. Does it really matter what day?"

"No, of course not," he lied, "but I feel badly for her. She was way too young to die, especially that way."

"Geezus, Brian, why did you disappear like you did? How could you leave your kids, your wife, and your job? What the hell? And what about your friends? Far be it from me to be judgmental, but how the hell did you just do it?" Jeff was very agitated.

"First of all, Jeff," he responded, "Margaret and I had a shit-ass marriage. It was a total sham. She treated me like shit." He felt himself getting worked up and tried to dial it down a bit. "I'm really sorry that she died, but don't get me wrong," he softened his tone, "she didn't care about me. It was the school board, being a lawyer, or saving the world. I was just an afterthought to her."

"I had no idea. But, then again, I had my own problems."

"Did you and Cindi get a divorce?"

"No, we didn't. We probably should have but didn't because of 9/11. That horrible day probably saved a lot of crumbling marriages," he lamented. "We all came together then and probably not all for the good. The unity for America was a great thing, but then after a while, life went on as it did before. And for some couples like Cindi and me, we got back to our old problems which were always there but had just been placed on the back burner for a few months. But what about Carol and Barry? Didn't you think of them?"

"That was the really tough part for me. That, and the guilt I felt about you. I love them unequivocally. Even though they are not my biological kids, I was extremely close to them. Are they okay? What are they doing? Have you heard?"

"They're doing great, no thanks to you." Jeff let that sink in. "Carol graduated from Williams and is now in real estate, and Barry is a senior at Lehigh."

"I really miss them!"

"Brian, I'm sorry that you were so unhappy that you felt you had to disappear. But seriously, what the hell were you thinking? You obviously couldn't have known about 9/11."

"Of course not," he agreed. "When I went to the city to meet with you, after our breakfast, I was ready to fake a mugging and my murder on the streets of New York, and then just drive away. I had even rented a car and obtained some false documents and was all prepared for a new life. Then 9/11 happened and altered my plans. The only downside in changing my scheme, and I hate to admit it, but that's what it was – a scheme – is what I did to you."

"I can't say it was easy, but I guess I do understand. I just wish that you had somehow let me know. I wouldn't have said anything."

"I should have, but I thought it would be worse for you if you did know. You would have become complicit in my crime. Once I began living the lie, I couldn't go back. I should have called you, and I'm so sorry I didn't."

"I'm okay now, but I can't tell you how pissed I was at you last night. Especially when you denied being you! I almost called the police when I got back to my room."

"Thanks; I'm sure glad you didn't."

"By the way, I don't think that you broke any laws."

"How so? The insurance company would be after my sorry ass if they knew I was alive!"

"No, they wouldn't," Jeff explained. "When I last spoke to Margaret shortly before her death, she said that the insurer had not paid out on the life insurance policy, nor would it until more evidence was available of your death."

"Those cheap bastards," Brian retorted.

"I even spoke to them on behalf of Margaret," Jeff went on, "but they were going to wait a while before paying up. Now it will go to Carol and Barry. Sorry, my friend," he added, "but then you will be plenty guilty of insurance fraud!"

"I was almost guilty of bigamy," Brian interjected, "until you told me that she died on September 21." His friend looked surprised. "I got married in Billings on September 28. I guess I missed being a bigamist by one week."

"The woman I saw you with?"

"Yes."

"I didn't get to see much but I saw enough to see that she was quite a looker."

"Thanks. She's a fantastic woman and sorry to say this, but every bit of the woman Margaret never was. I hate to say that since Margaret died so tragically," he felt a burst of remorse, "but it's the truth."

It was now close to 10:00 and the men were both enervated and yet energized simultaneously. Undoubtedly the alcohol helped Jeff to mellow out, but whatever the reason, he seemed to be sincere in his forgiveness. Brian felt relieved, a great and heavy burden almost miraculously lifted off him. They agreed to meet for breakfast the following morning, inasmuch as Jeff was leaving for the airport at 10:00. Both felt exhilarated, and Jeff was glad that his friend's fate did not match that of those poor souls on 9/11. They shook hands and exchanged a hug.

As they got up from the bench, Jeff staggered backwards for a moment, still wobbly from his earlier cocktails. Brian reached out to steady him, but his friend stumbled back for a few steps out of his grasp. Then he pitched straight down, striking his head on the stones below and rolled into the water. Shocked by the sight of his friend tumbling into the murky water, Brian wasted no time in easing his way down the stones to the water's edge. He reached into the pond hoping to feel something, but without success. At that exact moment, he saw someone walking by.

"Call 911 and the rescue people," he shouted at the top of his lungs, "someone fell into the water. Hurry!" With that said, Brian dove into the pond and tried to follow the gentle current in search of his friend. For three minutes he swam around the general area where Jeff had disappeared, hardly noticing in the frantic commotion how cold the water was. The water was dark and murky, and Brian's efforts were to no avail. *Clearly,* he thought, *Jeff must have died.* When he saw that rescue personnel were on their way and just several hundred yards away, he emerged quickly from the water, climbed over some rocks, and walked in the opposite direction. There was nothing more he could do. He was careful to walk on the grass to avoid leaving any footprints.

If admitting to his false identity was the only way to save his friend, he would have gladly done it. Fortunately for him, it didn't come to that. Fortuitously, someone was walking by when it happened. That person would have been able to summon help faster than Brian could have from the water's edge. It would have been foolish and unnecessary for him to have waited around after the accident to talk with the authorities, especially considering his own circumstances. It would have done absolutely nothing to help bring Jeff back to life. He had died in a tragic accident, and there was nothing else that he could do to help him.

"What the heck happened to you?" Kate shrieked when he returned to the room. "I was starting to get worried."

"Can you believe that I got too close to that beveled edge by the pond, and fell in?" Without waiting for a response, he went on. "When I realized that I could fall onto the rocks, I jumped in to avoid them."

At first, she had an incredulous look about her, but then she rushed over to him and delivered a bear hug. "Oh, geez," she exclaimed, "you're wet and cold. Get into a hot shower!" *Another bullet dodged,* he thought. But his thoughts were with Jeff, and he was worried. Really worried. He reasoned that he had done everything he could have done to save him. He couldn't feel guilty in that regard, but his spirits plummeted at the vision of Jeff perishing in the cold, gloomy water.

The next morning at breakfast, the restaurant was buzzing about the previous evening's drowning. Inasmuch as some stranger had alerted a passerby to summon the rescue squad and call 911, the authorities assumed that the tragedy must have been an accident. They recovered the body of Jeff Price under the bridge at the other end of the Broadmoor's pond. It had snagged on some debris near the water's edge.

The following day they determined that the body contained an extraordinary amount of alcohol in the victim's blood, and that he must have been tipsy and slipped onto the stones. There was only one mark on his body – a contusion on his forehead – consistent with such a fall. The official cause of death was drowning, which meant that Jeff Price was alive when he hit the water. While the police would like to have had an opportunity to talk with the Good Samaritan who had alerted the man walking by the incident to call for help, they didn't consider it vital to the cause of death. It may have been some guy who was there with another woman and didn't want to risk his wife finding out. Or perhaps someone who didn't want any publicity. Whatever it was, they were not unduly concerned because everything pointed to a simple accident, most likely caused, at least to some degree, by excessive drinking.

CHAPTER 31

On the way home from their honeymoon trip to the Broadmoor, Brian was thinking of his now dead friend and the circumstances surrounding the unfortunate accident. He thought that Jeff had been especially gracious to forgive him for his terrible transgression on 9/11. After all, he lived in guilt for well over a year, thinking that Brian had perished because of the meeting he had set up. *I don't think I would have been so forgiving,* he thought to himself. *The booze probably helped him to rationalize the terrible slight, but he was a very special guy and friend to forgive me so quickly.*

"Why are you so quiet?" Kate broke the silence.

"Just thinking," he responded.

"Thinking about what?" He could have told her how much he enjoyed their time together at the Broadmoor, but he didn't.

"About Charlie, I guess," he fibbed. "You know, Kate, he was the smartest man I ever knew."

"Where did he go to college?" she asked.

"Didn't. Couldn't afford to. He and his two brothers worked with their father in the logging business. Charlie said that they were too busy surviving!"

"Thanks to Dad," she weighed in, "I knew him but not well enough to know how he grew up. Yet, he was like the uncle I never had."

"Did you ever read *Paradise Lost*?"

"You mean that tome by John Milton? Why do you ask?" she responded.

"Actually, I looked it up," he smiled, "and it wasn't as long as I thought, but it was very difficult to read."

"Well, did you read it, smart guy?" she wisecracked.

"No, of course not," he laughed, "but Charlie did."

"Did he really? That must be a sign of great intelligence not only to read it, but to understand it, too."

"Apparently, he did. And he quoted something very cogent from it."

"Like what?" she asked, her interest piqued.

"The mind is its own place, and, in of itself, can make a heaven of hell or a hell of heaven!"

"That is really profound," she exclaimed. "That really explains human behavior better than any expression I've ever heard."

"That's what I thought," he agreed.

"Really, Brian, it explains why someone poor can be happy while a rich person is not. Brilliant!"

"Brilliant enough for you to read it?"

"No, smart ass," she laughed, "you just gave me the good part!"

"Kate," he said suddenly turning solemn, "Charlie also gave me the most thought-provoking quote that I've ever heard."

"What was it?"

"It was a Mark Twain quote. He mentioned the two most important days of your life."

"Well, what are they?" she inquired impatiently.

"Twain said the day you were born and the day you found out why."

"Wow, that is intense," she concurred.

"Have you found out why, Brian?"

"Charlie said I did when I phoned his kids and talked them into coming to see him when he was dying. He said that it was a very kind thing for me to do. But somehow, Kate," he continued in the same vein, "I'm not sure that qualifies as my knowing why I was born. Yes, I agree it was a nice thing for me to do, but it didn't require any sacrifice on my part. Shouldn't truly finding out why involve something more than just being kind?"

"I don't know, Brian, but I think you're now beginning to approach the twilight zone!"

"Yeah, I guess I am. But one thing for sure," he added, "my Holy Grail is to find out the real reason why I was born."

"Well," she responded after pondering the discussion, "we can both agree that Charlie Moore was a very bright and fascinating man."

"I was so lucky to know him," Brian said gratefully.

Just before they reached the city limits of Billings after their long trip from Colorado Springs, Kate asked him if he had ever caught up with the guy who had confronted him at their table on the terrace.

"Oh, you mean the mistaken identity guy?" he responded casually.

"Yeah, that one."

"No, he must have had a little too much moonshine."

"He didn't seem out of sorts," she commented, "but then again, I only saw him for a moment." She noticed that his face appeared drained of color. They were exhausted from the long trip and were thankful to sleep in their own bed.

CHAPTER 32

The next day at work would be a hectic one. Kate holed up in her office for almost four hours before emerging for a late lunch. He spent almost the entire day preparing for his opening remarks for an upcoming trial. The rest of the week they spent catching up on the numerous legal matters common in a law practice, and managed to grab an evening out at Barton's Steakhouse with friends, Steve and Sally Rosen.

The couple had two kids, Stephanie and Jimmy, and had been friends of the Harpers since they moved just a few blocks away from them some seven years ago. Ten-year-old Jimmy was almost family from Kate's and Brian's points of view, since he often appeared at the Harpers' house to do odd jobs for them. Sometimes he raked leaves, on other visits he would help clean the garage or wash the cars. Ever since Brian began living at 717 Pine Hollow Drive, the precocious boy seemed to enjoy hanging around him.

It was late October and Brian, while nursing a Crown Royal, was hard at work preparing a legal brief in the study well after dinner. Kate walked in with a stern look on her face, and he could feel the temperature drop. It was close to 9:30 p.m.

"So, what is Brian Miller up to tonight," she began, "or is it Brian Hart, or whatever it is you call yourself these days?" He put on his dumbfounded face, complete with a quizzical look and tilt of his head.

"Sorry, not buying it," she said sarcastically. "Whoever you are, can you please tell me something about you that is actually truthful?" He sat there wishing that he could be anywhere else in the world. The rug would do, if only he could crawl under it. He was at a loss for words.

"I looked up Brian Miller on the Cornell football and hockey team rosters, and do you know what I found?" Still there was no response from him.

"I found a Brian Hart, that's what I found," she answered her own questions. "And do you know what else? The only Brian Miller who ever played football for Cornell was in 1919. And you know," she continued her tirade, "you don't look quite old enough. As for hockey, there has never been a Miller except for Phil Miller who managed the team back in 1959. Do you see where I'm going with this, Brian? There is no record of a Brian Miller receiving a law degree at Cornell, but Brian Hart did in 1983. Try as I might," she ranted on, "I couldn't find a Brian Miller practicing law in Boston. But you know what? I found a Brian Hart practicing law in Rhode Island!" By now, for him, the room temperature had plummeted by at least fifteen degrees and traces of frost were almost visible in the windows.

Still... he said nothing. She stood there in his face, arms akimbo, signaling her considerable level of contempt for him. It was time for him to speak.

"I, ah, um, know how you must feel," he said barely audible.

"Seriously? You don't know anything about how I feel, you piece of shit!" she shouted and gave him a baleful look, slamming her hand on the pile of papers in front of him.

"Please hear me out Kate. Please."

"This will have to be really good, mister," she spat out with eyes almost popping out of her head.

"If you don't understand when I'm done, you can divorce me."

"Oh, that's very big of you." Her green eyes were now flashing with anger. "You can bet on it," she said with conviction. "The only truth that I've heard from you is your first name and that you were born in Buffalo, New York. Everything else spewing out of your mouth is bullshit!"

"Are you going to give me a chance to explain, or will this harangue go on all night?" That comment really pissed her off and she began pacing back and forth. "I'm sorry," he broke in, trying to recover from his error. "That was over the top," he conceded.

"Thank you at least for that," she replied acidly.

"Kate, let me start. Please sit down. If not next to me, please just sit and listen to me." She complied by taking a seat on the couch near him but definitely not next to him. "It's a long story, Kate, so please bear with me." She nodded.

"Do me a favor before I begin," he pleaded. Her eyes were full of questions. "Would you pour yourself a drink or a glass of wine?" he asked softly.

"Why?"

"I think it will help to calm us down, and we can have a better conversation," he said earnestly and she nodded her approval as she stood up and left the room.

"Do you want a refill?" she yelled to him.

"Yes, thanks." The coolness in the room seemed to be thawing.

"All those things you said about me are true. I did change my name," he admitted, "but there was a good reason for it."

"This should be rich," she said with a smirk.

"First of all, before I tell you my story, there is something I want you to know. I have never loved anyone the way I love you. I never dreamed in my wildest imagination that I could ever be married to someone like you." She just stared ahead while he went on. "You are so above me in every way," he said with his head slightly bowed. "I don't deserve you. I never did." He had her full attention now.

"I was so unhappily married; I was at best an afterthought to my wife."

"Then why didn't you just get a divorce, like other people do?"

"She had two kids from her previous marriage, and I didn't want to do that to them. They were probably the only reason I married her in the first place."

"Oh, come on Brian, you can do better than that," she snickered.

"No, honestly," he insisted, "I didn't want to put them or me through all that."

"Sounds like you needed some stones," she said without much empathy.

"Probably. I'm not proud of how I handled it," he allowed.

"Go on," she urged him. He took a large sip from his glass.

"She treated me with total indifference. It was like I didn't exist. The kids were in college those last few years and probably didn't notice it. I had all the responsibilities of marriage with none of the benefits. I mean zero benefits!"

"You mean there was no sex in your marriage?"

"Yes, that's what I was saying, but that was only part of it. Her total and callous disregard of me took a toll. You begin to think less of yourself if your mate ignores everything about you. I didn't mind making my own meals. It wasn't that, although it didn't help. We were polar opposites in every way. At first, she seemed to have been interested in me. Only one person had liked me before her, so I thought that she must be special. After all, she actually saw something in me that I didn't see."

By now, Kate seemed to be coming around and her obvious hostility toward him was subsiding. "Go on, Brian, I'm listening," she assured him.

"We disagreed on everything, from politics down to whatever else we would discuss. Kate, have you ever been with someone who not only disagreed with you on everything, but also always viewed the glass as being half empty?"

"Not really," she replied.

"I honestly thought that she took the other side of whatever we were talking about just to be contrary."

"Sounds like she had issues."

"Well, maybe, but it sure didn't help me feel any better about myself, let alone helping our marriage."

"Did she cheat on you?"

"Not to my knowledge. But you know something? I couldn't have cared less. In fact, my fondest desire was that she would run off with someone else."

"Not sure that would have been good for your ego, Brian."

"Maybe not, but I was going downhill fast anyway."

"What about you, Brian? Did you stray, or am I stepping over the line?"

"After what I've put you through, Kate, there is no line. Yeah, I did, one time. Not proud of it and managed to rationalize it, but she was a nice woman and she liked me. Interestingly enough, she was married."

"Sounds to me like the approbation of women is important to you."

"I guess," he admitted. "I imagine a shrink would have a field day with me," he opined.

"Tell me about your wife," she asked. "I've noticed that you never mention her by name."

"It's Margaret, and she was on the school board, going to law school, and doing pretty much anything else she could do to avoid spending time with me."

"Maybe she was just trying to fulfill herself," Kate reasoned. "Maybe she felt her own void."

"Maybe," he conceded, "but her book club, garden club, and community activities seemed to stretch even that line. And she was so hostile when we did speak."

"Sounds that way. Did you know that she died?"

"I just found out from that guy I pretended not to know. You remember? On the Broadmoor's terrace when you came back from the ladies' room...but, how did you know?"

"Brian, when I check into something, I am in all the way! I remember it well. I thought there was more to that incident than you would admit. It was part of what finally led me to do a back-ground check on you."

By now it was almost 11:00, but neither one wanted to end the conversation and go to bed.

"The guy's name is –or should I say, was—Jeff Price," he said sadly.

"Don't tell me," she interrupted with her voice rising, "that he is the one who drowned at the Broadmoor? Please don't tell me that!"

"Unfortunately, yes," he said with remorse, "he was the one."

"No, no, no!!!" she howled.

"Kate, he accidentally fell in. I didn't do it. I swear I didn't do it. In fact, I tried to save him. I swear to you that I had nothing to do with his death. He was drunk and he slipped."

Somewhat, but not thoroughly reassured, she reached for the

decanter of wine and poured its red liquid to the very top of the glass.

"Jeff recognized me at the Broadmoor, thinking that I had died on 9/11."

"My God," she exclaimed, "this gets more complicated with everything you say!"

"I'm sorry Kate, it is, and I'm barely getting started. Are you sure you don't want to go to bed and begin again in the morning?"

"Not a chance, Brian," she replied, her eyes gleaming.

"Well, here goes. I had been thinking for a long time about leaving Margaret – see, I used her name," he smiled. "I had decided to for sure. Jeff asked me to come to New York City and meet him for breakfast. He was having major marriage problems and wanted my advice on things, as his friend and as a lawyer. We agreed to meet in the restaurant atop the North Tower of the World Trade Center." She began to look like she was beginning to see where this was going, and nervously sipped her wine.

"It was Tuesday morning, September 11, 2001," he said with obvious distress. "Jeff and I were due to meet around 7:30 or so and I was there on time. I read the only newspaper kicking around the place while I waited for him. Finally, at 7:45 or thereabouts, he called and said his train was delayed and that he probably couldn't get there for another hour – around 8:50ish." Kate leaned in to him to fix on his every word. "I was annoyed, but what could I do? It wasn't his fault. I stuck around, talked with the waitress and had another coffee." Mention of the waitress brought tears to his eyes, which Kate noticed.

"I'm sorry," he said, noticing her reaction. "Every time I think about 9/11, which is way too often, I think of her. Her name was Penny, and she was a sweet young woman whose life ended so violently and so unnecessarily that day." Kate left her seat on the couch and sat down next to him.

"Well, anyway," he continued, "I left the restaurant at about 8:35 so I could buy a few more newspapers. By the time I had bought them and was on my way back to the elevator, it was precisely 8:46 and I heard a huge explosion above me. At the time, most people thought it was a light plane, like a Piper Cub or something like that, that had somehow flown out of its flight path. But I saw a huge gash in the building and an incredibly large fire. It had to be something much bigger."

"It must have been scary," she lamented.

"I was told not to go back into the building, and to tell you the truth, they didn't have any trouble convincing me. But I was worried about Jeff."

"You mean that he might get caught up there with the others?"

"No, I was relatively sure that his train was late enough that he wouldn't have been able to get up there. What I was desperately worried about was that Jeff might have thought that I was caught in the Tower. He didn't know that I went down when I did to buy newspapers."

"Well, didn't you call him after and tell him?"

"No, I didn't."

"You mean you didn't call him and tell him you were safe? What were you thinking?" Now her voice was beginning to get a little shrill, and her demeanor changed.

"That's where it gets complicated," Brian responded.

"No wonder the poor man was so angry with you, and now he's dead!"

"I know, and it just kills me. I felt so guilty for not telling him."

"I don't understand all of this, Brian."

"Kate, I had made up my mind to disappear by the time I got to New York City. I was going to fake my death by a phony mugging and planned to leave my license and wallet on a street corner. Before I could carry my plan out, the 9/11 attacks began." He paused, telling Kate he needed a few more ounces of Crown Royal. She got up and went to the kitchen for ice and then brought the bottle to him. He was getting very teary-eyed by now, and she saw his raw emotions surfacing.

"We don't have to continue this now," she said softly, "but I must admit that your story is a humdinger."

"No, I'm okay, and I want to get it all off my chest." He took a sip of his drink before continuing. "I rented a car, which I had worked out the night before, and was driving out of the city when the second plane hit the South Tower. I spent the night at a motel in Jersey or Pennsylvania, and watched the news all night on TV just like every other American." His eyes teared up again as he thought about all the firefighters, police, and other first responders who went into those buildings knowing full well that they probably weren't going to make it back. And, of course, the many other innocents who died that day.

"All of those brave men and women," he choked out the words," and their families." She stroked his hair to soothe him.

"I should have told Jeff, even if it would have messed up my plans. He was my friend and I owed him that. Instead, I saw an opportunity and took it."

"Don't be so hard on yourself," she tried to pacify him.

"I thought I was so smart," he admonished himself. "The phony mugging plan probably wouldn't have fooled a third-grader, but I had the perfect cover at the Windows on the World. With every passing day," he went on, "it was becoming more and more difficult to do the right thing and call Jeff. I rationalized it, Kate, that I would have implicated him in my scheme if he knew the truth."

"Okay, Brian, I'm starting to understand that pea brain of yours." Hearing her words, he couldn't help smiling. "I do have some good news for you, my husband."

"I could use some, that's for sure."

"You are not a bigamist...but it was close!"

"Yeah," he acknowledged, "just one week! Jeff told me she had died of brain cancer on September 21. Believe me, Kate, that was music to my ears – not that she had died, but that she passed before our wedding on the 28th."

"But if she hadn't, I would have married a bigamist. Would that have made me a bigamist, to have married one?"

"I don't think so," he responded sadly.

"Brian, I just thought of something else that might be a problem."

"I might already be ahead of you on that, but go ahead and shoot."

"Did you have life insurance, and could they have paid it to Margaret? If so, that would constitute fraud."

"I was worried about that, but Jeff told me that he had talked with her just a few weeks after our ill-fated New York breakfast, and that the insurance company needed more time to finish their investigation."

"Did he actually speak to the insurer?"

"Yeah, he told me that he explained about the breakfast and that there couldn't be any doubt about me being caught up in the Windows restaurant when the first plane hit."

"That, in and of itself, should have been compelling enough," she weighed in.

"One would think so," he agreed, "but this is an insurance

company we're talking about. I'm sure they'll delay the payment as long as possible...because that's what they do!"

"Unconscionable," she said caustically, "but their penuriousness actually works in our favor. The delay really helps us because once that check is cut, you will be guilty of insurance fraud."

"It is ironic. The cheap bastards actually helped me."

"Brian," she shifted to a related subject. "Tell me more about that next night you ostensibly went out to jog."

"After meeting him on the terrace, Jeff and I agreed to meet at 9:00 that next night. It was his suggestion just as you came back from the ladies' room. He threatened to sic the police on me if I didn't show."

"I did think it suspicious when you said out of the blue that you needed a jog."

"Well, as I arrived, he had obviously been drinking. He even told me that he was tipsy from the cocktail event he had attended. There was a financial planner type conference at the Broadmoor and that's why he was there."

"Okay, how did he fall in the water?" she asked expectantly.

"We had a really good and calm talk, and he actually forgave me. He told me not only that Margaret had died, but that the insurance company wasn't convinced that I was dead and hadn't yet paid off."

"That's all well and good," she said while nodding her head, "but how did he have his accident in the water?"

"I was just coming to that," he assured her as he took another sip of his drink. "After our conversation was over, we got up from the bench, shook hands, and agreed to meet for breakfast the next morning. We were all the way back to being good friends again. He stumbled as we got up, after we had given each other a hug, and he tried to regain his balance. That made it worse, and he reeled backwards. I reached out to grab and steady him but missed. You remember how close the stones were to the edge of the sidewalk, don't you?" he asked rhetorically. "He went straight down and hit his head on the rocks and rolled into the water." Brian paused with a heavy heart and a huge sigh as the sad memory of it all began once again to take hold of his psyche. He took another sip of the Crown Royal to help him regain his composure.

"I'm so sorry, Brian, that you have to go through this, but better with me than with the police. Go on," she urged him.

"I immediately worked my way down to the water's edge, but it took me a minute because it was so precarious with those rocks. Then I reached into the water," he said as his voice began quivering, "but I couldn't feel him. I couldn't locate him. The water was so dark and murky. At that exact moment," he went on painfully, "someone came walking by on the sidewalk. I yelled to him to call 911 and the rescue people because someone had fallen into the water."

"What happened then?" she asked as she moved to the edge of the sofa.

"I jumped in and swam after him, trying to follow the current. After about three or four minutes, maybe longer, I just couldn't find him and knew that he must have drowned. By that time," he continued, "the rescue people had arrived and were getting into the water at the other end of the pond to look for him."

"What did you do then?"

"Since there was nothing else I could do to help Jeff, I left the area rather stealthily, and came back to our room."

"Did anyone see you?"

"No, it was pretty dark. Honestly, I did everything I could do," he added. "If I had to talk with the police, everything would have come out about my deception. And none of it would have benefited Jeff.

There was nothing I could do to bring him back."

Seeing how tormented her husband had become in telling the story, especially about how his friend had died, she gave him a hug and tried to soothe him. "I know, I know," she tried to comfort him.

"Now you know every sordid detail about my past life," he said resolutely. "Now you can divorce me, if you want."

"Is that what you want?"

"No way. You are the best thing that has ever happened to me. I spent almost fifty years to find the love of my life. Now that I've found her, I'll be damned if I'm going to lose her!"

That was the right answer as far as she was concerned. She smiled and then held him tight. "I'll take that as a no," she said with a roguish smile.

That night in bed, he took her in his arms and they made love. Everything seemed good again. It was a Friday night, they were exhausted from the emotional events, and the couple looked forward to sleeping until at least 9:00 the next morning. Unfortunately, someone else had other plans.

The doorbell rang promptly at 8:45, and groaning loudly, Brian exited the bed and trudged slowly down the stairs. He opened the front door and was confronted by a smiling Jimmy Rosen, who was there to rake the leaves. Over the past two weeks, there had been a considerable build-up of leaves in their front and back yards.

"Looks like it's time to gather these leaves," the boy announced proudly.

"Thanks for noticing, Jimmy," Brian responded. "We'll have a cup of hot cocoa ready for you when you finish." He observed that the young boy was wearing a light jacket over his sweater. "Are you warm enough? It feels pretty cold out there."

"I'm fine, Mr. M," he insisted. He thought it was kind of cool to call him that, and Brian didn't seem to mind. In fact, he considered the moniker endearing.

It was a ritual at the Harper house after Jimmy had helped with the chores. He loved a cup of hot chocolate along with a chocolate chip cookie. When he was finished with his food and beverage, he asked Brian a few of his usual questions and then was on his way. But five dollars richer!

Five minutes later, after giving his sleepy wife a kiss, Mr. M jumped in his car and headed for the soup kitchen. He usually served meals but occasionally cleaned up after everyone was gone. This looked like a busy day, with three seatings instead of the usual two. The kitchen dining room accommodated only thirty people, and there were always a few folks who were too late for the first serving and had to wait their turn outside.

It was a blustery Montana day and more people than usual showed up for some hot sustenance. Every time he drove home after serving the needy, he was gripped with gratitude. He felt so lucky to be serving the meals instead of receiving them. *They do far more for me than I do for them,* was the way he described the experience to his friends.

Although still mourning for his friend Jeff Price, Brian was in a far better place than he had previously known. Kate had totally forgiven him, and the couple was counting their blessings. He felt truly liberated and complete as a man and with his God. Life couldn't have been better, although he would have to deal with the insurance matter soon.

CHAPTER 33

It was late afternoon on a brisk November day shortly before Thanksgiving, and Brian was home waiting for Kate so they could meet friends for dinner. He decided to go for a jog and slipped on shorts and a light windbreaker over his T-shirt since there was a nip in the air. By the time he reached the corner, the smell of smoke permeated his nostrils. His first thought was that someone must be burning leaves. He saw heavy black clouds of smoke billowing straight up and towering high in the sky. And then he spied several large flames. *This is no simple bonfire,* he realized and increased his pace. Getting to Highland Drive, he turned sharply to the right and continued until the end of the block. By this time, he sensed danger and began running at full speed.

The only people he really knew in the area were the Rosens. When he turned left, he saw a chaotic scene at the second house from the corner. It was the Rosen house and the structure was almost completely engulfed in flames. He sprinted up near the fire and saw Steve and Sally Rosen frantically pacing on the small hill in front of their home. She was trembling all over and appeared very agitated, her hands covering her face while screaming. Their daughter, Stephanie, sat nervously by her side. There was no sign of ten-year-old Jimmy. Three burly firefighters were blocking any entrance to the flaming building and had already turned back Steve's numerous efforts to enter the house to save his son. A fire truck stood nearby pumping a stream of water, but it wasn't making much of a dent in retarding the growth of the conflagration.

"Where's Jimmy?" Brian shouted repeatedly while breathing heavily.

Steve Rosen cried out, "They wouldn't let me go in!"

"He's in there, Brian, he's in the house!" Sally shrieked while Stephanie sobbed quietly in the grass next to her mother.

Brian looked up and thought he glimpsed a slight figure near the bedroom window facing the street. No one knew for sure whether that could be Jimmy, but three other firemen had assembled a safety net on the ground under the window just in case. They all yelled "jump," hoping that it was the boy. When Brian thought for a moment that he saw Jimmy's arm, he swung into action.

"I'm going to get him out," he assured the nearly hysterical parents. Without warning, he charged up the hill and was met by a phalanx of those three husky firefighters who had stopped Steve earlier. They braced for a collision while they yelled at him that the building was not safe to enter. Brian slowed down for a brief moment, acting like he was going to follow their instructions. They hesitated for a second and broke ranks. Then he lowered his head and raced toward the burning house, elbows flared out with a determination that nothing could deter him. He hit them hard and low, just like the former football player he was. The guy on the right side went down like a bowling pin and the other two were left trying in vain to grab him as he streaked by. One gigantic leap propelled him over the steps and onto the porch. The floor was hot to his feet but not yet actively burning. He tore off his jacket between strides and held it to his nose and mouth, and bolted through the open but flaming door frame.

Sparks and burning embers were raining down in every direction around him. He could hear the wood crackling and emitting a hissing sound. He mounted the stairs in four jumps and moved on relentlessly. A big mistake was trying to use the handrail. It was searing hot and his right hand immediately blistered. As he entered the bedroom with heart pounding, a smoldering chunk of wood flew by him and singed his left arm. He felt like his uncovered legs were burning up, but still he moved on. Suddenly a beam, flashing orange sparks, came crashing down directly in front of him. It was hard to breathe and even harder to see. Now in the middle of the room, he moved inexorably toward the window. He thought he could make out the form of the boy but wasn't sure.

"Jimmy, are you there?" he rasped, his throat parched. "It's Brian – Mr. M," he continued.

"Yes Mr. M," the boy responded weakly, fear evident in his voice. "I'm really scared."

"Are you hurt, Jimmy?"

"Just my right arm." Brian fought his way to the windowsill and saw Jimmy cowering in the corner. Flames from the raging fire shot out across the room, landing almost at their feet.

"I'm going to get you out of here, Jimmy," he choked out the words, "but you must listen to me carefully. Do you understand?" The small boy was huddled in the corner, afraid to move and too frightened to respond.

"Jimmy, look at me!" he commanded again as the dancing flames licked at his uncovered legs. "I want you to jump out the window. The firemen are there with a safety net, so you won't get hurt."

"I can't," Jimmy mumbled, frozen in fear.

"You have to!" Brian frantically implored, barely getting the words out himself. "I'm right behind you!" His mouth was dry and he couldn't stop coughing.

"I can't do it, Mr. M. I'm too scared!" With that exchange, and keenly aware that the sobbing boy was too paralyzed with fear to even move, he seized the boy, checked out the scene below to be sure the safety net was there, and threw him out the window. He listened to the boy's frightened screams, and then Brian could hear the loud cheers as Jimmy landed safely.

By this time, the hellish flames had covered the entire window-sill and began running up his shorts and the back of his shirt. He could smell the acrid odor of his own flesh burning. The excruciating pain was almost unbearable, but he knew that he had to get out immediately. He leaned forward to ready himself for the jump and placed his left foot on the burning sill, while hearing the cries of encouragement below him. Suddenly, and without any warning, the floor gave way and the entire bedroom ceiling above him collapsed, tossing him like a rag doll away from the ledge, pancaking him all the way straight down to the basement. The raging fire had already destroyed the first floor.

His neck and back must have been broken, because he couldn't move as he lay there helplessly. He couldn't catch his breath either. But he could still think. He felt no pain and strangely was at peace. "Charlie," he choked out the words in a hoarse voice, "now I know for sure why I was born. I'll see you soon, my friend."

Those were his last words.

All that remained of the three-story house was the concrete foundation surrounding the basement. The firefighters were determined to find and recover what was left, if anything, of Brian's body. He lay face up in the corner, the backs of his legs charred all the way up to his waist.

A firefighter came upon the body and called out to his captain.

"He's here in the corner..." Miraculously, his face and head were basically intact and recognizable, although very red and covered in soot. "You have to see this, Captain," the younger man shouted. "Despite his ordeal, this poor bastard actually has a smile on his face. Can you imagine the pain he went through? Do you think he knew he would die?"

"Yeah, Johnny. When he went in there, he had to know that he would never get out alive. But that's what we firefighters do."

"But Captain, he wasn't a firefighter."

The Captain nodded his head solemnly, "I know, Johnny, but that's what made him so special. He saved that kid; he's a hero... and that's what I'll tell his wife."

Outside the still smoldering ruins and less than 100 feet away sat the Rosens, all four of them, sobbing with little Jimmy safely nestled in his parents' arms.

ACKNOWLEDGEMENTS

We live in an incredible time when there are so many unprecedented and valuable resources available through the internet, television, and of course, the sometimes-forgotten actual written word. I am indebted to many of them, especially the Biography and History Channels, *The National Law Review*, and *When God Winks at You* by Squire Rushnell.

My gratitude is further extended to individuals who read the manuscript and offered constructive advice and encouragement. They include Clark Bell, Tony Romanovich, and Ed Smoragiewicz.

Special thanks to the people at Outskirts Press, especially Jamie Belt, our Publishing Representative, Rebecca Andreas our Author's Representative, and Joan Rogers our copy editor for their help in bringing this project to fruition.

I am especially indebted and give a special thanks to my wife, Michele, who not only typed the manuscript but made valuable edits to improve the text and dialogue during a number of edits and versions, making valuable suggestions, including finding the best name and cover photo depiction for my book. She was the important conduit with the publisher leading to this finished novel.

My little Trouper, who sat by me in her bed and let me pet her when I needed a little levity, also gets additional belly rubs and treats for helping me through this process!

ABOUT THE AUTHOR

Tim Norbeck worked in the healthcare arena for 53 years and was, most recently, the CEO of a national healthcare-related foundation. During his career, Tim enjoyed the opportunity to speak on behalf of physicians in all 50 states. His numerous writings, Op-Eds, articles, and speeches have appeared in a variety of industry related and other publications including Vital Speeches and periodic blogs for Forbes.com.

In the next chapter of his life, Tim began writing novels near his retirement and his first, *Two Minutes*, was published in 2018, while his second novel, *No Time for Mercy*, was published in mid-2022. *Almost Heaven,* his third novel, was published in 2023.

A Buffalo, New York native, Tim is an avid tennis player, dedicated gym goer, and a serious history aficionado. He lives with his wife, Michele, and their rescue dog, Trouper, in Estero, Florida.

Printed in the USA
CPSIA information can be obtained
at www.ICGtesting.com
CBHW021253120624
9957CB00007BA/97